FIRST KISS

"For all of our easy rapport and my delight in your beauty, my precious Angelique, you should not wed a man you do not love with all your heart. Truly, you deserve much more than this."

"As do you," she said hurriedly. "But Fate has not decreed as much for either of us. For the present, *my lord*, believe this—I have no intention of jilting you. So might I suggest you *amuse me* a little right now and kiss me? You haven't done so, you know, and I believe that a groom must at some point kiss his bride since I have always been given to understand that such is a man's duty to his wife."

She was being so brazen in asking for precisely what she wanted.

He hesitated.

"Kiss me," she said with a soft, encouraging smile, holding his gaze boldly with her own. "If you do, I'll let you pester me tomorrow about breaking off the betrothal. I might even listen to reason." She smiled and leaned into him.

He chuckled. "Very well, if you are sure you wish for it."

Angelique _____ *t* to kiss me, don't you Ch ____

He seeme _____ for the first time. He too _____ ngers lightly then warmly. _____ gloves were such an enemy in this moment. She wanted his lips sweetly against her skin.

"I should be a fool if I didn't want to kiss such a lovely woman . . ."

—from *The Bride's Gift* by Valerie King

BOOK YOUR PLACE ON OUR WEBSITE
AND MAKE THE
READING CONNECTION!

We've created a customized website just for our very special readers, where you can get the inside scoop on everything that's going on with Zebra, Pinnacle and Kensington books.

When you come online, you'll have the exciting opportunity to:

- View covers of upcoming books
- Read sample chapters
- Learn about our future publishing schedule (listed by publication month *and author*)
- Find out when your favorite authors will be visiting a city near you
- Search for and order backlist books from our online catalog
- Check out author bios and background information
- Send e-mail to your favorite authors
- Meet the Kensington staff online
- Join us in weekly chats with authors, readers and other guests
- Get writing guidelines
- AND MUCH MORE!

Visit our website at
http://www.zebrabooks.com

MY DARLING BRIDE

Valerie King
Judith A. Lansdowne
Marcy Stewart

Zebra Books
Kensington Publishing Corp.
http://www.zebrabooks.com

The Bride's Gift

Valerie King

One

Angelique Foxfield watched her betrothed pace the terrace of her father's country house for the third time. She knew he was agitated, she had even heard at least half the words he had spoken in explanation of his overwrought state. As always, however—as it had been from the first time she had laid eyes on the rakish viscount—she was utterly, completely, irrevocably besotted by the mere sight of him.

"You are listening to me, aren't you, Angelique?" he queried, stopping in midstride to capture her gaze, his face full of concern.

She looked into his eyes and felt her heart turn over. The massive oak behind him spread a canopy of ten thousand leaves over her papa's well-scythed lawn, framing his handsome countenance to perfection. He was tall, proportioned like Adonis and had eyes of the clearest most dazzling blue. His complexion was sun bronzed which made her think of the exotic lands of the Levant. He was loose limbed and lean, an athlete and so very strong. He had once picked her up as though she'd been a feather and saved her from an on-rushing carriage in New Bond Street.

No young woman could ever have loved a man as she loved Lord Charlton.

She sighed. "Of course I'm listening, Charlton. Do go on, for I can see that you have much to say."

He resumed pacing and her eyes followed him hungrily. He was speaking again about how much their forthcoming marriage of convenience was so very unfair to her because all that he could give her was a handle to her name. She deserved more, he said, she deserved a man who could propose to her out of the depths of his love. He hoped he did not give her offense but he didn't believe himself capable of loving anyone because for so long his duties had been directed exclusively toward the repair of his ancestral lands. He was convinced his soul was given entirely to Idstone House, his expansive country home.

"I know," she murmured, her heart swelling and swelling. To her, his words were nonsense.

"But are you certain you will be content in a marriage where you do not love nor are you loved in any romantical sense?"

Her words were rehearsed. How else could she carry off the sham of her part in their betrothal convincingly. "Of course I will be content. I am not a chit just out of the schoolroom. I understand perfectly the conditions of our marriage."

He did not seem much relieved and launched into another speech about how she ought to reject the whole of the bargain right now. Right now! He would release her, he would find some other manner of saving his lands than through the use of her fortune. He would take great pains to publish their joint decision oh-so-tactfully in *The Times* and *The Morning Post* so that no one would think he had jilted her.

Again, Angelique listened to only half his words. The rest of her mind floated backward.

What a devil he had been when she had first met him at Mrs. Shefford's ball. He had been so flirtatious and teasing, every word he had spoken a dare. Not that he had singled her out particularly in order to tempt her with an unusual mode of conduct. Not by half. He had been forever in the habit of flirting with anything in a pretty gown in just that roguish manner of his which set every maiden's heart to beating strongly in her breast.

And so, he had set her heart to beating.

She had been taken with him from the first and her interest had blossomed during the ensuing weeks. Of course, she was not a fool and knew that he had left behind him a string of hearts as long as the River Thames. Well, perhaps not quite that long, but certainly as impressive.

She had, therefore, taken great pains to search out every detail of his sordid reputation, asking a great many discreet questions about him and about the ladies who had made such a caterwaul about having been so thoroughly ill-used by him. In each instance, she had been satisfied with what she had found and felt that the bulk of his hapless reputation had been a result of extreme jealousy and uncontrolled gabblemongering.

No lady likes to be set aside in favor of another.

Her father had had an entirely different worry where Charlton was concerned. He knew that the eighth viscount's estate was all to flinders, burdened as it was with high-interest mortgages that should have sunk him long before now. But what her papa had uncovered was even more impressive than Charlton's ability to affect the feminine heart—only the viscount's masterful, studied care of his lands over the past eight years had kept the estate in tact. He was a gentleman farmer, a student of Coke of Norfolk and had made massive strides in improving his rentrolls because of it. The steadily increasing income had kept the cent-percenters at bay from the time he had come into the viscountancy.

In the end, her father had approved of him, warning her only, "My pet, you must understand that he's a proud man and will not like taking any heiress to wife, even one as pretty and delightful as you."

She allowed her society with him to increase after that, for she was charmed and she was able to charm him, only he wasn't aware of it because he was so poor and so proud and she so abominably wealthy. She had clear evidence of his interest for he singled her out at every ball, going down two sets with her each time. To her knowledge he had never paid a similar compliment to any other lady before. He called frequently at her house and several times a week drove her to Hyde Park at the fashionable hour. He always came to her box at the Opera and several times he had lost all track of time just talking with her, once at Vauxhall when her father had invited him to join them for supper, once at Richmond gardens under the supervision of her dear Aunt Felicity, and once when he escorted her on a shopping trip down New Bond Street.

That was the day, in mid-May, when he had saved her life after an out of control carriage had nearly run her down. He had held her tightly for a long moment until her trembling had passed, then he had looked into her eyes. She vowed he had almost kissed her for he had leaned into her in a breathtaking manner. How much she had longed for that kiss! Alas! He had caught himself on the brink of placing his lips on hers and had pulled back an expression almost of horror in his eyes.

The very next day he had announced his intentions of leaving London and returning to Idstone on pressing estate business.

She had not been fooled in the least for his next speech

had entailed her need to take greater pains in encouraging a larger number of beaux that she might very soon take a husband from among them. How sad he had looked. How utterly resigned.

Forthwith, she had pounced on her father to take action! If Charlton would not follow his heart then she would offer her fortune.

And so she had.

In the end, believing that Charlton's affections were engaged, regardless of his steadfast denial of it, she had done the unthinkable, she had persuaded her father to buy up all of Charlton's debts and to force his hand by threatening foreclosure, all anonymously, of course. Charlton must never know that Mr. Foxfield, who had made his fortune in India, was the owner of his mortgages. *Never!*

The day following the threat of foreclosure, her father had offered his daughter's hand in marriage as a means of extricating the viscount from his difficulties because— and this Angelique had insisted on above all else—*he* wanted a handle for his daughter's name more than anything on earth. In truth, her father had little interest in peerages and the like. He wanted his daughter's happiness which was what he believed he had paid for when he sought Charlton out.

Now, however, as Angelique watched her beloved pace and pace, even as she delighted in his earnestness, his beauty and his athletic grace, a wiggling of fear intruded into her present happiness. What if one day Charlton did discover her deception, her conniving? How then would he feel about his *innocent* bride?

She balled her hands into two tight fists and forced the unhappy thought away. She would be married in four more days and then she would be safe for he would never divorce her even if he learned of the truth. Besides, by then, she would have made him so enormously content that the truth would only make him laugh and bless himself that such a woman, his wife, had been so very foresightful.

If her logic seemed in anyway flawed she ignored her doubts especially when he turned and began walking toward her.

How soon, she wondered—her fears dissipating entirely —could she beg for a kiss?

His complexion was considerably heightened in his distress. He grabbed her shoulders. She wanted to melt into a puddle at his feet and wipe his glossy boots with long strands of her blond hair. How could he not see the truth of her sentiments? How could he ever think this was a marriage of convenience *for her*?

He was so very proud. "You don't have to do this, Angelique," he said softly. "I know your father is an ambitious man. I know that he wants this for you infinitely more than you do, but I fear in your innocence you will one day, and probably before the first twelve-month is out, regret your acquiescence to his schemes. You are far too young, too inexperienced to be driven to a marriage not of your choosing."

He stared into her eyes. She was so lost that it took every effort to put his words in a proper order so that her brain could comprehend it all.

"You don't have to marry me," he reiterated firmly.

Oh. He was at that again. She wanted to refute the nonsensical nature of all his arguments, but she had to sustain her part in the charade. She longed to tell him of the depths of her love for him. Her heart ached to speak the words, to let the truth hit the air and shatter into a thousand sparkling, beautiful pieces, but to do so would be to invite disaster.

How to reassure him, though?

Some of the truth might be of use.

"I am not so innocent as you suggest," she said. "Had I truly believed that our marriage would be so wretched as you suggest, I know that after a time I could have persuaded Papa against it. But you see, during the past three years in London I haven't found a single man who held my interest for more than a fortnight. And since I have no intention of dwindling into an ape-leader, for like you, I do have my pride, I prefer to be married. And I might as well be married to you as to anyone."

He chuckled and caught her chin with his hand, "My dear, you are only two-and-twenty, plenty of years to avoid spinsterhood."

"All of my friends have husbands and most a babe to dandle on their knee. I tell you, I've quite made up my mind."

His expression grew serious. "I am convinced you have entered into a betrothal that will not in the end suffice. There are a thousand gentlemen standing behind me, ready to win you and perhaps give you the love your beauty, your sweetness of temperament, your heart deserves."

"Hardly a thousand, surely," she teased with a smile. "As for my perceptions of our betrothal I would only defend myself by saying that you . . . amuse me. And if I must marry, I prefer to marry a man who *amuses me.* Do you know, for instance, that we always laugh at the same things and usually at the very same moment? Is this not hope of some kind that we will not bore one another to tears before our first anniversary?"

He smiled crookedly for a moment. He seemed pleased, his expression caught as he held her gaze. "You are so beautiful," he breathed. "At first it was all such a nightmare, the sudden demand that I pay the mortgages or sell my lands, but ever since your father came to me with his settlements the nightmare turned to this outrageously pleasant dream. I do enjoy your company, prodigiously, Angelique and yes I have noticed we laugh in a similar fashion to just about everything and . . . and I confess I find your beauty intoxicating. Do you know your eyes are the precise shade of emeralds? How is that possible?"

She smiled and melted a little more. His hand was still cloaked about her chin. He was so close to her and his words wondrously rich and portent of what she believed the best of their marriage would be. If only he would kiss her now, for the first time. Her mind bade him settle his lips on hers and seal their engagement once and for all.

Unfortunately, his expression grew somber again as his conscience warred within him. He released her chin letting his hand fall away resignedly. "You deserve better than this," he said bitterly. "For all of our easy rapport and my delight in your beauty, my precious Angelique, you should not wed a man you do not love with all your heart. Truly, you deserve much more than this."

"As do you," she said hurriedly. "But Fate has not decreed as much for either of us. For the present, *my lord*, believe this—I have no intention of jilting you. So might I suggest you *amuse me* a little right now and kiss me? You haven't done so, you know, and I believe that a groom must at some point kiss his bride since I have always been given to understand that such is a man's duty to his wife."

She was being so brazen in asking for precisely what she wanted.

He hesitated.

"Kiss me," she said with a soft, encouraging smile, holding his gaze boldly with her own. "If you do, I'll let you pester me tomorrow about breaking off the betrothal. I might even listen to reason." She smiled and leaned into him.

He chuckled. "Very well, if you are sure you wish for it."

She leaned a little more. "You do *want* to kiss me, don't you, Charlton?"

He seemed to consider the question as if for the first time. He took up her hand and kissed her fingers lightly then warmly. She drew in a deep breath. Her gloves were such an enemy in this moment. She wanted his lips sweetly against her skin. He said, "I should be a fool if I didn't want to kiss such a lovely woman."

"Humbug," she breathed softly. "Too prettily said, but kiss me anyway."

He slid an arm about her back. His brow grew furrowed as he drew her close to him. "This is still unfair. I should be madly in love with you before kissing you—and you with me."

"I have always been given to understand that the pleasure of kissing need have nothing to do with love."

He smiled, faintly. "Very well, then, my little wise one."

She closed her eyes. She breathed and dreamed. The first warm touch of his lips sent a lightning bolt of pleasure flooding her. He was kissing her at last, at last.

She leaned into him. She spread her hand over his chest, he kissed her more fully, she parted her lips.

She felt him gasp a little and hold her more tightly still. The kiss deepened and his tongue was a sudden, intense pleasure on the rim of her lips. She had never felt anything more wondrous or sensual. He invaded her and her soul lit on fire, shooting great sparks high into her mind. Her body became loose and parts of her trembled. She held him tightly. She kissed him back. A moan rose from deep within her throat and became a long, astonished, "Oh," as he drew back from her slightly.

She couldn't see his face, her eyes were so misted with her love for him. "You see," she whispered. "I was right."

"Angelique," he murmured, spreading more soft, sweet kisses over her lips in gentle, puffy wisps. "I must be dreaming—I never thought . . ."

The next kiss was hard and demanding which further reduced her knees to water and her soul to a place of liquid fire. She wanted to disappear into him and remain connected to him forever. Everything about the kiss, the embrace, proved to her that she was right about his sentiments toward her and about how perfect their life would be together.

Her mind drifted to elegant places of honeymooning and loving and the bearing of children. Ancient desires flowed over her and through her. She willed him to understand her thoughts, her purposes and her love for him. She wanted him to know the truth even though he wouldn't admit it.

After a moment, however, he released her. She could see him this time. Her vision seemed clearer than ever before. His brow was damp and his eyes dark with hunger.

She whispered, "There is something to be said then— a little something—for marriage to a confirmed rake." She couldn't help but tease him a little. She swallowed and ordered her legs to support her. "Do you kiss so well from much practice?"

He chuckled. "You are being very absurd," he murmured, staring at her as though she were a ghost and he was seeing her truly for the first time.

"Well," she said, forcing a brightness into her voice and hopefully her face, too. She was breathless, however, and her words came out in a string of wispy thoughts and intentions. "That was quite lovely . . . and I shouldn't be in the least disinclined . . . to permit you to kiss me again. Only . . . for the present I must leave you . . . to dress for Lady Peasemore's ball."

She walked quickly away and entered the house as

though she hadn't a care in the world. She glanced back only once and that to make certain he wasn't following her.

He wasn't. He was standing like a stunned statue on the terrace watching her leave.

As soon as she knew she was out of sight of him, she picked up her skirts and raced down the hall, up the stairs, down another hall, and another and finally dashed into her bedchamber.

Once there, she threw herself onto her bed, crushed her face into her pillow and screamed out her joy in muffled waves of utter bliss. Kissing him had been everything her innocent heart had dreamed it would be . . . and more!

Charlton remained on the terrace for some few minutes as one who had been given a heavy draught of opium. The sky above was the richest blue he had ever seen, and the massive, spreading oak a living being that shimmered laughter with every dancing leaf. The terrace, a rich rosy-red stone that heated up his boots.

Good God, kissing Angelique had been such a shock, such a severe, delightful, stunning, mesmerizing shock!

How eagerly she had fallen into his arms.

A certain suspicion trickled down through his brain. Could it be, was it in the least possible, that the chit was in love with him?

He felt oddly dizzy.

Oh-h-h, surely not! His suspicions were absurd for from the first she had spoken so sensibly of their contracted marriage.

He concluded that she merely liked kissing and evidently had had some experience at it for he had never known such a sweet, warm, malleable mouth as hers, so intoxicatingly sensual, so tenderly wicked.

He reviewed the kiss several more times, his body warming and flowing with newly discovered desire. For a first kiss, this one had been far and above the best he'd ever known and made exquisite promises for the future.

But what was he thinking! He had only one object now, one that had overtaken his presently guilt-ridden mind—to break off the engagement, and that, as quickly as possible.

In the beginning, when Mr. Foxfield had come to him with his outrageously generous offer, he had quickly grasped at the proferred straw. He had needed a veritable fortune to satisfy the owners of the company who had purchased his mortgages and who were threatening immediate foreclosure. He had seen Foxfield's offer as nothing short of miraculous in part because the figures were so perfect and in part because thoughts of marrying his daughter were wholly agreeable to him.

From the first, he had thought her a great beauty with enormous charm. He had spent several delightful weeks in her company, teasing her, flirting with her and even at times getting a little lost in conversation with her, just as she had said, for they seemed to be amused by the same things. Dancing with her had always been a pleasure for she followed his lead so easily. He had even taken to going down two sets with her at every ball, not entirely because he enjoyed partnering her but also because he liked to watch the odds increase at White's that he would soon be led to the altar by a young lady ten years his junior.

He had never had the least intention of offering for her—he had made it clear to her more than once that he was not searching for a bride since he was entirely unable to support a wife in any degree of comfort.

He remembered her response—so sensible!—the first time he had said something of that nature to her. "Of course you cannot marry," she had responded earnestly. "What man could bear to think that he could not care for his wife in the manner to which she was accustomed? And how much worse, were she an heiress!"

"Precisely," he had responded.

But that had been long before his hand had been forced by an anonymous company who had wanted his lands.

He had tried like the devil to uncover the identity of the company in hopes of reasoning personally with the owners, but to no avail. His solicitor had attempted numerous times, but the law firm representing the company was entirely unmoveable and kept insisting that they wanted his land for exploitation. His estate was known to have some coal deposits.

Rather than give Idstone over to the pillage of commercial interest, he had succumbed to a course as repugnant to him as cutting off his arm—a marriage of convenience to a great heiress.

His only solace had been that Angelique had been the first offering on the altar of his peerage. If he must marry, she was an unexceptionable choice of bride. If he must marry, she deserved by her sweet nature to bear the title Lady Charlton.

Only recently, since his arrival two days past at Foxfield Hall, had he started to comprehend the unfortunate ramifications of his decision where his bride-to-be was concerned. No lady, especially one so sweet and lively as Angelique, ought to be forced down such a heinous path. So greatly had he come to believe that he was mistaken, his sole intention had become to find some manner of extricating her from the impending marriage.

He was a little disappointed that she showed such a disinclination to be released from the marriage but such were her loyalties she would never set out to displease a parent to whom even a nodcock could see she was intensely devoted.

There was only one thing to be done, he mused. He must lay the matter before Mr. Foxfield and do all that he could to dissuade the fine, old gentleman from his present course of action.

Two

Angelique sat well forward on a smooth brown leather chair in her father's study. She was situated across from her beloved parent who stood by the window staring into the distance. "The gypsies have returned," he said. "I can see their colorful wagons through Ashley Wood. Hard to believe it is June already."

He huffed a sigh and ran a hand through his silvery white hair. He then turned and addressed the subject at hand. "I should never have let you talk me into this wretched scheme, m'dear. I knew there might be unforeseen complications but I hardly expected Charlton to come to me in this manner. He is deeply distressed, moreso when I absolutely refused to countenance a dissolution of your betrothal."

He had already told her of Charlton's request to end the engagement and now she had to reassure her father that all would be well. Her heart hammered against her ribs and she felt the spiderweb of her making growing more stickier with each passing hour.

She clasped her hands tightly together. "He is only feeling guilty for my sake. Somehow, though, I shall make him see that I am not adverse to the marriage—I will make him believe it."

Her father turned toward her, his hazel eyes warm with affection for her. "All the while pretending you are not head over ears in love with him when all the world can see that you are?"

She smiled tremulously. "Do you think that speaks ill for his powers of intelligence?"

Mr. Foxfield chuckled. "I think it speaks for your abilities which is what concerns me for I fear that you have deluded yourself about how happy this marriage can be. At the outset, you insisted his affections were engaged but I have yet to see otherwise. Yes, yes, he shows some evidence of it and perhaps it is as you say that he has never allowed himself to love because he has never considered taking a wife before now. But still, my darling Angelique, what do you expect of him, of this marriage, especially were he ever to learn the truth?"

"I expect that we should go on as we always have, conversing and laughing the way I used to see you and Mama do." She saw the concern in his eyes deepen. She added hastily as she rose to her feet, "In time I am convinced he shall grow to love me. No, no pray, say nothing more. I love him and he would never have accepted my fortune on any terms other than what we have dictated so in the end"—here she tossed her head—"the whole of the betrothal is the fault of his stubborness and pride."

Mr. Foxfield shook his head but chuckled again. "My dear little puss. How well I know you for I see nothing but bravado in that last speech yet I don't mean to regale you further. I have spoken my piece and I shan't say another word. You know my opinions and I believe I have acquainted you with the unhappy possibilities of the deception you are choosing to promulgate. Come and give me a kiss then, my daughter, and I will wish you well.''

Angelique rounded the desk and slid into his warm, fatherly embrace. "I do love you, Papa. And, and thank you for acquiescing to my schemes. Everything shall be all right, I promise you."

He hugged her. "I was never able to resist you," he stated. "I fault myself for that though I must blame my age. I married your mother so late in life that I always treated you with the gentleness of a grandfather rather than the more proper strictness of a father. I know I should never have agreed to buy up his debts as I did. Oh, my pet, what will the end of this be for, as Shakespeare so concisely put it, 'The truth will out' and then what will you tell the man you love?"

"I don't know," she murmured, but to herself she thought, So long as he marries me, all shall be well.

Lady Peasemore's ballroom was draped in elegant swaths of pink silk tied up with festoons of white satin and wreaths of ivy. Angelique had already greeted a hundred guests or so and received an equal number of felicitations on her betrothal to Charlton. He was heartily congratulated at having contrived an engagement to the prettiest lady to have graced England in the past decade and acknowledged his good fortune with elegant grace.

Angelique watched him carefully and noted the genuine pleasure writ on his face as he received so many warm wishes and was pleased. She knew she was right about their forthcoming marriage and very little she saw in his countenance bespoke an error of serious proportions.

Did she regret her manipulations? Of course.

Did she wish for the clock to be turned back? No, at least not precisely. Perhaps she ought to have managed the betrothal differently, but nonetheless she was content to be Charlton's betrothed.

Later, he guided her around the perimeter of the ballroom all the while pressing her about reconsidering the betrothal for the sake of her youthful heart.

"Are you at that, again?" she asked. "At our engagement ball? Oh, Charlton, pray desist for you are ruining my enjoyment of the party and you know how much I love a good fete."

His expression softened, "You do, don't you? I remember first seeing you at a ball, surrounded by beaux, laughing and teasing them all with such skill for one so young. I begged to be introduced to you and your Aunt Felicity, who has known me unfortunately far too long, rang a peal over my head about your sweetness and innocence, scolding me all the while about my reputation."

"She did not!" she exclaimed. "You never told me as much."

"I promised her I would keep silent on pain of death. But since we are to marry, I suppose she can no longer mind."

"She is half in love with you herself, you know. But then most of the ladies of my acquaintance are."

"What foolishness is this!" he disclaimed.

"Well, I am half in love with you," she stated, her heart begging him to hear the real truth behind her words.

"Are you, indeed?" he queried, smiling down at her.

A moment more and he was wearing that long-suffering, guilt-laden expression of his. She knew instinctively a speech was to follow about how it was not too late for her to break off the engagement.

She drew her arm from his and stopped him in mid stride. She planted her hands on her hips and glared playfully up at him. In a hushed whisper only he could hear, she stated, "If you dare to mention our circumstances once more, my lord, I shall set up a caterwaul, this very moment, in front of all these good people, so loud that the rafters will shake and groan and threaten to fall to the floor. Do you understand me?"

He laughed and smiled and she saw heaven in his blue eyes and in how easily she could charm him. She knew that her speech had drawn some attention toward them, but she didn't care, nor did he seem to, overly much.

He caught up her arm with his own. "What a baggage, you are!" he exclaimed, laughingly.

She overlaid his arm with her hand. "There! That is much better. Now, dance with me and then I shall be content for there are few things I enjoy so much as swirling about a ballroom floor with you."

A few minutes more, she had taken up her place on the dance floor alongside him and the orchestra struck the first notes of the waltz. She felt the pressure of his hand on her back and the lightness of his touch on her fingers. Together they lifted their feet and began to glide. Up and back, around and around.

Angelique settled into the dreamlike quality of the waltz with a deep sigh. The world was perfect in this moment. She was being cradled by the man she loved and twirled delightfully about an elegant ballroom. The chandeliers overhead glittered with a thousand sparkles of light, showering her with an increased sense that her life was indeed enchanted. He was telling her how pretty she was and how much he admired her hair done in just that fashion with so many curls atop her head and cascading down her neck.

She thanked him. She met his gaze and smiled. She felt dizzy and so completely in love that a sense of enormous safety and peace surrounded her. He looked into her eyes and his expression changed, softening tenderly.

"What are you thinking?" she asked. Up and back,

around and around. She thought she saw love shining in his eyes.

"I am thinking of the kiss we shared earlier," he murmured.

"If we were alone, I would permit you to kiss me again," she offered. "Would that please you?"

"I am intoxicated by the mere thought of it."

"You are intoxicated," she explained with a playful smile, "because we are waltzing and waltzing. I am so very happy, you've no idea, Charlton. For all your insistence I am throwing my life away, I am beginning to think my life has only begun."

"Perhaps," he murmured, his eyes raking her lips.

She would take him to Lady Peasemore's Conservatory. She would stare down anyone who dared to remain within the fragrant, earthy chamber until such time as they realized they were not wanted and quickly left the room. Then she would cast herself into his arms and kiss him until he finally understood that she loved him. And her love would be enough.

Oh, surely it would be enough.

"What are you doing to me?" he queried on a whisper.

Begging you to know me, to love me.

She said, "Dancing with you, my lord, as I intend to dance the remainder of my days."

"I feel as though I've been drinking wine for hours."

"That's not possible. You've been with me for the entire evening and I saw you have only a glass of Madeira with dinner—and that to make the venison a little more tolerable to the palate."

He smiled, appreciatively. "I believe it had been left on the spit a trifle too long," he remarked.

"You are being too kind. Poor Cook thinks it must be on the spit for a day and half to be properly edible."

He threw back his head and laughed.

She then brought forward a subject near to his heart—Coke's theories of farm husbandry. He accused her teasingly of flirting outrageously with him for what could be more romantic than a discussion of crop rotations and manure.

She smiled and gave her soul to him yet again. She was so pleased when she could make him laugh. It was as though her sole purpose in life had become to do just that.

She understood him, she had from the first, for they shared a similar past, having lost their mothers while still children. Only, Charlton's lot had been considerably worsened upon the death of his father eight years ago when, not only bereft of the last of his immediate family, he found that what had once been a prime inheritance had gone to rack and ruin.

She had great compassion for him. He had needed much laughter in his life and that was the one thing, she promised herself, she would always give him in exchange for the privilege she had purchased in becoming his wife.

The dance ended all too soon though for some reason, perhaps because they had been lost in conversation, they had continued the movements of the waltz for a few seconds after the orchestra had ceased playing. An enthusiastic round of applause had followed which caused her cheeks to warm with embarrassment. She knew that the observers had thought they were so romantically involved that they had stopped listening to the music but the truth had been far different. Charlton had been telling her that instead of turnips he was considering planting flax in his west fields.

Striving to force the heat from her cheeks, she let him guide her from the ballroom floor. Still holding his arm, she was about to pass into the antechamber which led to the music room, when a hand reached out to him, sheathed in an elegant gold silk and caught his arm. He was forced to pause as was she.

When she turned to see who had so abruptly halted their progress she looked into a bewitching feminine face surrounded by a shock of naturally red hair groomed into a Grecian crown atop her head.

"Your Grace," Charlton murmured, bowing to the lady.

"We have only just arrived, my lord, but I felt we should seek you out immediately to offer our congratulations and to be made known to your future bride. You remember Moulsford, of course?" She lifted her elegantly gloved hand and gestured behind her to a man with hard eyes and bushy silver eyebrows.

He stepped forward and in so doing, it seemed to Angelique that several persons were displaced by his presence. Many guests simply moved away as his booming voice blew her eyelids back.

"So this is the young chit that bought herself a groom and as pretty a piece of England as was ever fought over in a war. Congratulations, Miss Foxfield and my compliments to you. I daresay you will be very happy at Idstone."

There was something so offensive about this man that Angelique could only endure with wondering silence the formal introductions Charlton at that moment commenced. At the end of them, the Duchess of Moulsford addressed her husband, "You are being obnoxious and rude, my dear, as always."

"Nonsense!" he bleated. "A spade is a spade. No point in calling a purchase anything than what it is. She's got a good property and a title all bought on the backs of a million or so Indians I daresay. Ha!" He glanced at his wife who glared fiercely at him. He pinched her arm. "Bought you with a dukedom, didn't I?"

"Yes," she stated. "But unlike me, Miss Foxfield will not have to continue paying for her happiness until the day she dies." She turned swiftly to Charlton and offered him her hand, "I am happy for you, indeed, I am. As you can see, I made the lesser bargain eight years ago." She turned and nodded to Angelique. "My very best wishes for your every happiness."

Angelique was excessively relieved to see them go. She had had many persons whispering about her and some even loud enough for her to hear their condemnations of her betrothal, but nothing had come to her in so rude a form as the Duke of Moulsford's horrid pronouncements.

"What a beast of a man," she remarked. They passed into the music room where a quartet was playing quietly for the amusement of several aged ladies and gentlemen who were too old to take up a place on the ballroom floor. She fanned herself for she had grown quite heated in Moulsford's presence.

"More than a beast—a brute, I've heard tell."

"Then I am sorry for Her Grace."

"I believe she would have accepted of my hand had I offered that Spring, but my father had just died."

Angelique turned to look up at him and something of her dreams began to dim, crack, and splinter. "You had intended on offering for her?"

"Yes, I had. Of course, that all changed, as well you know. I found I hadn't a feather to fly with at the very moment I was ready to declare myself. I did tell her of my sentiments and she said she didn't care that I was suddenly as poor as a church mouse, but I knew the effect an existence of poverty would have had on her. She might complain publicly of her husband, but she is content to be a wealthy duchess, after all. Ah, here is your aunt."

A moment more and Aunt Felicity had whisked Angelique away from her betrothed toward the staircase. "If you must know," she whispered to her niece. "I can't find the lady's withdrawing room and I am grown quite miserable.''

"Oh, poor aunt. I shall show you where it is." She glanced back at Charlton who was watching her with a solemn expression on his face. Aunt Felicity began to chat, as was her custom, something for which Angelique was quite grateful. Presently, she found she could do little more than murmur in response to her aunt's observations. Her every thought had become fixed on the Duchess of Moulsford.

From the moment she comprehended that her betrothed had been on the brink of offering for another woman, even though the circumstance had occurred eight years past, her heart had come to an abrupt standstill.

What foolishness! she thought, berating herself. Why? How? When had it come to be that she had believed love had never once touched her Charlton's heart? All this time, contrary to what she had supposed, her beloved had known love, he knew very well what love was, which could only mean one thing—he did not love her.

The misery that flowed over her was so acute she nearly swooned as the door to the withdrawing room opened. Several maids were present ready to assist the ladies. While her aunt turned herself over to the care of the stoutest of them, she took a chair near the window and begged only that the window be thrown up and a little night air permitted to cool her cheeks.

She sat looking out at the stars, her heart weighted almost to her toes. So, Charlton had loved before. Her purposes, her plans, her schemes, everything seemed to turn upside down in that moment. Until now, she hadn't understood quite so clearly how much her betrothal had been based on a solid belief that Charlton *loved* her but simply hadn't yet recognized the depth of his love.

What foolishness! What agony!

No wonder he had been trying so very hard that entire day to dissuade her from marrying him. He wasn't thinking of her completely, but of himself and of his lack of love for her. He had even said as much but she hadn't listened to him. All that she had been able to see was how much she loved him and how much she wanted to spend the rest of her life with him.

What foolishness!

Even her father had tried to warn her. He had seen something of love in Charlton's manners toward her, but only *something* of love.

"What is it?" Aunt Felicity asked.

Angelique looked up at her, surprised to find that they were alone.

"You seemed so sad that I sent them all on errands so that we might have a little *tête-à-tête*. Is it Charlton? Has he said something to you, something unkind?"

Angelique looked into soft, loving, round eyes of a pretty shade of violet. Her aunt was well into her sixties and had beautiful silver hair. She was compassionate, sensitive and at times rather wise. For the most part she gave the appearance of a scatterbrained chatterbox, but not in this moment.

"Oh, no," Angelique responded. "He is never unkind to me. Never. He is always generous and sweet and for some really stupid reason I thought that meant he loved me. Instead, I am come to realize he simply has good manners." She chuckled, but tears began to trickle down her cheeks.

Aunt Felicity took on the expression of wise old age and drew a chair forward to sit beside her. "Now you listen to me, my little one. There isn't a man alive who was ever brought willingly to the altar and at the same time there isn't one that will confess it was ever anything but his idea. As for Charlton's tenderness with you being mistaken for good manners, I've never heard anything so absurd. Have you ever known a man to continue so sweetly once he's grown bored and disinterested? Trust me, if there wasn't something of love—even if it is just now blossoming—in Charlton's heart for you, he would have long since quit calling in Berkeley Square and he certainly would never have agreed to marry you."

"Why do you say that? He was desperate. We—I—made him desperate."

"You forget that I've known him a long time. I've been a friend to him all these years. You've seen how he teases me and more than once I've spoken my mind to him. He loves you, my pet. Follow your instincts and your heart." She peered thoughtfully at Angelique for a moment. "As for the Duchess of Moulsford—yes, yes, I saw her and that awful man she married—you mustn't think too much of her former attachment to Charlton. She had an enormous dowry and could have given him all the help he needed had she married him—"

"But he didn't ask her. His pride—"

Aunt Felicity nodded. "I contend that had she truly loved him, she would have kicked up a dust and insisted on the union. You would have done so without batting an eye had he come nigh to offering for you. No. I always felt there was something of the cat about Her Grace so don't repine on her behalf or his for having lost her. But I won't say anything more on that head. You had the great good sense to go to your father once you saw the salt escaping the saltbox."

"Then, then you approve of my betrothal?"

Aunt Felicity kissed her cheek. "I think you've a mountain of courage and my sole advice to you is to see this through."

Angelique looked hard into her aunt's beautiful eyes.

She saw strength there and something more, a lost love of her own perhaps. She drew courage from her aunt's firm convictions and with greater heart returned downstairs to rejoin Charlton.

She found him near the Conservatory speaking quite privately with Her Grace. He wore a tight, studied expression as he turned to greet her.

"We were just speaking about you," he said with a careful smile. "Her Grace was saying how lovely you are and I was agreeing with her."

"Thank you," Angelique said. The eyes she stared into, however, were as cold as glass. She shivered and knew instinctively that Her Grace's compliments had not all been happy ones.

Lady Moulsford remained in her company only a few more minutes then excused herself. "For I see Lord Peasemore waving to me. I cannot possibly refuse my host, now can I?"

Angelique watched her go, a sense of dread washing over her. She glanced up at Charlton and saw a haunted look in his eye.

"What's wrong?" she queried. "Did she malign my character, perhaps?"

"Not yours—your father's. She was telling me that the *on dits* that he was the one who bought up my debts all to give his daughter a title."

Angelique followed the line of his gaze and watched the Duchess of Moulsford flirt with Lord Peasemore. "Gossip can be so cruel," she murmured halfheartedly.

"Indeed. Well, we shan't permit the gabblemongers to spoil our evening. Do you care to go down a country dance with me?" he asked, offering his arm to her.

"I should like it above all else," she answered promptly, forcing a brilliant smile.

"Splendid," he responded.

As Angelique accompanied him toward the ballroom she wondered just how long she would be able to keep the truth from him for it would seem all the world already knew the terrible thing she had done.

Three

The traveling coach rattled slowly along the road back to Foxfield Hall some five miles distant. Angelique rested her head upon Charlton's shoulder, taking deep pleasure in the solitude of the journey. Her father had stayed on at Lord Peasemore's house complaining of the gout but she knew him well—he had proferred an excuse that she might enjoy a private hour with her beloved.

"Then, I cannot possibly convince you not to marry me," he said softly, taking up her hand in his own and kissing her gloved fingers.

"Not in a hundred years," she murmured in response. "I have given my word and besides, Papa adores you."

He placed a kiss on her forehead. "Oh, I nearly forgot," he said suddenly."

Her heart instantly began hammering against her ribs. What had he forgotten? More gossip that she must dispel?

She lifted her head and looked at him, his features barely visible in the moonlight which shone into the carriage. "What have you nearly forgotten?" she asked.

"You made a promise during our waltz together," he murmured and afterward kissed her soundly.

Angelique hadn't expected to feel his lips so suddenly upon hers and for a brief moment was stunned by the sensation. But since he lingered, she quickly adjusted to the experience and sank deeply into an awareness that the man she loved, so very much, was kissing her again.

Time slowed as he turned into her and slid an arm about her waist. His kiss became a search that deepened as she parted her lips. His hand gripped her waist and in that moment her body lit on fire. His tongue took sweet possession of her, a promise of the wedding night to come. A delicious agony overcame her, dragging her mind into a place of such desire, such hope for the future that tears sprang to her eyes.

She touched his face with her gloved fingers then drew back and said with a laugh, "One moment, if you please." She squirmed away from him and began removing her glove. As soon as he saw what she was about, he bade her stop and begged to complete the task himself.

She leaned back against the squabs and watched him as he eased the glove back from each finger then removed his own glove. He kissed her hand next, his lips soft against bare skin. She closed her eyes and reveled in the warmth of his kisses.

He drew away from her hand and placed his lips against hers all the while touching fingertip to fingertip. Again his kiss deepened until she thought the carriage might suddenly disappear and she would float in the air with him supported by the winds and the moonlight and her love for him. His bare fingers gently explored every line of her hand. He kissed her lightly, over and over as he did so. What sweet communion and gentle touchings these were, everything she had imagined her most private moments with him would be.

After a time, she drew back and said, "Charlton, will you promise me something?"

"Anything, my dear."

"Will you not speak of breaking off the engagement again? I know you mean well, that you want me to experience love in a way you cannot give to me, but you must understand that my heart is set on this marriage. I would not have allowed Papa to go to you that day, the day he learned of your troubles, had I had even the smallest reticence."

Charlton drew back and looked at her. He was silent apace and once again her fears surfaced for she could see a frown grow between his brows. "Just how did your father learn so quickly of my circumstances?"

Angelique had been prepared for this question but it was still a shock to see his suspicions. "Father has many connections in trade and our flirtations haven't precisely escaped notice. The man who came to him had heard the gossip and brought it directly to my father, as, as a favor."

"And he decided in that moment that we should wed, that his fortune should buy you a peer for a husband?"

"Yes, precisely."

He watched her with a considering look in his eye. "You know, I have been with your father for some time now, since the betrothal, and I have more than once been struck by how very little he seems to care for society, for going about and cutting a dash I mean. He treats everyone with a cordiality that is both pleasing and a little surprising given his ambitions for you. One would think that he would be more impressed with rank than he is, given that ambition."

"There is no explaining it then," she remarked, feigning indifference.

"He has always wished for it?"

"Always. I am his spoiled daughter, you see."

He caught her chin and looked into her eyes. "But Angelique, there is nothing about you that is spoiled, or petulant or demanding. Were I to observe the pair of you from a distance I would say you had no interest at all in peerages or titles or rank. There is simply nothing of the mushroom about you, either of you."

Angelique felt sick at heart suddenly. She was thrilled that he would think so nobly of them both, yet distressed that now she must perpetuate her lies. "Father has always been a man to seize an opportunity as he seized this one especially since he knew I had a certain fondness for your company."

"Ah," he murmured. She could hear his mind whirring and calculating and working out what she had told him. He looked at her again and smiled, "So, you are half in love with me you say?"

She smiled and felt herself relax once more. "Yes. But only half."

In the moonlight she saw him grow solemn. "What would it take, I wonder, to bring you the rest of the way?"

She heard in his words something marvelously seductive. She gasped as he nuzzled her cheek, her ear, her neck. "I . . . don't . . . know," she murmured in response. Another lie, of course.

His laughter was throaty and resonant as he once again sought her lips and began to play a melody over them with whispering kisses and sensual drifts of his tongue.

Lord Charlton would have forgotten entirely about the Duchess of Moulsford's gossip concerning his future father-in-law had he not begun to hear the same story repeated everywhere, that Mr. Foxfield had bought up his debts in order to secure a viscount for his daughter. The whispers reached his ears at the local inn while he was draining a tankard of ale, at a soiree the second evening at Foxfield Hall, at an *alfresco* luncheon served by the river the following afternoon and finally told to him directly by Lady Peasemore.

He had brought Angelique to her home in a round of several pleasurable social calls and was presently seated across from her ladyship and enjoying a *tête-à-tête*. Her daughter had taken Angelique to view a small table she had designed and which was presently gracing the music room.

He was staring now at Lady Peasemore who had just finished repeating the duchess's gossip.

"And who, pray, told you, my lady?" he queried. He would not have been surprised if Her Grace's name surfaced immediately.

"The vicar's wife who had it from her sister who lives in Upper Brook Street. The *ton* is all agog with the news. It is spoken of everywhere. I daresay, however, it means nothing to you since your marriage, after all, is a love match." Her smile was sincere and there was nothing of the gabblemonger about her.

He wasn't certain, however, which matter to address first but chose the latter since her opinion of his relationship with Angelique mystified him. "A love match—and who told you this?"

Lady Peasemore let out a trill of genuine laughter. "No one had to tell me it is anything other than a love match or were you not aware that the last waltz you danced with your betrothed continued a full minute past the moment the orchestra put down their instruments."

"What? Not a full minute, surely! I mean I know we had danced a few seconds after the music had ceased . . ."

She nodded, smiled knowingly, and sipped her tea.

"Good God, is that why there was a burst of applause once we had stopped?"

"What did you suppose had happened?"

"I don't know, a general congratulation upon our betrothal perhaps."

She chuckled again and sipped her tea once more. "At any rate, Charlton, it was completely romantic and sweet. We were all charmed."

"Though I realize I risk disturbing your lovely vision, as it happens we were discussing something quite unromantical in nature at that very moment."

"And what was that?"

"Crop rotations—some of Coke's theories. And turnips, too, I think." He took a sip of tea.

"Ah." She seemed to consider this then suggested, "But, my lord, do you always do so holding a lady so tightly about the waist?"

He sputtered his tea and choked. "I have no answer for you. Was I doing so?"

"Scandalously!"

"I begin to understand why you are speaking of a love match but I assure you ours is a marriage of convenience."

"I see. Well, if that is your notion of 'convenience,' I only wish you might explain it to my husband. We married for love and he will not waltz a step with me, nonetheless squeeze me tightly in public."

"Madame, you make me blush."

Again she trilled her laughter and he was charmed and mystified all at the same time. He smiled and shook his head. "I can't make it out," he said at last, "except," and here he paused since Angelique arrived at the doorway in that moment, "except that she is so beautiful."

"Are you telling secrets?" Angelique queried, glancing from one to the other. "Is that why you were whispering just now?"

"I hadn't meant to," he said, rising as she reentered the chamber and, along with Mary Peasemore, took up her seat again. "We were speaking of your beauty and suddenly there you were."

"Indeed?" she queried.

"We were also discussing that strange matter the Duchess of Moulsford presented to me the night of our hostess's ball, the rumors that your father had bought up my debts. She had it from sources in London."

He watched her blink and a sudden faint rush of color touched her cheeks. "It is no such thing," she said turning to Lady Peasemore, "I assure you. But I understand it is being spoken of everywhere. I can only wonder at how such a rumor began."

Lord Charlton felt as though he had been struck hard across the face. Not once had he truly considered the possibility that Foxfield had actually forced his hand. The man had no guile. Nor had his daughter. At least that is what he believed until now, when her blush bespoke a whisker.

When his mind resurfaced to attend to the conversation he found that the ladies had already introduced a new subject beyond his suspicious thoughts, and were now centered on a lively discussion of the wedding breakfast which would take place in two days time. "Papa has hired a string quartet which I think will be quite lovely and though the affair began as a quiet celebration the numbers have risen to at least fifty."

"Fifty?" her ladyship responded with a laugh. "Add a few more and we shall get up a ball afterward."

Angelique chuckled, a sound that was used to please him very much. Now, all he heard was the jingling of deception. Two days and he would be wed to this charming, elegant, beautiful creature who was in the habit of telling banbury tales.

What other lies had she told him?

* * *

On the journey back to Foxfield Hall, Angelique knew that something was amiss for Charlton had grown rather subdued and lost in thought, so unlike him. She would have addressed his silence had her own fears as to the source of his pensive state not risen sharply to immobilize her tongue. She knew precisely when his quietude had come upon him, shortly after he had brought forward the painful subject of his debts—and that so frankly in front of Lady Peasemore.

She knew she had blushed for the subject had been tossed to her like a hot coal. Yet, she had believed she had handled the prickly topic rather satisfactorily, even bringing forward a new matter for discussion—her wedding breakfast—with considerable ease, until she realized that Charlton was taking no part in a description of the coming festivity.

Now, as she glanced nervously at him, she wondered what she should do. If he was beginning to suspect her duplicity—or her father's—what was he likely to do next? Would this be sufficient cause before the eyes of the *ton* to break the engagement?

She turned this over in her mind several times and tried to imagine herself in his place. Within a scant few minutes she knew what she would do if she were him, and so it was that when the coach drew to a stop before the door of her home, she excused herself from Charlton's company by immediately complaining of the headache. As soon as she believed herself out of sight, she began to run toward the library where she knew her father frequently tucked himself away for an afternoon nap.

She thrust the doors open, breathing hard, then held her breath in order to listen for the gentle snorting sounds that indicated her father's sleeping presence. Nothing returned to her, not even the buzz of a fly's wing. He wasn't there!

His bedchamber.

Empty.

His office.

Empty.

The billiard room.

She heard the clatter of the balls and two masculine voices without the smallest need to press her ear to the door. She was too late. Charlton had found him first!

She placed both hands on the door and leaned her forehead against the cool oak wood. She was now panting from having run all over the mansion and her heart was racing like the wind. She pressed her ear to the door and tried to hear what was being said between the gentlemen, but she could only hear muffled, inaudible words intertwined with sharp cracks of the billiard balls.

With a heavy heart, she turned away from the door and headed toward the terrace, the oak, and the swing hanging from one of the tree's sturdy limbs.

"So it is true, then?" Charlton asked, watching Foxfield carefully.

"I shan't deny it, nor shall I protest otherwise. You've been listening to gossip. Make your own judgment."

The old man was being elusive and quite irritating. Charlton had found him snoring in the winged chair by the fireplace and with a tap on the shoulder had awakened the old man. Foxfield had sat up with a startled snort.

He had quickly explained his mission, to discover the truth about his debts.

Of all things, Foxfield had eyed him for a long moment then suggested sleepily a game of billiards.

Charlton had acquiesced impatiently only because there

had been something in Foxfield's eye that brooked no refusal. He began to see his father-in-law-elect in a new light, the light Moulsford had hinted at when he had said that Idstone had been purchased on the backs of a million Indians. Quick fortunes were made by quick men.

So, here he was, losing at a game of billiards to a man with silver white hair, a congenial smile and eyes that now ressembled a falcon's observant, piercing stare.

"Would it matter?" Foxfield asked. "Perhaps that is the pertinent question. Let's say I did buy up your debts— maybe even to ensure my daughter had a handle to her name—what difference would that make at this hour?"

"Every difference," he responded coldly. "My lands were prospering and in another ten years I would have been able to—"

"Hardly ten—" Foxfield interjected strongly.

"All right, in twenty years, the rentrolls would have paid off the mortgages."

"Not at the current rate of interest. I had my clerk do the computations. Thirty years and not a day sooner."

"Then you admit you bought up the debts."

"I admit nothing. When I saw how much you were sitting in my daughter's pocket—and that was in early April, mind—I had your situation thoroughly investigated." Here he rose up with his cue stick in hand and eyed Charlton narrowly. "I don't hesitate to say, my lord, that I was quite impressed with what I found. Your father left you with hardly a feather to fly with, but you did something about it. I don't mind saying that sort of character is uncommon. *Uncommon* and don't argue with me on that score. I've seen the world, I know men. You've a brain and a bit of tenacity and you've used them both. For that reason I determined you deserved having my daughter as well as my fortune."

"I shall pay back every penny you've spent settling the mortgages."

"I'm not speaking of the mortgages, Charlton, I'm speaking of the fortune I made in India. I have no intention of marrying again, or trying to produce an heir and I have no other relations to speak of, except my sister, Felicity, so that the entire fortune will go to Angelique and thereby to you. Those that have come to claim a connection aren't worth a flea's arse. No. Angelique is my sole heir, a fact I made irrefutable in my will the very day we agreed on the marriage settlements. You'll have it all one day, Charlton, and I hope you've enough sense to comprehend precisely why I'm content to leave it that way."

Charlton was stunned. The implications of Foxfield's announcement were overwhelming. The old man had half a million on the 'change alone.

Foxfield leaned over the table and slapped his cue in a quick jerk sending another ball home. "I suppose now," he continued in the face of Charlton's silence, "I've made your situation a bit more difficult to sort out."

"I won't deny it."

At that, Foxfield tossed his stick on the table and approached Charlton. He clapped his hand on his shoulder. "Come, lad. She loves you."

"No, that is not true. She has confessed to being only half in love with me."

Foxfield laughed outright. "Very well, believe as you wish. But know this—I have every confidence in you and I mean that with all my heart. So do all of us a favor and let sleeping dogs lie."

Charlton met his gaze squarely. "This isn't fair to Angelique and well you know it."

"You are speaking of love?"

Charlton nodded.

"I see. Then you are willing to end the betrothal, humiliate my daughter besides breaking her heart, all for the sake of what you believe to be the protection of her sensibilities?"

"Yes. Angelique deserves a man who would rise up like a dragon to protect her."

"And you wouldn't?"

"Not in the true chivalric sense."

"Ah. But you would do it for duty's sake, though?"

"For duty's sake—yes."

Foxfield shook his head and turned away. He picked up his cue stick and again attacked the billiard balls. "You are far too romantical for me. Well, do as you wish, but one thing I will insist on, Angelique must agree to end the betrothal wholeheartedly. I'll not have her browbeaten just to satisfy your absurd sense of what is right in this situation."

"I understand."

"One more thing, Charlton, I've never given a fig about titles. Just thought you should know."

He mulled this over and realized precisely what Foxfield was saying. "The betrothal was *her* idea—not yours."

"Yes," was his succinct answer.

Charlton turned on his heel to go in search of his bride-to-be. Angelique it would seem had lied—about many things.

Four

Angelique sat in the wooden swing which hung from a branch of the spreading oak. The sun was a warm afternoon glow on the red brick of the house and the terrace. The old rhythms as she swung back and forth were comforting to her as she considered the likelihood her father had confessed the truth to Charlton. She felt as though her every happiness was being slowly drained from her. If what she suspected was true, that Charlton had been informed of her role in the betrothal, he would undoubtedly despise her, hardly a basis for even a mite of joy in a marriage.

What to do? She had to think, to plan, to ponder. She didn't want to speak with Charlton just yet. She wasn't ready to confess her misdeeds and to see the hard look in his eye as he accused her of having bullied her way into the engagement.

She slid suddenly from the swing and set off to the south, near Ashley Wood. She would go to her favorite dell, stretch out in the low, mossy turf and give herself to pondering her dilemma. She had always found peace in her secluded, secret place for no one had ever troubled her there or even found her when she had been missing for a time.

Her heart lightened the more distance she placed between herself and her home. Perhaps in the quietude of the dell she would find the answers she sought.

Charlton observed his betrothed's sudden departure from the terrace lawn with a strong sensation she was running away. He had been watching her for some few minutes knowing he should go to her and confront her beneath the oak. Yet, something had stayed him.

Twice he had determined to push the glass door open and cross to her. Twice he found he couldn't seem to lift his hand in order to see the task done.

Now she was leaving but where was she going and on such a quick tread?

When she passed through the arbor leading to the formal gardens, he acted swiftly, giving the doorhandle a quick turn and crossing the threshold. He ran across the terrace and down the steps sensing she would soon disappear into the meadow which was carpeted with numerous shrubs and dotted with thick stands of woodland.

When he entered the formal gardens he caught but a whisper of light blue fabric as she disappeared through a gate. Just as he suspected, she entered the wood near the farthest yew hedge.

But where was she going in so purposeful a manner? In the several days he had been ensconced at Foxfield Hall she had yet to take him into the dense wood to the south.

He set himself at a brisk walk, keeping his steps on the gravel light and even. He didn't want her to hear his pursuit. His heartbeat quickened. He began to feel as he did during a fox hunt when the hounds had been released and his mount was fresh for the chase.

The gate creaked as he passed through. The path diverged. Left, right, straight ahead. He chose the path in front of him because it led away from Foxfield Hall which seemed to be her purpose. She had seemed none too content while swinging beneath the oak.

He started down the path and every now and then caught glimpses of heel marks. Much of the pathway was overgrown and he found himself frequently caught by small, leafless branchlets that wanted to hold him back. When the heel marks disappeared entirely, he retraced his steps and stood in a glade that sloped to the east but became woodier and more dense to the west. He headed east for a hundred yards, following a narrow foot track which took him increasingly into open country. There was nary a heel mark to be found.

Again he retraced his steps.

The path leading into the woods offered up a boot impression within fifteen feet. He walked for what seemed a quarter of a mile in fairly rugged terrain. The path was only visible occasionally between outcroppings of rock and moss, yet continued to provide him with signs that Angelique had passed that way.

The wood grew dense and the shade so deep that he nearly lost his way since the trail seemed to disappear. He found it however and began pushing his way southeast again. When at last he broke through, he found himself on the edge of a farm and staring at a hundred quiet, dozing sheep tended by a young shepherd reading a book. Bordering the pasture was a drystone wall nearly shoulder height which served to contain the encroaching wood.

"I say," he called to the shepherd who had been regarding him with mild curiosity. "Have you seen a lady pass this way?"

"Nay," the lad responded. "I've seen no one, except the gypsy children now and again."

"Thank you," he said, then turned to stare back into the wood. Where had Angelique gone?

Once more he retraced his steps and paused at the thickets which pressed tightly against a group of large gray boulders and found what he had been seeking—moss scraped from one of them in two places.

She had climbed the boulders.

He followed suit, dipping his body to slide beneath the overhanging branches. He heard a splash of water and as he dropped from the boulders onto the grass he saw Angelique wading in a shallow clear pool shaded by birch, willow and alder. The late morning sun sat on her bonnetless locks and cast a glimmer of gold from her hair which was now dangling about her face in charming country simplicity.

She took another step into the water oblivious to his presence.

How reluctant he was to disturb her, to announce his arrival when his very soul was overcome by the verdant beauty before him. She had discovered a treasure of a dell, surely her private place for contemplating the transgressions of her life, for ordering her thoughts, for enjoying a stretch of solitude.

He knew he should leave, that he was standing on the threshold of a sanctuary meant only for Angelique. But for the life of him, he couldn't. His gaze drifted over so much beauty in the low turf scattered with moss of every shade and littered with flowers that sparkled like jewels against their green bed.

Ferns clung to the rocky walls, teasing out bits of soil now and again and planting more ferns with their long tendrilled fingers.

A spring bubbled from the gentle rise to his left and his

eye was drawn along its path back to the pool and ...
Angelique.

She slid a portion of her hair back behind her ear and
bent over to gently skim her fingers along the water's
surface. Her gown, tucked between her knees, sank slowly
into the water. She didn't seem to care but began moving
in a careful circle until the entire hem of her gown was
soaked and swirling about her ankles. She smiled and
laughed, playing at her child's game.

As he watched her, he was suddenly overcome with a
sensation so powerful that he thought his chest might be
crushed because of it. He saw her as a child with all of her
playfulness and innocence. He realized that with every
opulent wish at her command she would choose the pleasure of playing in a pool of water over excessively fine gowns
and ribbons and expensive dolls.

He realized with a start that he had been drawn to her
simplicity from the first. Even though she was a great heiress and though she was always gowned fashionably, she
avoided every excess of fashion that so many ladies found
irresistible—ropes of fine jewels, yards of billowing lace,
intricate embroideries that overtook a skirt or spencer. He
had always credited her Aunt Felicity or perhaps a superior
governess for such control and judgment. Now he saw that
she was the source of her splendid elegance for her soul
was rooted deeply in the beauty of the land surrounding
her and in her father's love.

She twirled a little more and now faced him completely.
She saw him and froze, like a deer before a strong lantern.
Her arms were raised in the pose of a beautiful alabaster
statue which put him forcibly in mind of a Madonna gracing a holy fountain. Before she could recollect her former
unhappiness, an expression of joy at seeing him spread
over her face. He knew then that what Lady Peasemore

had said about her was true, what her father had said was true—*Angelique was in love with him.*

He understood her in that moment and recalled especially the day of the shopping trip in New Bond Street when he had caught her and saved her from an out-of-control carriage. He remembered looking down into her face and wanting to kiss her more than anything.

The memory became shockingly vivid, of how her green eyes had nearly mesmerized him, begging him to see into her soul. But he had refused to have any of it, for to enter her soul would be to go down an impossible path. The next day he had told her he would be leaving London and he had heard himself as one observing from a great distance tell her she ought to find a husband. How strange to think that he had never once questioned why he had decided to leave the Metropolis so quickly, why he had lied to her about needing to return to Idstone because of pressing estate problems, why he had pressed her about finding a husband.

She had understood, though, and she had taken matters into her own hands. She had persuaded her father to buy up his debts and, as Moulsford had so crudely yet accurately put it, she had bought herself a husband.

How could he marry her now, though, under such conditions?

How could he not marry her?

These thoughts had traveled through his mind in lightning succession so that only now, a few seconds after her recognition of him, did the sudden joy of her face begin to dim.

He didn't want her happiness to be diminished by his presence so he smiled, though the effort seemed to hurt several muscles in his face. He doffed his hat, he bowed to her and cried out, "You've been discovered, Miss Foxfield."

She sighed deeply. "I have, haven't I?"

He ignored the double meaning of her words. He didn't want to speak of the unhappy things between them. He wanted something else, something different, something more.

He looked about him and began walking toward her. "You've found the heart of Albion, I see. How long have you known of this place?"

She seemed uncertain as she watched him. "I liked having adventures, I guess, from the time I was a child. I explored all of my father's lands. I pushed my way past the boulders when I was eleven."

"Does anyone else know of your secret dell?"

"Only one—a gypsy named Igor."

"Ah. I have seen their colorful wagons from the window of my bedchamber. Does Igor visit you here often?"

She shook her head. "I brought him here only once and he said the dell disturbed him. He felt he was marching across sanctified land and refused to return. But that was a long time ago when we were both very young." She sighed. "Igor was my first love and quite, quite handsome though several years older than I." She lifted her chin slightly. "Alas, our lives were too disparate to allow of a deepening of our love."

He chuckled for she was playacting delightfully. "No, I don't suppose that your father could have ever countenanced your having married a gypsy out of hand. A peer, perhaps, but never a gypsy." He watched her glance at him sharply.

"Never," she murmured, some of the sadness again creeping into her eyes.

He could bear many things in this moment, but not her sadness.

"You have known the gypsies a long time, then?"

Her expression lightened. "Yes. They camp here every

June for a fortnight before making their way in slow stages north to Cumbria.''

He smiled at her. How odd to have been in her company for so many weeks and only now to have just begun comprehending her or her parent. ''How generous of your father to permit them to stay.''

She nodded. ''He has great compassion, I think because he saw so much of the world before building his home in England. From the time I was a child I have heard such stories as would shock you.''

''That would explain it, then,'' he said quietly.

''What?''

''The air you have about you of worldliness and simplicity.''

She frowned at him slightly. ''Is that how you see me?''

''That is how I am beginning to see you. I've been blind for a long time though I suspect you already know as much.''

Her serious expression remained for a moment. ''It is possible I learned too well at my father's knee. He was never a man to hold back but took what he wanted from life, acting first and considering later.''

''He seems to have profited by it.''

''But will I?'' she asked, holding his gaze steadily.

Another powerful sensation ripped through his chest. His lungs felt squeezed by strong, unrelenting hands. She was asking hard questions, not of his mind, but of his soul.

He wanted to draw near to her, perhaps even to touch her, but she was still standing to her ankles in the pool.

''Would I defile your waters overly much were I to join you?''

She seemed surprised and a smile approaching delight soon overtook her face. She teased him. ''Your valet will not like to have your boots ruined.''

''I wouldn't think of putting him through such agony.''

"Are you saying you intend to remove your boots and . . . and your stockings?"

"I believe it is permitted during a betrothal."

She laughed outright at the absurdity of it. He sat down on a rock nearby and began the arduous task of tugging off his exceedingly well-fitting boots. She glanced at him several times in the process but beyond wearing a wide smile of amusement she said nothing.

When at last he had removed his stubborn boots, his brow damp from the effort of it, he slid off his stockings, pushed up his pantaloons and began slowly wading into the pool. He knew now why she had been so careful in her own steps for a slick layer of water moss covered the entire bottom of the pool. Infant trout could be seen in the shallows.

"This is a birthplace then," he remarked staring into the clear waters. He heard her sigh.

"Yes. And at the far side, where the branches overhang the edge of the pool so thickly a moor-hen has built her nest. She is presently hiding from us."

He glanced about the walls. "This must have been a quarry at one time."

"That is what I think, though I was used to imagine it to be the grotto to which Eros brought his beautiful Psyche. I am not so romantical anymore."

"Aren't you?" he queried, turning to look at her. "I am more and more convinced the opposite is true."

A blush was quickly on her cheeks, but not of embarrassment he realized.

Good God, why hadn't he seen it before, the sparkle in her green eyes, the bloom on her lovely, youthful cheeks, the way her lips frequently parted when she looked at him as though she couldn't breathe.

She said nothing and he finally read her thoughts, her mind, her heart. She held nothing back from him but reached toward him with every tendril of her being, like the ferns on the rock wall, searching for a bit of soil in which she might plant herself and grow. All these weeks she had looked at him in just this manner and he would look back as one mesmerized yet blind and lacking understanding of even the smallest kind.

What a nodcock he had been not to have seen it before, the depth of her love for him!

Only now did he truly comprehend the unfairness of his betrothal to her, for he could never return such a love. His heart was a rock wall with no crevices of fertile soil into which to plunge a living root.

He resolved within his rational mind, then and there, that he would open his mouth and tell her that he couldn't marry her because he couldn't love her. He would place his tongue at the back of his teeth, he would let the air pass through his throat, he would move his lips and he would tell her that theirs had been a grave mistake, that he could never in good conscience take such an innocent, such a beautiful, adoring, loving innocent to wife—but nothing came forth.

Instead, his right foot moved closer to her left foot. His left foot followed suit. His arm wrapped itself about her small waist, his hand found the softness of her cheek and touched her lovingly. The next moment he was kissing her fully, richly, deeply, drinking in her love for him, robbing her of her heart's innocence, cheating her and stealing from her.

She relinquished her soul. He felt it fly from her chest and sink into his heart. He groaned as he kissed her. The sudden fire in his body began to consume him. She responded in kind. She clutched at his shoulders and back, she took his tongue deeply into her mouth, she leaned desperately into his body. She was panting for he was holding her too tightly and she couldn't breathe. She took in his breath, he breathed in the sweet apricot fragrance of her exhalations and in that moment, soul to soul, breath to breath, he stole her love from her and knew he would keep it with him forever.

Somewhere in the midst of kissing Charlton, Angelique understood how deeply she had cheated him. The embrace, which had first taken her high into the heavens, now began plummeting her into the bowels of the earth. Her conscience became a living snake that worked and worked inside her until she was writhing in agony.

Gone were the sweet sensations of love and of being loved that had at first assailed her when he had taken her so forcibly in his arms. Replaced, was a painful awareness that she had cheated him of ever loving her by her deceptions and conniving.

She drew back from his embrace. She saw the replete warmth on his lips and countenance. She saw that he was full of her love, indeed, her soul was even now encircling his heart and surrounding him with love and pleasure. He tried to take her back into his arms. He was speaking nonsense, "We'll honeymoon for a year. I want you to myself for that length of time with no one to bother our heads and make demands of us. I want to kiss you from morning until night."

How long had she waited for him to speak these words to her? How long? Only the dull, agonizing breadth of every interminable second that had passed between them since she had first exchanged words with him at Mrs. Shefford's ball in London.

That long. An eternity, two eternities. But now that words of his passion for her were striking her ear, they struck with a force that shattered her heart for they were false words spoken in a false moment.

She turned from him and slipped on her half-boots. She fled her sacred dell which was now defiled, not by his presence but by the machinations of her unworthy heart. Moulsford had spoken too clearly, too shrewdly in saying that she had bought herself a husband, for she had and in her cold purchase she had lost her soul and he, his ability to discern that what seemed like love blossoming was nothing but a sham.

"Angelique, wait!" he cried, calling after her. But his voice had the empty quality of one who was desperate and not one who loved deeply and richly.

She caught her long, loose locks on sharp branchlets as she scrambled back up the boulders. She had one last view of him struggling to put on his boots. She could escape him then!

Still, she hurried. She cut her arms on a tangle of bramble. Shameful water seeped from her eyes. She tumbled off the boulders on the other side. She picked up her feet and ran and ran. She pushed herself to return home before he could catch up with her, before she could ever fall into his arms again.

When she arrived home, she locked herself in her bedchamber proclaiming a raging headache which would not permit her to join her father and Charlton for dinner that night.

The following morning, she rose early, dressed in her riding gear and rode ten miles to Reading where she searched out her father's solicitor.

That evening, Angelique's heart was lighter than it had been since the day Charlton had agreed to her father's terms of betrothal. She had settled all the necessary business of extricating herself from her engagement to him and could now be at ease in her mind. Only one thing remained, to hide from Charlton until he left Foxfield House for good. But where to go?

Five

"What do you mean, she is not to be found?" Charlton asked. He stood by the mantel in the crimson and gold drawing room stunned by his host's announcement concerning Angelique.

Mr. Foxfield's brow was pinched with concern as he stepped into the long, elegant chamber. His voice echoed back from the lofty ceiling painted a celestial blue. "Earlier today she returned from Reading, for the head groom took her horse from her at three o'clock, but no one has seen her since, not even her abigail. I daresay I would have known nothing about it except that Cook is in a state since she cannot serve dinner which has been kept waiting this half hour and more."

Charlton considered this speech for a long moment. "What did her maid have to say? Surely a lady will confide some things to her maid which she will not to her bridegroom or to her father."

"Ginny was apologetic. She felt she should have informed the housekeeper that her mistress had not sent for her at the usual hour to dress her hair, but she knew nothing of her arrival at three. She supposed that she was returning late from Reading for the last thing Angelique had said to her was that she would be gone for the day."

Charlton took a step toward his future father-in-law. "Ought we to be concerned?"

Mr. Foxfield sat down on a chair of gold silk damask and drummed the arm with his gloved fingers. "I don't know. It is very unlike her to have disappeared in this manner. Of course I would be sick to death with worry had she not returned at a timely hour. But to have not been seen since three o'clock!"

"What of kidnappers? She is worth a king's ransom. Have there been threats in recent months or years?"

He shook his head and pursed his lips. "I am more likely to believe her disappearance has more to do with you than with strangers. Last night, when we were informed she would not be joining us because of the headache, I felt certain something was amiss. I didn't ask at the time, but now I feel I ought—did you quarrel with her yesterday? You had every right to, of course . . ."

Charlton wished now that he had followed his first inclination yesterday when Angelique had fled from him at the dell. He had hurriedly sunk his feet into his boots and meant to chase after her, to catch her and to force her to hear the confessions of his heart. Instead, his mind had sensibly ordered the situation. He had decided in a very rational fashion that she should spend some time alone working out the troubles of her heart and conscience, then later, perhaps, they could gently come together and resolve everything.

What an error that had been for a full day had elapsed and he had not yet seen his bride to tell her that all had changed! He had finally opened his heart to her when he had embraced her and kissed her in the dell. Love had finally been born—or perhaps merely recognized—in that moment. How much he wanted her to see that the purchase of her bridegroom had turned into a love which every poet at some point in his career immortalizes with sonnets and plays, couplets and epic poems that go on for days.

Damme, he was ready to be her husband, her companion, her friend, her lover but how could he do so if he never saw her again?

This afternoon, his heart had been a pulsing, beating thing, tingling with anticipation for her return from Reading. He had rehearsed a dozen speeches all designed to melt her heart. He had listened for a horse in the drive for hours on end.

When he had finally seen her come in from the stables, he had tried to intercept her but apparently she had slipped up the servants stairs and eluded him. Regardless, he had slid a missive under her bedchamber door begging her to meet him in the formal gardens to the south if only for a few minutes.

He had waited in the gardens for an hour, then another, but she had never come.

Now, with dinner cooling to Cook's infinite distress, she was nowhere to be found.

"We did not quarrel, precisely," he murmured, responding to Foxfield's original question. "Though I fear I may have caused her some distress by, er, kissing her." How could he possibly explain to his beloved's father all the changes of his heart in recent hours.

Foxfield leaned sympathetically toward Charlton and in a hushed tone, said, "You do realize my daughter is an innocent. I mean—and I don't like to interfere in this manner—but perhaps you were a bit too forceful in your attentions. Perhaps you gave her a fright, that sort of thing. Without a mother to, to impart the general womanly knowledge of marriage—and God knows I hate to think what Felicity might have told her!—well, I can see how my daughter might have responded were you a bit too *urgent* in your, well, you know, embraces." His face had taken on the hue of a ripening peach.

Charlton held up a hand and politely refuted Foxfield. "No. I may have only kissed her twice, no, thrice, but there was no shrinking in her. I don't fear in the least that I was *too urgent* as you have suggested. I believe she is suffering from a great deal of unnecessary guilt because of having orchestrated the purchase of my debts." He met his future father-in-law's gaze. "I want you to know that I believe now she was right to have done so. I would never have tumbled in love with her as I have otherwise. No, that's not accurate. I would never have grown aware of how much I love her, otherwise."

This was the truth then. He had loved her from the first.

Mr. Foxfield leaned back in his chair. "Angelique and I argued the matter for an hour but she won me over, she always does. I'm happy for you, Charlton, only where the devil do you think she is?"

Charlton thought for a moment, started and laughed at his own stupidity. "The dell, of course! I know precisely where she is. I'll go after her now, but I'll need a lantern and I'll have to put on a pair of boots. These shoes will be of no use in the woods."

"I'll see to the lantern and have it ready for you, if you're sure?"

"I'm positive."

"Very well. I'd offer to come along but I fear with my bones being as old as they are I'd likely stumble in the dark then where would we be?"

"Don't trouble yourself in the least!" he cried. "No, this must be my doing."

Charlton met his gaze steadily and saw that faint tears

were brimming in the older man's eyes. In this moment, though he was two and thirty, he felt more of a man than ever. He was being passed a responsibility that had for two and twenty years belonged exclusively to the man before him but would no longer.

"Yes," Foxfield murmured. "I believe the duty to be yours now." His smile was tremulous as he nodded for Charlton to go.

"I won't be but a few minutes. Have the lantern ready. I'll find her, never you fear."

By the time Charlton had changed his black superfine coat to a sturdy russet stuff, his knit pantaloons to a pair of buckskins, and his drawing room patent shoes to a pair of Wellington's, evening was settling deeply on the downs. The woods were dark and eerie the further he marched along the path leading to the dell. After twenty minutes had elapsed, he reached the boulders which he carefully climbed, catching his coat only three times on prickly branches before sliding into the beautiful depression below. He was smiling as he came to an upright position fully expecting to find Angelique huddled by the far stones and awaiting his rescue.

She was not, however, anywhere to be seen.

His disappointment was severe and accompanied quickly by a panicky sensation. He was so certain she would be here! Why wasn't she?

He walked further into the dell and listened to the quiet sounds of nightfall. His small lantern cast a dull, yellow glow all about the walls of the old, mossy quarry. The moorhen skidded across the pool and slunk into the shadows. For a moment, he allowed himself to remember the kiss he had shared with Angelique on the day prior and how his heart had been fully awakened to love in that moment.

He had thought he would speak to her of her lies, instead he followed the thrum of his heart and kissed her. His eyes had been opened and, like a blind man seeing for the first time, he had been overcome by the newfound joy rising in his chest. He had wanted to hold her forever but before he could even begin expressing the swell of his feelings for her, she had twisted from his arms and run from the dell.

Now he was here, trying to figure out where she had gone, if not to the dell. He turned to go, but something caught his eye, something rolled up near the stone on which he had sat the day before to remove his boots. He turned back and slowly made his way down the slippery mossy bank.

There, on the stone, was a sheaf of papers tied up with a maroon silk ribbon. So, Angelique had been here and had wisely divined that he would return to the dell in search of her.

He settled himself and the lantern on the wide, flat stone and cradled the packet on his lap. He untied the ribbon and discovered that the uppermost paper was his original missive, the seal unbroken. His heart thudded dully against his ribs. Then she hadn't even permitted herself to read his request to join him in the gardens earlier that afternoon—she had been that overset.

He quickly scanned the remaining papers. One was a letter from Angelique, the rest were remaining documents—all of the mortgages discharged at the time he and her father had signed the marriage settlements. Her letter was brief.

Charlton,

　　by now I believe you are fully acquainted with how very much I love you. I have adored you from the first only I was so stupid as to have let myself get caught up in a scheme that was as ignoble as it was hopeless. Please believe that I am deeply ashamed at having forced your hand as I did and know that my father was entirely innocent. His heart was always too generous toward me and whatever I wished for, he has long since been in the habit of granting. You will be glad, I am sure, to be rid of such a spoiled female. Accept your mortgages as my gift to you as penance for my silliness and in hopes that one day you will find a proper bride.

Yours, abjectly,

Angelique Foxfield.

Life without Angelique was the only terrible thought that went through his mind in this moment. He didn't think of the mortgages at all, or his bride's silly conduct, only that her overly sensitive conscience could possibly ruin his life forever.

He reread her letter several times and loved her for every word she had written. Only where was she now?

Lady Peasemore's? Perhaps, but then she would know he or her father would search first for her there.

With Aunt Felicity? He shook his head as he carefully folded up the documents. What he knew of Felicity, she had little doubt that good lady would have fallen into a swoon had Angelique asked her to call off the wedding breakfast and steal her away to some remote part of England.

The vicar's wife? She had an equally sensitive conscience and though she might have taken Angelique under her wing she would have probably sent a secret message to Foxfield letting him know where his daughter could be found.

His mind worked in this manner for a quarter of an hour. Each personage he brought forward he found entirely unsatisfactory. No one would conceal Angelique from her father, no one. Angelique, it would seem, had the grave misfortune of counting among her friends only people of high and estimable character.

He smiled and wondered at his own great good fortune to have met and fallen in love with such a sweet, generous, albeit, misguided young woman.

In the distance, he could hear music of a style as far from Mozart as England from China. The strains were exotic and strummed out languidly on a guitar. A rich, baritone voice began a ballad that intrigued him.

The gypsies.

The gypsies!

Of course! Igor and his family. They would easily have taken Angelique to their fireside and possibly promise to steal her to the other side of England if she wished for it. Their loyalties, though as deep as any Englishman's, were entirely individual. Angelique's desires would be their sole concern.

He knew the encampment was but a few hundred yards from the dell, so he quickly slid the papers into the waistband of his breeches, picked up the lantern and headed toward the concealing boulders.

He recalled the low stone wall to the southeast and immediately turned in that direction. Once he arrived there, he followed the wall which circled to the southwest for a quarter of a mile.

Sounds of the gypsy encampment grew louder and louder until the wall broke off to the south and a meadow opened up. Beneath the shade of several ancient elms, a circle of wagons was grouped. In the center was the brilliant light of a large fire on which were being thrown chunks of dead wood. Near the outer circle was a pile of branches the height of the wagon and Charlton suddenly could see the benefits of a Gypsy encampment for all the woods in a several mile radius of the camp would benefit immensely from the removal of dead and rotting trees, diseased shrubs and fallen branches.

He knew enough of the Gypsy nature, however, to call out loudly before approaching the fire with the strict purpose of announcing his presence. He had little doubt that a knife would have been at his throat had he done otherwise for the Gypsies were highly protective of their families.

Several wiry young men quickly ran from the encampment, surrounded him and demanded to be told his business.

"I have come to speak with Angelique if she is here."

They fell silent and even though the glow of the lantern did not illumine their faces entirely he could see the knowing looks exchanged one to the other. He breathed a deep sigh of relief, for though he had been convinced she had gone to Igor, he didn't know what he would have done had circumstances proved otherwise.

Angelique sat near the campfire with a toddler asleep on her lap. She had asked to borrow a rocking chair in order to attempt to comfort the babe who was teething and miserable. As she crooned the songs of her childhood to him, he had fallen fast asleep. Even the usual raucous noises of the camp could not awaken him.

She had been with Igor and his wife for several hours now and had even supped with them on a delicious stew made in a communal pot. She had conceived of the plan of staying with the Gypsies because she was certain no one would think of looking for her here.

Only . . . the longer she stayed at the camp she came to realize that yet again she had worked her way into a ridiculous situation. For one thing, to have simply vanished meant that her father would be beside himself with worry.

She had therefore spent the past hour trying to contrive some manner in which she could reassure her parent that she was perfectly safe but would not return home until such time as Charlton left for good. Yet how to do so without alerting him to her whereabouts since she would naturally have to make use of one of the Gypsies as messenger.

Then, there was the truly horrible realization that the camp was in no way prepared to accommodate a lady of quality. Besides a number of great inconviences which she could not even fathom enduring, how thoughtless of her to have dispossessed Igor's eldest son, who was only eight, from his bed for the night.

She had also noted that though the Gypsies were a clean people, many of them scratched at bugs.

She had been bitten alive by bedbugs at an inn in Worcestershire once. She dreaded the thought of trying to sleep with the small creatures gnawing away at her flesh the whole night.

Finally, however, she simply couldn't bring herself to ask where they kept their chamberpot. She was nearly in tears as she watched members of the encampment simply melt away into the woods now and again and return hitching up trousers and reordering the beautifully woven and colorful skirts so popular among the women.

So it was, that when she heard Charlton call out to the camp, she nearly screamed with relief that he had found her. She remained in her rocking chair however as several of the younger men went out to scrutinize him while Igor came to stand over her. He put his hand on her shoulder and said, "Not to worry, Miss Angie. We'll not let him take you."

She looked up at him. "Igor, you've been most kind this evening, but, indeed, I think I ought to speak with him."

"You are being too gentle," he reprimanded her. "Never fear. I shall send him away. You may rely on me."

His heavy accent and the firmness of his words boded ill for Charlton. When the young men escorted her betrothed into the light of the campfire, she quickly called to him, "I am here, Charlton, quite safe I promise you. Igor has been my friend for ages."

"How well I know it," he responded, catching sight of her yet pausing in his tracks.

Angelique's heart turned over at the sight of him. Forgetting her current distress, all she could see for the present was how handsome he was, and tall, and manly. The child stirred on her lap and she once more set the chair to rocking gently.

Igor descended on Charlton, his powerful shoulders set firmly like a wall against an onrushing wave. "You must go," he stated firmly. "Miss Angie does not want you. When you leave Foxfield House, she'll return."

"I would only beg a word with her," he said quietly.

Igor turned around uncertainly. Angelique nodded for him to let Charlton pass.

"Please, Igor," she said. "I need to speak with him. He will not harm me, nor will he force me to do anything against my wishes."

Igor finally stepped aside but not without a menacing stare which Charlton acknowledged with a nod of his head.

With each step her beloved took toward her, the flutterings of her heart increased like butterflies flitting from leaf to leaf. All her love for him rose up like an ocean swell, sweeping her heart toward him. He came to stand in front of her and she looked up at him, her entire body trembling with the simple of joy of seeing him.

"How beautiful you look," he murmured, "with a babe on your lap. The only thing wrong with this portrait of you right now is that the child is not mine. Angelique, please be my wife that we might raise a family together, that we might kiss the sun good morning and argue the moon to bed at night, that we might discover just how deep our love will grow.

"I was a fool not to have understood your love for me sooner and an even greater fool not to have allowed myself to fall in love with you long before the kiss we shared in the dell."

Angelique's throat constricted painfully. She could not credit that he was actually speaking the words she had waited so anxiously to hear yet believed she never would. She could only conclude that her father had kept her secret after all, that Charlton still did not know the truth of what she had done.

"Did you go to the dell first, before coming here? Did you find the packet along with my letter?"

He nodded.

"Did you actually read my letter?"

Again he nodded.

She truly did not understand. How could he be insisting he loved her if he now knew of the truth? Perhaps she had not been clear in her letter, that he still didn't understand her wretched conduct. She took a deep breath and began solemnly. "There is something you must know, Charlton. Papa was the one who bought up your debts but not because he wished for it. I begged him to."

"Yes, I realize that now," he said quietly, a warm smile on his lips.

"You do?" she asked, disbelieving him. "Why, then, aren't you as mad as fire? Why haven't you come to ring a peal over my head instead of staring down at me as though I was presently sporting angel's wings? You ought to give me a dressing down, you know. Oh, Charlton, I behaved so very badly! How will you ever forgive me?"

"Because I no longer give a fig about who bought up

my debts or when they were purchased. They've led me into a betrothal with you and that is all that matters to me in this moment."

Tears trickled down her cheeks. "Oh, Charlton," she breathed. "I thought you would hate me forever."

"Never," he murmured, dropping to his knees on the grass beside her.

"Your breeches!" she complained instantly.

He laughed outright. "What nonsense is this! A man ought to address his beloved on his knees."

"I am convinced the buckskin will become hopelessly stained, ruined in fact!"

"Then I will ruin them with pleasure if only I might be able to dry the tears from your eyes." He touched a thumb down her cheek but more tears appeared. He scoffed playfully, "If you continue to weep, my breeches will be worn through at the knees before I am done!"

She chuckled. "Then stop making me cry."

"I don't want you to cry, my darling. I want you to laugh and to be happy. Please say you'll marry me, that you'll forgive me for being such a slow-top. I love you, Angelique Foxfield. Will you do me the honor of becoming my wife?"

She looked into his eyes and she believed him. "Yes, I will but only if you are very certain you wish for it."

"I am."

Her heart melted into a pool that took every strength from her limbs. Over the top of the child's head, he placed a kiss on her lips sealing their betrothal upon which the caravan of Gypsies began shouting at the night sky, yelping and shaking their tambourines. Afterward a general singing ensued along with a passing round of a skin of wine. Even Angelique tilted her head back to let a few drops flow into her mouth before sputtering and laughing and passing the skin to Charlton.

The child continued to sleep on her lap until Igor's wife

took their babe in her arms and carried him to her wagon. Only then, did she rise to her feet and begin her farewells.

Charlton had just picked up his lantern preparing to leave, when he said, "Oh, I just remembered. I have something for the fire." He withdrew the mortgages from his waistband and showed them to Angelique.

She stayed him, however, with a quick thrust of her arm over his. "It is not too late for you to act on these," she assured him. "I meant the gesture whole-heartedly." She waited breathlessly.

"I know you did," he responded. "But my darling, there is only one thing I intend to do with your gift." He then marched to the fire and with a swift flick of his wrist threw the debts into the crackling blaze. The papers browned and curled and finally burst into a brilliant ball of flames.

Angelique watched as sparks flew suddenly upward into the night sky. A fitting end, she thought, for something so ignominious as these debts.

Charlton turned back to her, caught up her hand and with a final wave to the Gypsies, began leading her toward the drystone wall by which long and circuitous path she could see her beloved meant to guide her home.

His true intentions became fully evident when, once he had taken her some distance from the camp, he paused her in midstride, settled his lantern carefully on the wall, and took her in his arms.

It was at this moment that Angelique truly realized all that had happened with Charlton's arrival in the camp. She now knew her love to be returned in full measure. She fell into his arms, receiving his violent kiss as one who had been starved for just such a gesture all her life. She devoured him, returning kiss for kiss, until he was clutching her so tightly she could hardly breathe.

"Oh, Charlton," she murmured. "My darling, my darling." A fire crept through her body until her lips were burning as he pelted her with kiss after kiss.

"I was such a fool," he whispered into her hair, his breath teasing her ear and causing a spattering of goose-flesh to steal down her neck and side. "I must have loved you from the first, from that moment at Mrs. Shefford's ball when I saw you flirting with a dozen beaux. Your green eyes teased each of them with more merriment than I had ever seen before. I was charmed and dazzled. Later, you never once seemed the least afraid of me and I was further charmed."

"How could I have carried any fear in my heart, Charlton, when I tumbled so completely in love with you that first second of looking into your eyes."

"Angelique, Angelique," he whispered throatily as he devoured her once more.

The cool June air swirled over Angelique's shoulders. Overhead stars twinkled their laughter and the night droned its safety and pleasant slumbers. She reveled in the love that had come to her at last, at last.

The Parson's Mousetrap

Judith A. Lansdowne

To Drew, Thank you

One

The Reverend Mr. Jason Farley collapsed into the wing chair and laughed uproariously as billows of dust puffed up about him. It was the gloomiest, most begrimed room he had ever seen. Spider webs dangled from the ceilings and the drapery rods and the paintings on the walls. The only chair whose stuffing remained intact was the one in which he sat.

"You are not hysterical, are you, Jay?" asked a quiet voice from the parlor doorway. "You may change your mind, you know. Lady Farnsmoor will understand. All we need do is bring her to look at this place."

"Never will I change my mind," grinned the cleric, straightening. "Have I not plagued you ceaselessly to obtain this living for me, Duke? I mean to have it dirt, dust and grime not withstanding."

"Well, I cannot think why," murmured the Duke of Weyland with a shake of his gleaming black curls. "You shall have Mr. Tanner's living at Weyland Hall in a few years. That old gentleman cannot go on forever. And I always thought you were perfectly content to bide your time at St. Cyril's. It is not as though you need the money. It is not, is it?" added His Grace, his brow creasing abruptly. "You have not had a falling out with Adderleigh? He has not cut you off without a penny?"

"James? Of course not. It is—there is a specific reason why I—Devil it, Duke, stop gazing at me as if I am a lunatic."

"You are a lunatic. I knew so the very moment I told you that I intended to marry Eloise and you jumped up from the sofa and began to do a jig in the middle of the parsonage parlor."

"Yes, well, I was happy you had discovered true love at last."

"Balderdash! For all you knew, Lady Eloise was stupid, ugly, a complete shrew and I was marrying her simply to gain possession of Twilight Hill."

"Not so. You will not have Twilight Hill. It is entailed and belongs to his little lordship, Charles Ashbury Arthur Exeter Danbury Hanforth."

"You know my little brother-in-law?"

"By thunder, listen to that, Duke. There is something the size of a deer stomping across the ceiling," offered Mr. Farley, abruptly changing the subject.

David Adamson Mallory, the eighth Duke of Weyland, leaned his shoulder against the door frame and gazed questioningly down at his cousin who, though seven years his senior, had been his best friend for all of his twenty-six years. "Do not attempt to divert me, Jay. How do you come to know little Charlie?"

"I do not know little Charlie. I merely know his name. Nothing odd in that. I know any number of names."

"Uh-huh. You are not going to confide in me, are you? And after I practically begged Lady Farnsmoor to give you this living, too. Took disgusting advantage of my coming relationship to the poor woman, I did. Called her my dearest mama-in-law-elect and spun her a tale of a poor relation who was too stubborn to accept charity at my hand."

"Good God, did you?"

"Indeed. Poor Mr. Farley whose only wish was to have a small living of his own so that he might support himself in the life he has chosen. Though why you wish to have this particular living, especially now that we have seen the place, I cannot for the life of me understand. You are the brother of a marquis and the cousin of a duke, and James and I between us could use our influence to raise you to the highest of positions within the church if only you would let us do so. I vow, it is the queerest sort of pride to be working yourself to distraction as a mere curate at St. Cyril's and then to choose to come here when you might easily become one of the assistants to the Archbishop of Canterbury."

The parson's eyebrow cocked the merest bit as he studied the gentleman in the doorway. "An assistant to Canterbury? Me? I think not, Duke. I have not the least ambition in that direction. And I particularly wished to have this living because—because—"

"Because you have a passion for spider webs in the parlor and great somethings clumping across the ceiling?" The duke's eyes lit with humor. "Never mind, Jay. I shall not force you to tell me. But you will not abide in this rectory until it has been cleaned and polished and some decent furniture got for it. I assure you of that. That far I will not indulge your need for humility or whatever it is. And if Eloise and I are to be married from that outrageously neglected church—and in little more than a fortnight, too—we shall need to call upon the entire village to help us clean up the place."

The Reverend Mr. Farley extricated himself from his

chair, strolled across the room, took his cousin by the arm and tugged him into the corridor. "Let us look about the rest of the establishment, eh? Farnsmoor must have done something quite extraordinary, don't you think, to have sent his rector running off into the night and compelled all of his dependents to let their own church fall to ruin while they traveled a full hour to Crossfields for services? There are good reasons for me to take this living, Duke. The villagers and the tenants will be grateful to have the church open once again and your Lady Eloise will have her fondest wish—to be married in her own parish. You did tell me that was her fondest wish, did you not?"

The Duke of Weyland nodded. Eloise had told him as much time and time again. She wished to be married from her own little church right here in Farns Moor. "But you need hardly sacrifice yourself, Jay, upon the altar of my betrothed's wishes. I must, but it is not necessary that you do the same. And you might just come and do the deed and then go back to St. Cyril's again, you know. It is not in the least necessary that you consign yourself to this rats' nest for the remainder of your days."

Lady Farnsmoor sat down upon the tent bed hung in rose silk draperies and dabbed with a dainty lace handkerchief at the tears that rolled silently down her rosy cheeks. Really, it was the outside of enough! She ought to be singing, not crying. Eloise was to be married—and to the Duke of Weyland, a gentleman of rank, noble family and considerable fortune who had always behaved as a perfect paragon toward her; who claimed to be tail over top in love with her; a gentlemen whom Eloise loved in return. What more could a mother wish? Nothing more. For the past month she had been the envy of all the mothers with marriageable daughters. Even Lady Truley envied her. She had to pull herself together and cease this nonsense. The duke had sent word that he and Mr. Farley had taken rooms at the Bull and Butter in order not to inconvenience her and this very evening the two of them would be coming to dinner.

And I must act the perfect hostess, she told herself on a tiny sniff. I cannot do the least thing to embarass Eloise before His Grace. But I cannot seem to come around. The merest thing sends me right into the dismals. And there is no reason for it. None at all but my wretched imagination. "Well, but I will be most welcoming and jolly when they arrive," she whispered. "I will. And I will not say or do anything untoward."

"Mama, what on earth is wrong?" asked a sweet voice. "You are crying!" And with a swish of skirts and the hushed whisper of kid slippers across the carpeting, Lady Eloise hurried to her mama. She pushed aside a most becoming day dress of sprigged muslin and plopped down in a most unlady-like fashion upon the counterpane, taking Lady Farnsmoor into her arms. "What is it, Mama? Has something dreadful happened?"

"N-no," managed Lady Farnsmoor, tears once again rising and grief threatening to close her throat entirely. "It is merely—merely that—oh, Eloise!" she managed around the choking sensation. "I shall miss you so! Must you marry His Grace?"

Eloise, whose wide blue eyes glistened with good humor, bestowed a kiss upon her mama and tucked her more comfortably into her arms. "I knew it would be so the moment Prissy told me that you had come to my chamber and sent her away in the midst of her packing. No, Mama, I must not marry His Grace, but I wish to do so very much."

"B-but marriage is so very hard, Eloise. And how can you know that you will be happy? You are happy here with Charlie and me. You do not need His Grace's money. I made certain from the day you were born that you would not need any man's money. You are to have the property my Aunt Augustina left me and I made your papa set aside a fine competence for you as well.''

''Which I greatly appreciate, Mama. But I love David and I wish to share the rest of my life with him. I can think of nothing I wish to do more. I shall love and cherish him just as you loved and cherished Papa.''

Lady Farnsmoor lowered her eyes and stared at the fingers twitching in her lap as if they must belong to someone else. ''But I did not love and cherish your papa,'' she whispered.

''You did not?'' Eloise stared at her agog.

''Once I thought I did because I wished to love him more than anything, you know. But then I was forced to live with him day after day and I could not continue imagining him to be someone he was not, Eloise. The charming, daring, exciting gentleman I thought I had married was not your papa at all. Your papa was an inconsiderate, selfish boor.''

''Mama!''

''He was!'' sobbed Lady Farnsmoor. ''He was a rogue and a scoundrel and once we married, he did not care about me at all! Oh, I ought not to be saying these things to you, but it does not matter that your banns have been read and the wedding guests are expected within a fortnight. It is not too late, my darling, to change your mind. It is not!''

''You did not love Papa?'' Eloise repeated, staring at her mother in considerable shock.

''I thought I loved him. He was handsome and titled and wealthy and an intriguing scoundrel to boot. All the young ladies of my day wished to capture your papa, Eloise. But then I did capture him and had to live with him, and I discovered that I had made a terrible mistake. The only kind, thoughtful, considerate thing your papa ever did for me was to fall off Banbury's back and break his neck.''

Lady Eloise's pretty little lips rounded into a perfect O.

''I am so sorry, Eloise,'' sighed Lady Farnsmoor, at last recognizing her daughter's shock. ''He was your papa and you loved him just as you ought to have done. I should never have said the least word. I do not know what has come over me, but I shall pull myself together and be happy for you and your David, I promise.''

Streaked with soot from a successful attempt at unclogging a chimney and brandishing a much overused broom in a fashion resembling an Italian fencing master, the Duke of Weyland shouted, ''Take that and that, you raggedy villain! A pox upon ye!''

''I'll put a pox upon ye,'' chuckled Mr. Farley, himself covered in mud from a brief but fruitful encounter with a recalcitrant pump in the yard. ''How the deuce do you think to subdue the thing in such a backward manner, Duke? Anyone would think, the way you are flailing about, that you had never before encountered a rodent. You need to smack the blessed thing upon the head with the business end of that broom, not lunge and jab at him with the stick.''

''I beg to differ,'' replied Weyland in a most refined drawl. ''That wretched mouse has challenged me to a duel and I am determined he shall have a proper one and not a mere clunk upon his pointy little skull. Look how he stands and stares at us. Just waiting for my next lunge. An honorable mouse, Jay, due an honorable end.''

''You have lost your mind,'' groaned the parson, his eyes brimming with laughter. ''Chimney soot did it I expect. Why does the little villain not flee, do you think?'' he added, staring down at the tiny brown mouse who had risen upon his haunches and was gazing at the two of them inquiringly.

"Thinks he owns the place," grinned Weyland. "Most likely bred and born in this very bedchamber. In this very bed. Never forced to put up with interlopers the size of us before. Oh, there he goes, Jay, behind the clothes press. Stand back, I shall flush the villain out and engage him once again."

"No, have mercy upon him, Your Grace," cried Mr. Farley most dramatically. "He is merely a misguided creature of The Almighty! Love and caring must be his redemption, not a clout by such a demon as yourself."

The Duke of Weyland, broom in hand, collapsed upon the sagging mattress in gales of laughter, sending dust and feathers flying in all directions. "And ain't that just like you, Jay! Love and caring must be his redemption! I cannot discover them, but there are likely more mice in this rectory than people in the parish and you will never bring yourself to kill a one of them no matter how you talk of smacking them on the head. You will never sleep alone in this place, I fear."

"I have grown tired of sleeping alone," murmured Mr. Farley.

"You wish to sleep with mice, Jay?"

"No, I do not wish to sleep with mice. I am thinking in terms of a wife."

The duke picked his way off the mattress in a considerable silence and when he had gained his feet, leaned upon his broom and cocked an eyebrow at his cousin.

"I am not an antiquarian," announced Mr. Farley with considerable aplomb. "I am still young enough to wish for a wife. Thirty-three is all. In the very prime of life. Do cease staring at me in that particular manner. I am not joking."

"No, I can hear you are not. But I have never heard you mention marriage in all my life. Is it because I am marrying

Eloise? Has that made you think of taking the leap yourself? Or is there some lady you have met who has caught your eye? I am sorry to be so curious, Jay. It is just that the idea is so very new to me. You married. You, who never once would glance at any of the London ladies, no matter how many set their caps for you before you decided to take orders.''

"I am not interested in any London ladies. It is a lady in the country I should like to make my wife.''

"A lady in the country? A particular lady? Who?''

"A lady who stole my heart once, a long time ago, and never gave it back. But I have not the least idea if she knows or cares that she did so. She married someone else. She was a mere miss when I knew her but now she is a countess.''

"A countess?''

"Um-hmm. You think I am aiming too high, do you not?''

"What countess? Who? Jay, do stop nibbling at your lip and speak up. What is she like? She is a widow now?''

"Oh, yes. Been a widow for two whole years. But I have not seen her or spoken to her since I was sixteen.''

"You were sixteen? You are wearing the willow for a lady you loved when you were sixteen?''

"Foolish, is it not? But there it is. I met her; I loved her; I love her still.''

"You are a hopeless romantic, Jason,'' sighed the duke, leaning more heavily upon his broom and surveying his friend seriously. "I know you have developed a heart of pure mush over the years, but I never once guessed that you were wearing the willow for anyone. You must only tell me what I may do to help and I shall do it. Country parson or not, even a dowager countess would be privileged to be your wife. Does she live hereabout? Is that why you pressed me so hard to gain this living?''

"Yes, as a matter of fact. She lives quite close by."

"Within a day's ride?" The Duke of Weyland's mind was whirling through the population of the near countryside. A countess? A widowed countess? Somewhere near Farns Moor?

"Less than a day's ride from this very rectory," replied the parson, a slow smile rising to his lips. "A half hour's ride at the most. She was Miss Meredith Cottesmore when I knew her. Now she is the dowager Lady Farnsmoor."

"My mother-in-law-elect?" Weyland's jaw dropped in amazement.

"Do not look so astounded, Duke, a gentleman may be in love with another gentleman's mother-in-law. I assure you, there are no commandments forbidding it."

"But—but—Jay, are your attics completely to let? She is much too old for you. She is at least—at least—" Weyland paused to count upon his fingers seriously.

"Thirty-eight on the fifteenth of July," provided Mr. Farley. "And I do not give a fig how old she is."

"But Jay, she will give a fig and more."

"Do you think so? Even now? Deuce take it, I have not given one thought to that. I did not think for one moment that the difference in our ages could possibly matter now. All that has worried me up to this moment is that she may—may—"

"May what?"

"Put my name and my face together," sighed Mr. Farley with a frown. "Of course, she may not. There are any number of Farleys. Five of us in my family alone. And I went off to join the cavalry so she will not be expecting me to be a parson. And I have changed, Duke. I do not look the stripling anymore."

"Jay, what the devil are you babbling about?"

Two

It was in the midst of the second course and mere seconds after Mr. Farley had decided that all of his apprehensions about meeting the countess had been for naught that Lady Farnsmoor, a portion of guinea fowl raised to her lips, paused abruptly and stared down the table at him. He could feel his heart wrench free and thump agonizingly against his ribs as the smooth, silken ivory of her throat reddened. He watched in dread as the blush swept upward and into her cheeks. And when her ears began to glow at their edges, he choked on his peas so badly that it took both a footman and the duke, himself, and a full glass of wine to quiet his coughing and to get him to breathe normally once again. And still Lady Farnsmoor stared.

She knows, he thought, swiping at the considerable number of tears the coughing had forced to his eyes. She remembers. She has recognized me. Oh, God, he prayed in silence, his gaze falling to study what remained upon his plate, please let it not be so.

But Lady Farnsmoor continued to grow redder by the

moment and returning her guinea fowl to her plate, she leaned back in her chair and fanned herself vigorously with her napkin. The delightfully drawn lips that he had never once forgotten gasped like a carp out of water and the fine, flashing black eyes that had roused him from sleep night after night attempted to hide behind wildly fluttering lashes. The bosom he did not remember as being quite so upstanding, heaved dramatically upward to an even more impressive height. And Mr. Farley knew beyond a doubt that Lady Farnsmoor not only recognized him but was remembering *Everything*.

"Mama, whatever is wrong?" asked Lady Eloise with a trembling voice. "Shall I fetch your vinaigrette?"

"No," managed Lady Farnsmoor in the most pitiful voice and with a tiny shake of her head. "No. I must—I am—"

"Air!" exclaimed Mr. Farley before he could stop himself. And without the least will to do it, he stood and went to help Lady Farnsmoor from her chair.

She batted his hands away.

"No, but Meredith, you must," he murmured. "You are dreadfully in need of a cool breeze and privacy to pull yourself together."

"Not with you," hissed Lady Farnsmoor in reply. "Are you mad?"

Mr. Farley's knees felt like melted butter and his hands shook and his collar was tightening around his neck like a noose, but he pulled back her chair and offered her his arm in spite of it all.

With hands shaking quite as violently as the parson's, Lady Farnsmoor rose and allowed him to lead her through the lovely French doors out into the mildly approaching night. There was no moon and not the least twinkle of stars in the sky. It was merely seven o'clock on a June evening after all. But all around him Mr. Farley saw flashes of fireworks bursting across a black sky and heard the booming of cannonade and the roar of thunder in his ears.

He led her as far as the delicately carved wrought-iron rail. She removed her hand at once from his sleeve and clutched at the frail balustrade in panic.

"Do not," Mr. Farley murmured, his face grown as white as hers was red. "Do not, Meredith. I did never intend to—I would never—Oh, God, what was I thinking to come knocking upon your door after all these years?"

"You were thinking that I would not remember you," gasped Lady Farnsmoor, gulping for air. "But you were incorrect, you dastardly villain!" And with a fury quite beyond anything she had felt in years, Lady Farnsmoor slapped Mr. Farley's cheek so hard that it grew instantly red and she could see the imprint of her hand clearly in the fading twilight.

"They have gone back to the Bull and Butter," announced Eloise as she entered her mama's chambers. "Mama, what is wrong? Why did you slap the Reverend Mr. Farley's face?"

"Did he say that I slapped him?" asked Lady Farnsmoor, staring from her window at the two gentlemen riding off across the park.

"He did not need to say it, Mama. Your handprint was quite apparent. David was horrified to see it and so was I. I cannot guess what has gotten into you these days."

"He called me Meredith!" exclaimed Lady Farnsmoor abruptly. "How dared he call me Meredith?"

"Well, that must have seemed brazen. But you ought not have slapped the poor gentleman for merely thinking to appear fatherly."

"Fatherly? You think he made free of my name because he wished to appear fatherly?"

"Some clerics, Mama—"

"Some clerics? Do you tell me that he is truly a cleric? No, it is all a ploy upon his part to gain admittance to this house!" declared Lady Farnsmoor, turning from the window.

Eloise was completely baffled. "But of course he is a cleric, Mama. He is David's cousin and took Holy Orders almost five years ago. And when David told him that my dearest wish was to be married from St. Agnes of the Moors, he offered at once to come and do it."

"He c-came here because of you?"

"Yes, Mama. And because you told David to offer him the living. Though why he wishes to accept it I cannot imagine. The church is in a frightful condition, David says, and the rectory is falling to wrack and ruin. The two of them spent the entire afternoon unclogging chimneys and working upon the pump and chasing mice from the bedchamber."

"There are mice in the rectory bedchamber?"

"Indeed."

Lady Farnsmoor lowered herself onto the tiny cherrywood bench before her dressing table and studied her reflection in the looking glass. "Jason Farley has come to Twilight Hill to marry you to the Duke of Weyland," she murmured. "And all unknowing, I have bestowed the Farns Moor living upon Mr. Jason Farley in little Charlie's name. Your papa must be spinning in his grave."

"Mama, you are not making a bit of sense," sighed Eloise. "And now that you have slapped the poor gentleman, I doubt he will wish either to perform our wedding ceremony or to keep the living. He is likely on his way back to London this very moment. The Reverend Mr. Farley may have been willing to put up with spider webs and rodents and clogged chimneys and broken pumps, but I doubt even David's cousin, no matter how loyal he is to him, will wish to remain in a place where his patron's mama has slapped his face for him.''

The Duke of Weyland was one of the most courageous men in England, but he was not stupid. There was no way on the face of the earth that he was going to ask his cousin what had occurred upon the balcony. They rode in silence to the village of Farns Moor and entered the little inn without a word having passed between them. They climbed the stairs to the first floor and entered chambers directly across the hall from each other. And once Bottswell had helped him out of his boots and coat, the duke ordered his stalwart valet to Mr. Farley's chambers to see that his cousin was made comfortable. ''Because he is in a wretched mood, you see, Bottswell. He must be. She slapped his face.''

''Who slapped his face?''

''Lady Farnsmoor.''

''Slapped Mr. Farley's face?'' Bottswell's eyebrows lifted in unison. ''Is she a madwoman?''

''Why do you ask, Bottswell?''

''Well, it is our converted Mr. Farley, Your Grace. He has not been the brazen, audacious gentleman he once was in five years or more. What in the name of all that's holy could he have done or said to cause a lady who is a perfect stranger to slap him?''

''I have no idea. That is precisely what I should like you to discover for me, Bottswell.''

''Me, Your Grace?''

''Indeed. *I* am not going to inquire.''

''Nor I,'' intoned Bottswell with a slow shake of his head. ''I have known Mr. Farley, boy and man, for thirty years.

And I know he has greatly changed and inexplicably so, too, but—"

"But what, Bottswell?"

"But I am not trusting enough of his new character to be inquiring into a lady's reasons for slapping his face any more than you are, Your Grace. He would likely box my ears."

"Never. He eschewed violence from the moment he turned to the church," offered the duke encouragingly as he settled into a wing chair and accepted a brandy from Bottswell's hand. "He is no longer a gentleman with fists of iron, but a parson with a heart of mush."

"Would you care to lay odds upon it, Your Grace?"

"At this particular point in time? No. You are quite right, Bottswell. Heart of mush or no, Jay is likely to slip back into his old ways if he is as angry as I fear. So you will simply help him into his night clothes and see that he is made comfortable. And if he should happen to speak to you of the matter, well, there is no reason you may not return here with the information."

Mr. Farley, however, did not speak of the matter. Instead he accepted Bottswell's help in doffing his boots, muttered something completely incomprehensible, and then dismissed the man.

With a sigh, he sank down upon the edge of the feather bed and allowed himself to fall backward across it, staring up at the old red velvet canopy that hung between himself and the ceiling. Meredith had slapped him. And not a missish, tentative little whisp of a slap either. A regular jaw buster of a slap that had sent his head spinning. Not that his head had not been spinning from the very moment he had entered the drawing room and laid his eyes upon her at last. Thunderation but she was beautiful. As beautiful as he remembered her to be, though not in the exact proportions. Her eyes were still as dark and glistening and her hair as fiercely red, but where once she had been sleek and sylphlike, now she was possessed of alluring curves, seductive rises, and incredibly inviting valleys.

And she had remembered him with all the passion of a woman possessed. With an odd degree of satisfaction, Mr. Farley saw again the blush rising to her face, the napkin she waved so energetically to cool the flame that had burst into flower within her. She remembered me, berated me and slapped me, he thought, a slow smile crossing his face. But she did not withdraw the living on the spot. Quite likely she simply expects me to give it up. But I will not give it up without she forces me to do so. I have waited near twenty years to make Meredith Cottesmore my bride and I am deuced if I will abandon my only opportunity to do it and scurry back to London with my tail between my legs. I am not such a poltroon as that. No, if she wants me gone she must order me from the place, because I will not take a hint. Not even a hint as broad as the one she laid upon me tonight. Charles Ashbury Hanforth may rise up in his grave and shriek for all I care, but I will have his wife for my bride and I will use every device at my command to have her, too.

"I can see you, Charles, popping right up out of your grave," growled Lady Farnsmoor, turning upon her side beneath the covers and staring across the room at the empty hearth. "Yes, and I can hear you shrieking too. But I had not the least idea that His Grace's Mr. Farley would turn out to be that—that—stripling! But you will have peace again soon," she muttered, turning onto her back. "Eloise is most likely correct. Jason Farley is already on his way back to London."

The vision of Jason Farley riding in the dead of night back to London popped immediately to the forefront of

Lady Farnsmoor's mind. He would ride heavy now, sixteen stone at least. It will take a tall, barrel-chested beast to carry him, thought Lady Farnsmoor. He is no longer the willow-thin, gangly youth I knew. He has most definitely achieved his full growth.

Mr. Farley's straight back and broad shoulders and well-rounded calves, his muscular thighs and arms, had not gone unnoticed either. No more than had his hair which was still the color of autumn leaves and his remarkable eyes that sparkled like living emeralds from between thick dark lashes.

"I have not given him one thought in near twenty years," Lady Farnsmoor whispered into the stillness. "Not one thought. How could that wretched rapscallion have slipped so easily from my mind the moment he left my sight? What a scourge he was to me. What a plague. I am itching to slap him again right this very moment at just the memory of the travail he put me through! And he thinks he shall become my rector? Ha!"

But it is Eloise's fondest wish to be married from St. Agnes, she thought then, woefully. And from what she tells me, the rectory and the church are in terrible condition. There is likely no other cleric will set foot in the place. Why did I never suspect that Charles had let all fall to ruin? I thought merely to open up the church and hold the wedding. What a peagoose I am not to have suspected that after his terrible row with the Reverend Mr. Gorsuch, Charles would not spend one more penny upon St. Agnes. I ought to have known! I ought at least to have gone and inspected the place. Now Eloise will not have her fondest wish and it is all her father's fault. Men! Even two years after they are dead, they make your life miserable!

Eloise will not be married from St. Agnes, Lady Farns-moor thought again soberly. The entire wedding party will need to travel to Crossfields from Twilight Hill. And the tenants and the villagers of Farns Moor, who have known and loved Eloise for all her life, will not be waiting outside the church to sing her and her duke into their carriage.

The thought that the singing would not happen brought the threat of a tear to Lady Farnsmoor's eye. In her little home village of Dusbury the people she had known all her life had sung her and Charles to their carriage. It did not happen everywhere. It was a tradition peculiar to only a few tiny places. And it was a lovely tradition of which she had now deprived Eloise with one slap of her hand. "But Jason Farley is a rogue and a scoundrel," she hissed, "and it is far better that Eloise be disappointed than that *that man* be allowed anywhere near—I am as selfish and pig-headed as Charles!" she gasped suddenly. "I am willing to sacrifice the dearest wish of the daughter I love, the daughter I am about to lose, to my own spleen!" And with a sigh, Lady Farnsmoor made the decision. "I shall send Windemere to the Bull and Butter the very first thing tomorrow," she muttered to herself. "And if Jason Farley has not already gone off to London, I shall summon him to attend me here. And I will keep my temper tucked nicely away and speak to him in the most straightforward manner and we will reach some agreement. I expect I shall be able to put up with the sight of him for little more than a fortnight. And once the wedding is over, I shall never need to see his face again. He cannot possibly hope, now that I have recognized him, to keep the living. Not even Jason Farley can be as audacious as to hope for that."

Eloise was mystified. She tossed and turned between the sheets, her mind awhirl. Who was the Reverend Mr. Jason Farley other than David's cousin and friend? Why should her mama hold the gentleman in such abhorrence? And why should his appearance to officiate at the wedding and to take up the living at Farns Moor send her papa spinning in his grave? Did David know anything at all about it? No, he could not. David had looked just as confused at dinner as she had felt. Really, it was all most intriguing.

"Not that I will ever be granted the least opportunity to learn the truth," she grumbled to herself. "Most likely Mr. Farley is half-way to London by now. And mama will never tell me."

It did occur to Eloise as she lay pondering in the darkness, that mama had admitted that very afternoon that she had fallen out of love with papa. But she was quite certain that that revelation could not equal what must be the truth about Mr. Farley. And while the lack of love between her parents had given Eloise a shock and had made her quite sad for a good hour, still she knew—she absolutely knew— that nothing so appalling could happen to her and David and that her mama's fears were unfounded upon that point. She would love David until the day she died and he would love her equally as long. But now, in the darkness, her mama's words returned to confront her again and they took on quite a new significance.

"Mama fell out of love with Papa and into love with Mr. Farley!" she gasped in sudden enlightenment. "That is why she blushed so heartily when she recognized him at last! He came into her life at the verimost vulnerable moment and took her sobbing into his arms and comforted her and Mama fell in love with him!"

Yes, that must be it, she thought, sitting up in the bed and hugging her knees, pleased with her own sagacity. And Mr. Farley being a noble and honorable gentleman— and a cleric besides—absolutely knew that their love could not be. Mr. Farley, quite rightly and despite his feelings for mama, refused to insert himself between a gentleman and his wife. He refused to have an *affaire* with Mama and most properly took himself off to some distant parish where he was lived in grim despair for years and years just so that Mama might reconcile with Papa. Which she never did. But how could he know? And Mama slapped him because—because—because she still loves him! But Mama thinks he merely took advantage of her all those years ago. She does not realize that Mr. Farley did the only honorable thing and has suffered gravely for his nobility. She believes herself to be the only one who has suffered. She believes he went off and lived his life merry as a grig while all the while she was forced to put up with Papa.

"Oh," sighed Eloise, a haze of romance rising up to encompass her. "And Mr. Farley has returned at last in the hope of ending the anguish of his heart and soul, in the hope of regaining Mama's esteem now that Papa is dead and love between himself and Mama is no longer forbidden."

Three

"More than the church requires attention. The rectory must be made livable again," insisted Mr. Farley for the fifth time. "You cannot actually think, Meredith, that I am going to live for an entire fortnight at the Bull and Butter. It is not going to happen. Either the rectory is restored to its former state or I marry the pair of them at Crossfields. And it will be me who marries them, sweetings, because Weyland will have no one else and your Eloise will insist upon pleasing him."

"How dare you refer to me as sweetings!" exclaimed Lady Farnsmoor, her dark eyes flashing. "I am Lady Farnsmoor to you and my daughter is Lady Eloise."

"Neither here nor there," Mr. Farley replied offhandedly. "We are discussing the rectory."

"And you are taking disgusting advantage of me."

"Yes, I know. But I am not going to live at the Bull and Butter for one day longer than next Sunday. And on next Sunday, I am holding services in St. Agnes, too."

"You? I think not."

"Whether you care to believe it or not, Meredith, I *am* a cleric. And the parishioners of St. Agnes have been forced to abandon their own church long enough. I have not the vaguest idea what Farnsmoor was thinking to leave the living empty and to pay not the least attention to the upkeep of the buildings and the grounds and the glebe, but the neglect is at an end. Your people have every right to their own church and their own rector and well you know it, too."

"And you think that you are going to become their rector?"

"You have not yet rescinded the living."

"Even you cannot be so very stupid as to think that I will allow you to keep it."

"Bishop Mallory instituted me when he received your presentation last week," Mr. Farley stated, his voice growing suddenly quiet as he rose from his chair and began to pace the room. "All that is left to make me rector of St. Agnes of the Moors is to read myself in and ring a few bells. You would not have blinked twice at it, Meredith, if you had not put my face together with my name and come up with a dreadfully unfortunate memory."

Lady Farnsmoor stared up at him, speechless.

"I know what you think of me. I hoped you had ceased to think of me at all after twenty years, but it was not to be. Still I *need* this living, Meredith, and your people need a rector."

"You *need* this living? You? You are the younger brother of the Marquis of Adderleigh. I doubt you stand in need of anything."

"No, not anything one can buy with monies. But a man has other needs. Needs he does not—does not—generally discuss."

It was the most amazing thing! Lady Farnsmoor, who had been about to lose her temper regardless of all her previous good intentions, studied the tall, handsome figure pacing nervously back and forth across the space of her morning room and felt a serious sympathy for him. Ever since he had arrived in answer to her summons this morning, she had not once thought of Jason Farley as a gentleman who stood in need of anything. "What needs?" she asked quietly, setting her temper aside.

"You will laugh," grumbled Mr. Farley, bringing his pacing to a halt before her chair and staring down upon her, a most disturbing light in his wide green eyes. "You will laugh and call me a fool and think I have gone mad besides."

"I thought you mad years ago," murmured Lady Farnsmoor. "Certainly you do not give one fig for that."

"No. But this—this is different. I find I cannot go on, Meredith, as I was used to do. I do not care to be Adderleigh's pampered younger brother. No, nor the supposedly glorious war hero either. There is a thing gnawing away at my vitals."

"What thing?"

"Fear. I call it fear at least. Fear that my life has been meaningless and might well continue to be so. Fear that all the money and fame and glory I have is without the least worth. Fear that when I am dead and buried, Meredith, my having been on this earth will not have made one jot of difference."

Lady Farnsmoor's jaw dropped.

"Just so," muttered Mr. Farley, turning away and stuffing his hands into the pockets of his dove grey breeches. "You think I am mad. But it is there all the same, this great fear gnawing at me day and night. A man cannot ignore such an overwhelming thing. A man cannot simply set it aside and go on with his life as he always did. So five years ago, I took orders. Adderleigh wished to use his influence to secure me any number of prominent positions within the church. He does not understand, you see. At least—I have not told him—but I do not think he would understand."

"You wish to be of service to the poor," murmured Lady Farnsmoor.

"No, not the poor. I wish to be of service to God. And I thought that at last, at long last, I had found a place to begin; a place of my own from where I might reach out to other hearts and soften them and make them see each other as they were meant to be seen, as God meant them to be seen, with understanding and empathy and love. Bah! I have developed a heart of mush, just as Weyland says and a mind of mush as well to think that you might have forgotten me and my indiscretions or if not, that you could be brought to overlook the stupidity of my youth. You win, sweetings. I shall marry your chick to Weyland and be gone the next day. But I will not relent about the rectory. Some cleric will live there and it ought to be restored for him if not for me."

"It is because you do that," exclaimed Lady Farnsmoor, her hands becoming fists upon the chair arm, "that you set my teeth on edge. I am not your sweetings; I am not Meredith to you; I am Lady Farnsmoor!"

"No, you will never be Lady Farnsmoor to me. And I am sorry for it too, because I should like more than anything never to set your teeth on edge again."

Lady Farnsmoor rose and crossed the room to stand beside him where he had paused before a window to stare out into the deer park. "I expect you will always set my teeth on edge. I had not given you one thought for twenty years until last evening and then when I recognized you at last—"

"—the first thing I did was set your back up," finished Mr. Farley for her. "I know."

"You will read yourself in next Sunday," muttered Lady Farnsmoor.

Mr. Farley looked down at her, his eyes sparking with something she did not recognize.

"I shall most likely live to regret it. We will likely be at each other's throats before the end of summer. But I shall attempt civility if you will do likewise. It is not for me to deprive all of Farns Moor of a gentleman who wishes to do them only good."

Lady Farnsmoor in a wide white apron, a rag tied inexpertly about her curls, waved the business end of a broom cautiously at the cobwebs adorning the little parlor of the rectory while the Reverend Mr. Farley, stripped to his shirtsleeves, stood in the little garden beyond the window, his muscles rippling beneath thin muslin in the sun as he beat enthusiastically at the parlor carpet. Dust flew about him in all directions and every so often he was forced to cease his efforts and sneeze loudly. Each sneeze took Lady Farnsmoor's attention away from her task to center her gaze upon him.

This is truly outrageous, Lady Farnsmoor thought, gazing out upon the parson's most recent sneezing fit. *He* is truly outrageous! I must be growing addled with age to have agreed to such a thing. A countess and her daughter and a duke of the realm, too! How could we all have fallen in with such a plan? Of course, it is true that my entire staff is overwhelmed with the preparations for the wedding guests, and that not one of the tenants can spare the time at this moment. Good heavens, even the villagers all had some excuse as to why they could not take on the task until a good month from now. And really, it would be disgraceful to hold Eloise's wedding in such a filthy church and no one could be expected to reside in a rectory covered in dirt and grime and overrun with spiders and rodents, not even Jason Farley. But that he should have the temerity to suggest that *we* do the thing ourselves! What is wrong with the man? And for the duke to agree to it and convince Eloise to do likewise. What could I do? If the duke and my daughter can lower themselves to clean the church, then they must certainly expect me to add my own efforts to the task of making things right.

"Think I am a slacker, do you?" asked Mr. Farley, approaching a window and raising the sash to sit for a moment upon the sill. "I assure I am not, but apparently I cannot beat more than three or four times without sneezing. I begin to think, you know, that you and I have drawn the worst of this bargain. We ought to have chosen the church for our own and set the children to work in here."

"You ought not call them children, Mr. Farley. And none of us had ought to be working in here. Why you cannot reside at the Bull and Butter until someone of the tenants or the villagers are able to apply themselves to this task, I cannot for one moment understand."

"No, I expect you cannot. But that is just the way it is. I cannot do it. It would not be right. If I am to be the rector, then I belong in the rectory, not diddling away my time at the village inn. It would appear quite extraordinary, I assure you."

The Reverend Mr. Farley cocked his eyebrow at her in such a way that it made Lady Farnsmoor quite jittery. Though why it should do so she could not in the least understand. It was merely an eyebrow after all. Everyone had eyebrows. And everyone cocked them this way or that at one time or another too. Still she felt, with a certain amount of shock, a blush rising to her cheeks and her hands tightening considerably upon the broomstick.

"I say," drawled Mr. Farley, "you are not intending to hit me with that broom are you, Meredith? The way you are clutching it is most intimidating. I do thank you, you know, for lowering yourself to such a task as this. And I admire you as well—extremely much—because I know you are doing it for someone who is most undeserving of your effort."

"Well," gulped Lady Farnsmoor, "well, that is not so, Mr. Farley. Even you deserve to live in a place free of dirt and bugs and mice."

"Even I?" grinned Mr. Farley.

"Yes, no, I did not mean it precisely in that way."

"No, of course you did not. You have been everything kind since once you agreed I was to keep the living and I am a beast for teasing you."

"Teasing me? Is that what you are doing?"

"Indeed. And it is unforgivable of me to do it, but I cannot resist. You look so very—homely—in your old round gown with a rag tied about your curls. I could almost think you one of the cottagers making her home cozy for her husband and not a countess at all. You are so very comfortable looking when all your consequence has been tossed to the far winds."

"Comfortable looking? My consequence tossed to the far winds? I will have you know, Mr. Farley, that—oh, you are teasing me again, are you not?"

"The merest bit." The gentleness of Mr. Farley's tone caused Lady Farnsmoor to gaze up at him in the most confused way, her wonderful black eyes filled with questions and doubt. Mr. Farley's heart ached to see them so. *She would not look like such a frightened little deer if I had carried her off to Gretna Green and married her as I planned,* he thought with some asperity. "You have a smudge," he said then and tugging his handkerchief from his pocket, he gave it a lick and applied it gently to the tip of Lady Farnsmoor's pert little upturned nose.

It was the oddest sensation. Lady Farnsmoor had never felt anything quite like it in all of her thirty-eight years. "I—

I expect I have more than one smudge,'' she murmured, overwhelmed.

"You are a perfect treasure, my lady, to allow me to keep this living. And to actually come and help me with this rectory is beyond anything kind.''

"Well, and it is kind of you not to have run off to London after I—after our dinner last evening. Eloise wishes more than anything else to be married from St. Agnes.''

"And she will be. I promise you. Married in the finest style a parson can manage and sent on her way with songs of joy.''

"You know about the singing?''

"Yes. I came once to a wedding here. But that was years and years ago. It was a sergeant of mine married a girl from the village. Dorothea was her name.''

"Dorothea Manford? The potter's daughter?''

"Yes, now that you mention it, I do believe that her father was a potter.''

"He is still a potter. He sells his wares in the square on market days. I had no idea you had ever been to Farns Moor.''

"Only that once. Only because it was Sergeant Thompson. He was my batman, you see, and we were close friends. He saved my life once, in fact. And a bit later I returned him the favor.''

"You *were* in the army. I thought you had gone to be a soldier.''

"I ran off to join the cavalry, yes. The very day your wedding announcement appeared in *The Times* as a matter of fact.''

"The day my—''

The small vertical line between Lady Farnsmoor's eyebrows deepened and Mr. Farley knew he had said exactly the wrong thing. "But that is neither here nor there,'' he interrupted her thoughts quickly. And then he smiled his most charming smile and saying, "if you will permit me," and licking his handkerchief again, he scrubbed gently at another smudge, this one upon one of Lady Farnsmoor's work-rosy cheeks.

"Kindly cease your laughter, Eloise, and help me up," drawled the Duke of Weyland in his most aloof tone.

"I—I—" Eloise could not begin the sentence much less finish it, so very hard was she laughing.

Her eyes sparkled and her cheeks glowed and her short red curls floated out from under the most becoming little mob cap with the most adorable ruffles. Really, thought Weyland, his bottom growing wetter by the moment as he sat, legs outstretched, in a puddle of water from his overturned bucket. Really, she is the most amazing creature. I have not heard one angry word or had one sour glance from her all morning despite how foreign all this scrubbing and polishing must be to her. "How lucky I am to have discovered her," the duke murmured to himself.

"What?" asked Eloise, subduing her laughter into mere chuckles and crossing through the row of pews to him. "I did not hear what you said, David."

"I love to hear my name upon your lips."

"David," repeated Eloise promptly. "Do you think we shall truly be married in less than a fortnight?"

"Of course. Why would we not?" He took the hand she extended to him and let her help him to his feet.

"Because we shall never get this church clean in time. I have not the least doubt that on the very morning of the twenty-third of June, you and I shall be inside this place in our wedding clothes polishing the pews."

"No, do you think so?"

"It is quite likely if you do not cease to play about in the water rather than scrub with it."

"Unfair, Eloise. I slipped."

"Yes, so I heard."

"You ought not be doing this," Weyland murmured then, one finger playing with a ruffle on Eloise's cap. "You are the daughter of an earl, not a chamber maid."

"And you, sir, are a duke."

"Yes, but Jason is my best friend and my cousin besides."

"And there is no one else to help him," completed Eloise with a thoughtful gaze at her intended. "I cannot think *why* there is no one else to help him. Certainly the staff at Twilight Hill cannot, but the tenants and the villagers cannot all be so very busy."

"But they are. Extremely busy. We asked about, you know. Your mama even sent footmen out to beg for assistance."

"Yes, and everyone declined. That is what I do not understand. I know for a fact, David, that everyone is not overwhelmed with other work. Why is it they would not come? They cannot possibly dislike Mr. Farley. They do not even know the man as yet."

"Well, it turns out that some of them do know Jason," sighed the duke. "I thought I could keep up with this Banbury story of my cousin's but I cannot. I find I cannot lie to you, my dear. I have just discovered in the last few days what a devious devil Jason Farley can be when he is determined to have his way."

"David, whatever are you talking about?"

"About a potter named Manford and myself and Jason. We spent an entire day riding about the village and the farm lands, not asking for assistance, but begging everyone not to offer us their aid. And by the time your mama sent her footmen out to request people to help us, they had already promised not to do so."

Eloise was flabbergasted. "You did what? But why?"

"Well, it is all part of Jason's plan. I cannot explain the

108 *Judith A. Lansdowne*

whole of it, Eloise, because I do not understand it all. But you already know that your mother and Jay are known to each other."

"Yes. I did notice that first evening at dinner that they were not perfect strangers," nodded Eloise, tongue in cheek and eyes glistening with laughter.

"Exactly so. And though I still do not have the story myself about why she slapped him, I do happen to know that Jason is in love with your mama."

Eloise stared at the duke dumbfounded. She had been correct in her musings. Oh, it was all too romantic to be believed!

"I, myself, thought we should be riding back to London that very night," continued the duke, "but Jay would have none of it. And the very next morning after he had spoken with your mama, he came riding back to the inn in ecstasy. 'I have the living,' he said. 'She'll not take it back from me. And I have just thought how to make the wretched state of that rectory and church work in my favor.' And then he rushed me into the saddle and took me pounding upon this potter's door, and off the three of us rode to beg everyone not to help us. All of our scrubbing and cleaning and polishing in this church is part of a devious plot for Jay to keep you mama alone with him in the rectory and win her heart. It is the strangest way to go about courting a lady that I ever heard—forcing a broom into her hand and a rag about her curls—but who am I to gainsay the man? He, after all, is the one who has worn the willow for her for twenty years."

Four

Bottswell mumbled over the state of the duke's clothing and cast an accusing eye upon that gentleman as he stood before the looking glass in the midst of tying his cravat.

"What, Bottswell?"

"If you persist in returning to this inn in such a state, Your Grace, you will run out of clothing before the end of the week. There is little to be done with these but consign them to a fire."

"Yes, I expect you're right, Bottswell. And no one else departed the place in any better stead. Eloise's dress was a wretched mess and from what I saw of Lady Farnsmoor—covered in cobwebs she was from head to toe. You were extremely lucky to be playing ill, Bottswell, or it might have been you sitting upon that stone floor soaking in dirty water and covered in a considerable amount of mud."

Bottswell flushed guiltily. "I—you did say that I was not to accompany you, Your Grace."

"Yes, I did say that, but you will tomorrow. Because tomorrow, while Mr. Farley and the countess and Lady

Eloise and I continue our ablutions of the church and the rectory, you and Lady Eloise's abigail must search through the attics at Twilight Hill and discover what furniture lies in them that may be of use in the rectory. Hopefully you will find a mattress that has not been nested in by mice because the one presently upon the bed in the parsonage has seen innumerable litters of the little beasts."

"It is not at all my business, Your Grace," began Bottswell, brushing a piece of lint from the back of the duke's jacket, "but can you not use your considerable influence to procure Mr. Farley a more prominent living than—than—this mouse-ridden rectory and abandoned church? Surely he is worthy of—"

"He is worthy of St. Paul's, London, Bottswell. But he does not care for St. Paul's. He has assured me that this is where his heart's desire lies."

"I cannot think what has got into him."

"Love, Bottswell, has got into him."

"Love, Your Grace?" The valet's usually placid countenance began to glow with pleasure.

The duke, abruptly recalling that at one point in his many years of service Bottswell had been groom of the bedchamber to the old Marquis of Adderleigh, spun about to face his valet squarely. "Bottswell, do you know what occurred between Jay and a Miss Cottesmore years and years ago?"

"Miss Cottesmore? Miss Cottesmore is here? Great heavens!"

"You do know! Tell me, Bottswell—"

"If you so much as mumble one word, Bottswell, I will see you flogged on the steps of St. Paul's," interrupted Mr. Farley, poking his head into the room. "When I decide it is time to inform His Grace of the intimacies of my love life, I shall do the informing myself. I am sorry to be a bother, but I cannot seem to get into this deuced jacket without a bit of help."

"I shall come at once, sir," nodded Bottswell readily. "If I may, Your Grace."

"Yes, yes, go and help him. We have not eaten since breakfast and I am rapidly becoming ravenous."

Bottswell, with a slight bow, followed Mr. Farley across the corridor and into the parson's chamber where he helped that gentleman ease into a coat of midnight blue Superfine that had to be urged very gently over broad shoulders.

"Is it true, Master Jason?"

"Is what true, Bottswell?"

"That your Miss Cottesmore lives somewhere near to hand."

"She lives extremely near to hand. We have been invited to dine with her tonight as a matter of fact."

"Lady Farnsmoor? Miss Cottesmore is Lady Farnsmoor?" gasped Bottswell. "And you came upon her without giving her the least warning? It is no wonder she slapped your face on Monday night."

"Yes, well, I did hope that she would not recognize me, Bottswell, but then, of course, she did. We have got by that now however, and I have convinced her, I think, that I am not a buffleheaded halfling any longer. And when she sees I have grown out of all my freakish starts and am become a respectable gentleman, I dare say she will be inclined to forgive me the past entirely and in time may be brought to listen to my hopes for the future. How do I look?"

"Like a most respectable gentleman," smiled Bottswell, "and not at all like a buffleheaded halfling."

Lady Farnsmoor could not keep her eyes from him. Her heart wobbled the merest bit when he spoke and though she attempted time and time again to focus her attention upon the duke and Eloise, she was incapable of doing so. His hair glistened in the candle light and curled carelessly down over his wide brow, and his fine emerald eyes sparkled with intelligence and good humor, and each time he gazed her way, his incredibly interesting face crinkled into a smile that set her pulses to pounding. Never had Lady Farnsmoor been more disturbed by the mere presence of a gentleman at her dinner table.

I am putting up with the scoundrel merely because I have developed a sympathy for him, she told herself when he glanced at her over the trout and she felt her cheeks grow warm.

One misstep upon his part, the least indication that his reasons for acquiring this living are a sham and out he goes on his ear, she reflected when he spoke to her over the roast beef and she heard herself giggle like a schoolgirl in reply.

I must remember that he is *Jason Farley.* I must never forget, she warned herself as he lifted his glass to her with the arrival of the syllabub and she realized that she was lowering her eyes in the most disconcerted fashion.

Great heavens! I am the Countess of Farnsmoor and the mother of his benefactor and he is but a cleric. His living here depends upon my beneficence and he knows it to be so. Certainly he cannot be flirting with me. He dare not. I will part his hair with a carving knife if he does.

"You are looking most pensive," Mr. Farley's soft, pleasing voice interrupted her thoughts. "Are you feeling a sight more easy about your daughter's coming nuptials?"

"What? Oh, yes. Yes, I expect I am," murmured Lady Farnsmoor, and then she frowned. "How on earth do you come to know that I feel uneasy about the wedding? I did never say a word to you."

"I merely guessed. I expect you did not wish Eloise to marry at all, did you?"

"Mr. Farley, I cannot see that my feelings in regard to this marriage are of the least concern to you."

"Your feelings will always be of concern to me, Meredith. And it cannot be easy to lose your only daughter to a gentleman, any gentleman. Especially when—well—never mind that."

"Especially when what?"

"Nothing."

"Especially when what? Speak up, Mr. Farley," sputtered Lady Farnsmoor. "I should like to know what you were about to say."

Mr. Farley shrugged his broad shoulders and shook his head slowly. "I was about to say, especially when one has been married to a man like Farnsmoor for most of twenty years. But I did stop myself. You must admit that I did. It is only at your insistence that I complete the thought."

"Of all the impudent, cheeky, presumptuous things to say!"

"I know. That is precisely why I halted in the midst of it. But it could not have been easy for you, my dear, being married to Farnsmoor. And such a relationship as you must have endured must needs make you fearful for your daughter."

Lady Farnsmoor did not know whether to stalk from the table in righteous wrath, to order Mr. Farley gone from her sight, or to slap his face for him once again. "Of all the—of all the—I will have you know, sir, that my marriage was everything proper and joyous," she proclaimed in such a voice that Eloise and the duke could not help but hear."

"Oh, Mama, what a bouncer!" exclaimed Eloise from down the table. "Why you told me only Monday that the most considerate thing papa ever did for you was to fall and break his neck."

The two footmen in attendance reddened considerably, their cheeks puffing out with guffaws they dare not release. The Duke of Weyland hastily applied his napkin to his lips to hide a wide grin. Lady Farnsmoor glared at Eloise while Mr. Farley bestowed upon the young lady a most charming smile and then helped himself to a sip of wine.

"I think we ought to leave them to themselves," the duke whispered as he followed Eloise into the withdrawing room, both he and Mr. Farley having declined to remain at table with a bottle between them once the meal was completed. "Let us settle at the pianoforte. If you play loudly enough, they will think we are not paying them the least attention and feel free to scrap with each other as much as need be."

"But why must they argue at all?" asked Eloise sweetly, following Weyland's lead and taking a seat upon the piano stool. "They are in love with one another."

"Yes, but your mama don't know it."

Eloise looked up at him. "She does not?"

"No, I do not think so."

"Oh dear."

"Just so. Here, this is a rousing number," the duke proclaimed, setting a piece of sheet music before her.

"But ought I not to play something romantic? To put Mama into a better mood?"

"No, you ought to play something energetic and loud. Very loud," grinned Weyland, "because Jason has set your mama's back up and he is about to do it again. I can tell from the tilt of his lips and the way he has just crossed one knee over the other."

"Loud then," agreed Eloise, striking the first chord of the chosen composition with great enthusiasm.

"Great heavens," muttered Lady Farnsmoor. "What is the child thinking to play as though we are all quite deaf?"

"Weyland's idea most likely," responded Mr. Farley. "If I know my cousin, he expects there to be another row between the two of us at any moment. Is there going to be another row between us?"

"I—I don't know. Are you going to say something utterly audacious again?"

"No. That is, I hope I am not. I am greatly in your debt, Meredith. You know I am, and I have not the least wish to plague you about anything."

"I wish you will remember that," sighed Lady Farnsmoor, smoothing the skirt of her delightful forest green gown. "I ought to have sent you packing the moment I recognized you, you know."

"I know. I did never find an opportunity to apologize to you for all the nonsense I put you through all those years ago, Meredith. Let me apologize now. I was a mere stripling and quite bowled over by you. You were everything I ever thought to dream of in a woman and I was hopelessly in love."

Lady Farnsmoor glanced at him in disbelief. "Love? Never say it. You were set upon plaguing the life out of me."

"Only because I loved you and wished you to take notice of me."

"I could not help but take notice of you, you villain. You were everywhere I went."

"I was, was I not?" laughed Mr. Farley.

"It was not at all amusing."

"Come, Meredith, perhaps it was not then, but after all this time? How can you not think it humorous that I made a perfect spectacle of myself by standing upon the bench in the pit at Drury Lane gushing poetry up at you in Farnsmoor's box?"

"Is that what you were doing? Reciting poetry? I did not hear a word of it. I only thought you quite mad balancing there and waving your arms all about like a monkey with fleas."

"You did not hear a word? What a pity, and it was such dreadful poetry too! I think I compared you to a sweet pansy amongst weeds or some such thing."

Lady Farnsmoor smiled a bit. "You did it over and over again, at Drury Lane, at the opera house, at Covent Garden. Charles wished nothing more than to rush down there and strangle you."

"I can imagine. But you prevented him from doing so?"

"Yes, though I cannot think why. I should like to have seen you strangled before my eyes."

Mr. Farley grinned so boyishly at her words that Lady Farnsmoor's heart skipped a beat and she lowered her eyes in consternation. Really, she could not understand why this gentleman affected her so. Yet he had always affected her in one way or another. He had never been a person she could merely ignore—though she had attempted to ignore him time and time again.

"Come, cry *pax*, Meredith," he urged now, one finger gently tickling her chin to get her to meet his eyes. "I admit I was wretched and you admit I was wretched as well. We are in agreement upon it."

"Remove your finger from beneath my chin this instant!" sputtered Lady Farnsmoor, grabbing at the offending digit and giving it a twist.

"Ouch!"

"How dare you to touch me in such a way! How dare you to touch me in any way!"

"Ouch," muttered Mr. Farley again, staring at his finger.

"You will say more than ouch if you cross such boundaries again, Jason Farley. Is that any way for a parson to behave? And after all you said to me about your new purpose in life and wishing to serve God. I am quite certain that service to God does not include tickling my chin to get me to look at you."

"No, it does not!" growled Mr. Farley, rising. "And I shall remember that in future, believe me. Damnation, Meredith, but you are the most—the most—"

"The most what?"

"The most unseeing woman I believe I have ever met."

"Unseeing? And just what do you mean by that? I see perfectly well, Mr. Farley. I see everything."

"No, not everything," mumbled Mr. Farley with a shake of his head. "Barely anything at all."

She had not sent him out into the night with a sneer and a rigidly pointing finger, and she was very glad that she had not. Lady Farnsmoor sat before the looking glass in her nightgown, brushing languidly at her hair. Truly, she thought, I do have the most vile temper of late. Well, perhaps not just of late. I have always had a vile temper. But it grows much more unmanageable the closer this wedding comes. I am jittery is all. Once the guests have arrived and all is in order, I will be much more the thing. Though I do feel quite sorry for Mr. Farley. I do believe I am taking every worry I have out upon that poor gentleman.

"Poor gentleman," she whispered, gazing at herself in the looking glass, a smile twitching at her lips. "What an absurdity to refer to Jason Farley as a 'poor gentleman.' He has never been poor in his life and he is a gentleman only by birth. Though he does appear to be attempting to act a gentleman these days. He is not very good at it but I must admit that at least he is attempting the thing." With a soft sigh, Lady Farnsmoor set her brush aside, rose and wandered into her bedchamber.

The truth was that, despite her wrenching of his finger, Mr. Farley had remained in conversation with her until tea was served. And he had put any number of her concerns for Eloise to rest. He had, in fact, convinced her that the Duke of Weyland and her daughter were truly in love and likely to remain so forever. He had avoided any further reference to her own misbegotten marriage and yet pointed out all the positive signs in favor of Eloise's future happiness, not the least of which was the manner in which the young couple had survived an entire day of cleaning and scrubbing and generally getting in each other's way in the church.

"And not one complaint or tantrum or sign of anger from either of them," he had said with satisfaction. "No better way to tell how a team will go on together than to throw them into double harness and make them work. And we did that today, Meredith. And just look at them. They are as pleased with each other as ever they were. How can you ask to know more than that? When they are able to perform unexpected and completely foreign tasks which are most definitely beneath them, and still they smile and laugh and cannot seem to have enough of each other's company, one can only draw the conclusion that they were meant to be joined."

I did not think of that at all, she told herself, as she settled between the sheets. I did not give it one thought. Thank goodness Mr. Farley pointed it out to me. I feel so much better about it now. If only someone had put Charles and myself into a similar situation, I would have known— I would have known that—no, I will not think upon it and make myself sad. I will not! I have not been so content in years as I am tonight and I will not allow thoughts of Charles to ruin it for me.

"But Jason Farley is still the most impertinent, presumptuous, cheeky person I have ever known," she added in a

whisper. "And if he does not cease to refer to me as Meredith, I shall—I shall—I shall begin calling him Jason, that
is what I shall do. I shall give him back tit for tat. He will
not like me to be free of his given name before the entire
parish when he hopes to gain their respect and impress
them with his abilities as a rector. Yes, that is exactly what
I shall do, and he will undoubtedly realize how I feel when
he does it to me and cease immediately.

"The thing of it is, Duke," muttered Mr. Farley over a
glass of brandy in the inn's public room, "that every time
I think I am finally turning the lady up sweet, I do or say
something to make her despise me again."

"No, never say so," replied Weyland, leaning far back
in his chair. "My mama-in-law-elect does not despise you."

"She does not? Has she told you so?"

"No. She has not said one word about you to me."

"Oh. Eloise? Has Eloise said—"

"As far as I know, she has not said one word about you
to Eloise either. No, I am certain she has not. Eloise would
have mentioned it to me. Come, Jay, do not look so very
mournful, eh? She smiled upon you when you departed."

"Because she was pleased to have me go."

"Perhaps if you behaved toward her with just a bit more
deference."

"Toadeat her, you mean?"

"No, not at all. But I must tell you, Jay, that rarely if
ever have I heard any cleric refer to his patron's mama by
her given name. It ain't done. Nor have I ever noticed a
parson tickle his patron's mama under her chin. Do not
raise your eyebrow at me. Of course Eloise and I were
watching. What did you expect of us? We are both anxious
to see how you will bring Lady Farnsmoor around."

"I shall bring her around. You may count upon it."

"Oh, I do. We both do. Do you know, Jay, it might be of some help if you were to meet little Charlie and win him to your side. He is top of the trees with his mama."

"Well, I intend to do that," sighed Mr. Farley as if anyone with a mind would know his intentions had been such. "I am not a perfect nodcock. But I doubt Meredith will allow me to set eyes upon the fledgling. She has not once suggested that I ought to make the rascal's acquaintance. The fact of the matter is, Duke, I expect she has given the boy's nurse a blunderbuss and convinced her to stand guard over him from morn till night, just in case I should somehow discover my way up to the nursery."

Weyland chuckled and the sound of it lit a spark in Mr. Farley's most speaking eyes.

"What? What are you laughing about?"

"You and Lady Farnsmoor. I cannot for the life of me guess what went on all those years ago to set her against you with such a passion, Jay. Nor I cannot guess why you are so set upon having the woman. You do never appear to do anything but rub each other raw when you are together. I will lay you odds that when the two of you first met, Cupid was totally befogged with Blue Ruin and shooting those little arrows of his at anything that moved."

Five

Eloise sighed and fell upon the flowered settee in a most unladylike manner. "At last we are done, Mama. We have cleaned and scrubbed and polished for four whole days. Are you not exhausted?"

"No. I do not know what it can be, but I feel younger than I have in years. The rectory is looking much better, do not you think? And the furniture from the attics is just the thing. Mr. Farley has a rectory of which he can be proud."

"And a church of which he can be proud too," nodded Eloise. "David leaves tonight for London. He will meet his mama there and escort her to Twilight Hill on Wednesday, he says."

"Yes, and Mrs. Grimshaw has agreed to become house-keeper-cook at the rectory and will begin by making Mr. Farley's dinner for him this very evening. We shall have an early dinner in the nursery with Charlie, shall we, Eloise?"

"Oh, yes, Mama. That is a splendid idea. I have missed the little ruffian these past few days."

"Mr. Farley has been asking to meet Charlie. I expect that is quite proper. Charles is his benefactor after all, not I. I shall take him to services tomorrow and introduce the two of them then. It will be nice, Eloise, not to be forced to ride all the way to Crossfields every Sunday. It will be very nice."

"And you will not mind that Mr. Farley will be preaching?"

"Mind? Whyever should I mind?"

"Because you are always angry with him, Mama."

"No," mused Lady Farnsmoor, "not always. Less and less, in fact. He has been on his good behavior of late. Why, not once today did he say or do anything at all cheeky."

Eloise could not help but laugh, but she was highly surprised when her mama laughed right along with her.

"Mama, will you not tell me about Mr. Farley? It is no secret that you were known to each other before he ever appeared in our drawing room."

"Known to each other? Oh, yes. Everywhere I went in my third Season, there the scoundrel was. I could not be shed of him. We met first at a card party at his brother's town house. And from that day on, he scampered after me like a puppy dog, always under foot, always tugging at my skirts. And when your papa began to develop a decided interest in me, Jason Farley did everything he could think to annoy me to pieces."

"He did, Mama?"

"Yes indeed."

"Oh."

"Oh?"

"I just thought—that is to say, Mama—I thought perhaps you and Mr. Farley had—were—that there may have been some bond between you at one time."

"Oh, there was a bond between us. He was set upon

plaguing the life out of me and I was set upon murdering him.''

"You did not—you never loved him?''

"Loved him? Jason Farley? Whatever put such a notion into your head? I was twenty-one and a Diamond of the First Water, a Belle who had reigned supreme for three years, and he was a mere child. Why he could not have been more than seventeen.''

"He was sixteen, Mama. He told David so.''

"Ha! Sixteen! No wonder he was such a dolt!''

Flowers filled the little church in the middle of Farns Moor village on Sunday morning. Vases and jars and jugs of flowers stood in every possible place, making the inside of the old stone building brighter and warmer and more colorful than the outside. Lady Farnsmoor could not imagine why every villager and tenant and even the servants at Twilight Hill had taken it in mind to welcome the new parson with such a show of enthusiasm. "Are they all so very grateful that they need not travel to Crossfields any longer that they have plundered the gardens in celebration, Eloise?'' she whispered.

"Perhaps," replied Eloise softly, though she suspected that the flowers had appeared in a massive outpouring of guilt on the part of the people who ought to have volunteered to clean up the church and the rectory but had not. Of course, she reminded herself silently, the rector himself had begged them *not* to help.

"Charlie, do be still,'' Lady Farnsmoor murmured, putting an arm around the little boy who wiggled and bounced upon the pew beside her. "The Reverend Mr. Farley will be most distracted to see you leaping about right before his eyes and he will likely forget everything he means to say. You are a big boy now and must learn to sit still in church.''

"I am sittin' still," declared the Earl of Farnsmoor with a most petulant look in his great dark eyes and a voice that carried all the way to the very rear of the chancel and through the entire nave. "It is Donald makin' all the ruckus."

"Donald?" Lady Farnsmoor stared down at her little gentleman with a most bewildered expression; Eloise turned her head toward him and smiled widely. The entire Sommers family and Mr. and Mrs. Terrance and Granny Kitchen and Livvy Hill and old Mr. Faber and his sons and indeed the remainder of the occupants of the various pews continued to stare reverently straight ahead, but their lips rose upward and their eyes glowed as they sought to catch her ladyship's response.

"Who is Donald?" Lady Farnsmoor asked, glancing about. "I see no one here beside me, Charles, but your sister and yourself."

"Yes, Donald!" declared the earl with a shake of his curls. "He is invis'ble and he is actin' up somethin' awful! He is right there, Mama, an' he is pokin' at me an' will not stop."

Lady Farnsmoor was about to suggest that the invisible Donald had best cease his poking or both he and little Lord Farnsmoor would find themselves out in the carriage in nurse's custody when Reverend Mr. Farley entered the chancel and strolled with a rather admirable nonchalance to the pulpit. "Good morning to you," he said with a most captivating smile. "I am the Reverend Mr. Farley and I should like to welcome all of you back to St. Agnes of the Moors, including you, Master Donald, though I shall be forced to make you come up here and stand beside me through the entire service if you do not cease poking at Lord Farnsmoor this very moment."

Little Charles, who was in the midst of squiggling across to the very end of the pew, froze and stared up at the gentleman.

Mr. Farley, his emerald eyes alight, stared a bit to his lordship's right. "Now that is much more the thing, Donald," he said nodding. "Just right and nicely done too. Now we can begin."

Eloise found it all she could do to contain her laughter. Her brother sat through the reading-in entirely agog, his eyes never leaving the rector. And when, in the midst of his sermon, Mr. Farley took leave to comment upon the pleasure he would have in coming to know each and every one of his parishoners, visible and invisible, and he smiled charmingly in Charlie's direction, Eloise was forced to stifle a full-blown giggle by clapping her hand over her mouth. She then glanced tentatively to the side to see what reaction the whimsical words had drawn from her mother and discovered Lady Farnsmoor fanning herself vigorously with her prayer book, her cheeks blooming like wild roses.

"I cannot think what came over me," sighed Lady Farnsmoor as she and Eloise sat alone in the north parlor that evening, she at her embroidery and Eloise gazing dreamily into the dusk beyond the window. "He was so very kind, really. Any number of clergymen would have glared at Charlie until we were all of us squirming in our seats. And did you see how Charles grinned from ear to ear when Mr. Farley bid him good day at the church door and called both Charlie and Donald inveterate young scoundrels? Why, I thought Charles would pop his buttons, his little chest puffed out so."

"Yes, and Charlie was even more impressed when Mr. Farley reached down and shook Donald's hand so heartily. I thought I should choke to death on my own laughter,

Mama. And yet, I could not laugh and make Charlie feel any less than extraordinary, which he did feel. Everyone could tell it."

"Indeed. He was so very proud of himself and so agog that someone as grown-up as Mr. Farley was quite willing to pretend with him in front of everyone in the parish that there really was an invisible Donald. I should never have thought it of Mr. Farley."

"Never have thought what of him, Mama?"

"Why, that he would be so ready to lend himself to the games of a three-year-old. Though why I did not, now that I come to think on it, I cannot say. He is likely the most whimsical gentleman I have ever known."

"He is, Mama?"

"Quite. I never did appreciate whimsy—not until today."

Eloise's eyebrows rose the slightest bit and she turned her gaze from the twilight beyond the window to her mama's face. "Was there nothing about Mr. Farley that you liked, Mama, when you were young? Did he never do anything to please you?"

Lady Farnsmoor was about to declare that he never did, when she halted with parted lips and her eyes grew most gentle. "Yes," she murmured then. "He pleased me exceedingly once."

"How, Mama?"

"I had a dog," murmured Lady Farnsmoor, remembering. "A little pug named Titus. He was the dearest thing. I loved him with all my heart. But one day, he escaped the house as I was leaving with your papa to drive in the park. And he came barking after me. And—and—your papa would not stop for him, and another carriage hit him in the street."

"Oh, Mama!"

"I was looking back over my shoulder and I saw it happen

and I begged and begged your papa to stop and go back, but he said that Titus was merely a dog and an ill-behaved one at that and he would buy me another and he drove on."

"Mama! How could he!"

"Gentlemen are not like ladies. They seldom conceive an affection for dogs—unless they are excellent hunters of course. And poor Titus did not hunt at all. Well, I cried all the way to the park and all through the Promenade, and finally your papa grew so very tired of my tears that he turned around and took me home. I looked for Titus everywhere. I thought to bury him, you see. But someone had already removed him from the gutter into which he'd been thrown."

"And that someone was Mr. Farley?"

"Indeed. He appeared upon my doorstep the very next day. I was amazed that Gilding admitted him, because he had standing orders to refuse Mr. Farley. But before I could so much as blink, Mr. Farley was standing before me with a wicker basket upon his arm. And he bowed and presented it to me. And inside, nestled warmly amongst any number of Mr. Farley's neckcloths was my Titus. Oh, he had a bandage wound 'round his little head and a splint upon one of his forelegs, but he gazed up at me and wagged his little tail ecstatically. I was so very happy."

"What did you say, Mama, to Mr. Farley?"

"Why I said thank you and he said I was welcome and then he called your papa an unfeeling wretch with not a thought in his brain box for anything or anyone but himself. And I—"

"You what, Mama?"

"I slapped him. Well, he was quite out of line to disparage the gentleman I loved—the gentleman I thought I loved—right in my own parlor."

"Oh, Mama," laughed Eloise. "I am amazed Mr. Farley

does not cringe in fear every time he sets his eyes upon you."

The Reverend Mr. Farley paced back and forth across the rectory parlor, his hands clasped behind his back. His dinner sat cold and untouched upon a small table beside a brocade wing chair recently retrieved from the Twilight Hill attics.

"And now what am I to do?" he mumbled, glowering down at the flowered carpeting. "Not only do I love Meredith and find her daughter delightful but now Charlie, despite the man who sired him, proves to be a most engaging rascal. If I spend any time at all in his presence, I am bound to lose my heart to him too. It is not at all fair," he growled, glancing upward. "I have prayed for years to have another opportunity with Meredith Cottesmore, and what do You do but provide it in a most aggravating fashion—and increase the stakes besides. Is it not hard enough that my heart cannot be whole without a lady who thinks me a dastardly villain? Must I now chance giving what is left of it to a sweet young bride and a regular rapscallion of a boy and run the risk of losing them too? There will be nothing left of me if I fail. I warn You of that."

He spun on his heel when he reached the windows that overlooked the garden and paced back again, muttering all the way. "There will be no Reverend Mr. Farley left for You to order about if Meredith will not have me. And You will regret that. I warn You so. I am a tremendously good parson. I am a better parson than I was a cavalryman and I was a damnably good cavalryman," he added as he came to halt at the hearth and rested his arm along the mantelpiece. "And I would make an even better husband and father than I do a cleric. You know I would! Why will You not help me? What is it I have done that I deserve to have my heart torn to bloody shreds again?"

Frustration flowed through every vein in Mr. Farley's body. I have done *nothing* wrong, he thought angrily. I have been loyal and steadfast and true to You and to Meredith. And I will be likewise to her son and daughter both. "I am not like that scoundrel Farnsmoor. My God, she suffered through seventeen years of marriage to that selfish boor," he shouted, pounding his fist upon the mantel. "She deserves to be well and truly loved! She deserves to be loved by me!" At which point the mantel trembled, then gave way and toppled to the floor.

"Oh, devil it!" shouted the parson, staring down at the enormous piece of carved oak that had barely missed his toes. "Is everything in my life to go to wrack and ruin just like this confounded rectory? Why will You not give me the least help? I can make life wonderful for Meredith and for Charlie, just as wonderful as Eloise's life will be with David. What the deuce?"

Mr. Farley's gaze had lifted from the fallen mantel to the one brace that remained upon the wall. On the thin, flat surface of it a small brown mouse sat wiggling its whiskers and twitching its nose inquiringly at him.

"Now where the devil did you come from and why do you not skitter away this very moment? I am speaking to you, sir," he added, a smile stealing slowly across his countenance.

The mouse sat upon its haunches and began to rub at its nose with its forepaws.

"You are very forward for a mouse," smiled the parson.

"Tch," the mouse replied, ceasing its ablutions to blink uncomprehendingly at the parson. "Tch-eek snipf."

"Yes, well, and I thought we had discouraged the lot of you from attempting to remain inside this parsonage. Obviously you, sir, did not take the hint."

The mouse grinned a perfectly charming mouse grin at him. And then, with what Mr. Farley observed to be a tiny mouse bow, he turned about and scampered into a small hole that apparently led down into the wall behind the brace.

"Devil," murmured Mr. Farley, crossing to fetch the candelabra from the table beside his chair and going to study the remaining brace more closely. "What a remarkable place to think to build one's house. We did none of us think to look for a hole to stop up beneath the mantel. Not even Bottswell. And how nicely done it is, too. I must show it to Meredith."

And then a most preposterous idea occurred inside Mr. Farley's brain and he began to laugh. "God," he asked, laughing upward at the freshly dusted ceiling, "is this Your idea or mine?"

Lady Farnsmoor gazed with some perplexity at the bare wall above the hearth in the rectory parlor. "But where has the mantel gone?" she asked in barely a whisper. "Is this why you bid me come, Mr. Farley?"

"No, not actually. That is, it is merely part of the reason. It fell from its moorings on Sunday night, but it is what I discovered after it fell that I wished you to see. Do me the honor to be seated. He has not arrived as yet, but he will."

"Of whom do you speak, Mr. Farley?"

"Oh, you will discover that soon enough." Mr. Farley, with a wisp of a smile, led Lady Farnsmoor to the flowered settee that years ago had adorned her own morning room and now stood before his parlor windows and settled her comfortably upon it, then sat down directly beside her, an action which sent her hands to fluttering about in her lap.

Must he sit so close? she wondered, unconsciously pleating the material of her skirt. Surely he would be more comfortable in that old wing chair.

"I am quite happy that you asked me to visit," she murmured, her breath coming awkwardly, in short gasps. What was wrong with her of late? "I did mean to stop in and thank you for your kindness to Charlie on Sunday."

"My kindness?"

"You know very well of what I speak."

"Donald?" asked Mr. Farley with a grin. "Oh, you should not thank me for accepting Donald into the parish. I am very glad to have every parishioner I can get."

Lady Farnsmoor smiled. How like him, she thought, to make a joke of it. And then she wondered why she thought it like him at all. It occurred to her quite forcefully that she had not the least idea what Mr. Farley was truly like. She only remembered how he had seemed to be twenty years before and because she had chosen to believe her ancient observations, she had set about treating him in a most irritating manner from the very first. Perhaps— perhaps a good deal of the animosity that always arose between them was exactly because she did not know anything about Jason Farley. Perhaps a good deal of their arguing grew from a misunderstanding on her part. "Oh, my goodness," she whispered to herself. "I have been dreadfully at fault."

"Pardon?" asked Mr. Farley, not quite grasping her words. "Ah, there he is now, the rascal!"

"Who? What? Great heavens!" gasped Lady Farnsmoor, her gaze following Mr. Farley's pointing finger.

"That is why I bid you come, my lady. That very gentleman."

"But I thought that we had rid the place of mice. We tossed legions of them out with the mattresses and the furniture. And His Grace's valet spent an entire day hunting out their hiding places and laying bait for them."

"Indeed, but it appears that Andrew is much too intelligent to be tossed out or baited, are you not, sir?"

"Snick tch," replied the tiny brown mouse from his perch upon the brace and then wiggled his nose in the most forward manner.

Lady Farnsmoor giggled girlishly to see it. "Oh, what a bold fellow he is. Look how he sits there so calmly. Now he is washing his ear."

"Exactly. Bold as brass he is. Ever since the mantel gave way he has come to the parlor at least three times a day to converse with me."

"To—to converse with you?" Lady Farnsmoor's eyes sparkled with laughter.

"Indeed. And he has a good deal to say, too, though I do not understand him quite yet. I am not fluent in mouse. He has built himself a home in the wall behind that brace, and he comes to me now when I call for him. A very intelligent mouse, Andrew. Learned his name after only three days of bribing him."

"I shall send one of the men over to eliminate him immediately."

"No!"

"No?"

"Tch-eek sqwipf."

"Hush, Andrew, no one is going to eliminate you."

"Sqush-tchf," observed the mouse, stretching to the very end of the brace and staring down as if to see the two people on the settee more clearly.

"What I hoped, Meredith, was that you might be in possession of a trap—the kind that will catch him without doing him damage. I should like to trap the fellow and give him to little Charlie as a pet. You would not mind him to have a mouse for a pet?"

"How stupid of me, of course you would not wish to kill the creature. Not when you have made friends with it already. My brother Theo had a mouse in the nursery when we were children and we built a most magnificent house for it. What fun it was! How very odd of me to have forgotten it. And Theo is coming for the wedding! He will gladly help us build a house for Charlie's mouse."

Lady Farnsmoor clapped her hands in the most innocently excited way and Mr. Farley gave silent thanks that she had not screamed at the very thought of her darling boy having a mouse to play with.

"You will stay for tea, will you not?" asked Mr. Farley, clearing a number of books from the low table before them so that Mrs. Grimshaw might set a tray upon it. "Andrew is staying. Aren't you old fellow? Fond of having tea with me, Andrew is. That much I have learned about him."

Six

Lord Farnsmoor's dark eyes opened very wide and he crawled out from beneath the sofa and did a happy little dance right in the middle of the parlor carpet. "A mouse, a mouse, I am to have a mouse," he sang as he jiggled and jigged about, and both his mama and his sister clapped for him and laughed.

"We shall get your dollhouse down from the attic, Eloise," Lady Farnsmoor decreed merrily. "And when your Uncle Theo and Aunt Aurelia arrive, we will get Uncle Theo to make it safe for Charlie's mouse. He once made my dollhouse into a house for a mouse," she giggled girlishly. "I do hope he has not forgotten how he went about it."

It is the oddest thing, Eloise thought, as her mama took Charlie's hand and led him off to the nursery. I cannot remember ever hearing Mama giggle and she has done so any number of times since Mr. Farley arrived. And she has not fallen into tears over my marriage since his arrival either. And she smiles more and more of late and is not at all jittery about the arrival of the wedding guests. Why, less than two weeks ago, Mama was bemoaning Uncle Theo and Aunt Aurelia's arrival and wondering what she would do to entertain them and she could not even face the thought of playing hostess to David's mama. I do think Mr. Farley has changed her attitude toward all. He is so very good for her. How can she go on naming him a villain and holding the past against him?

The sheer ecstasy of her younger child at the very thought of having his own mouse was not wasted upon Lady Farnsmoor. The fact that Mr. Farley should think of the idea was not wasted upon her either. It was most kind of him to suggest it, she thought as she handed Charlie into the care of his nurse and wandered down to her own chambers. I do hope he can actually catch the mouse. Charlie will be most disappointed if he cannot.

"But of course he will catch it," she murmured, turning into her sitting room. "Unless I am sadly mistaken, once Jason Farley has determined to do something, he does it. I do believe he is the most stubborn man I have ever known."

Not that I truly know him, she reminded herself as she sat down before her writing desk and tugged a lovely lacquered box from the drawer. I do not think I have ever truly understood the man. She opened the box and began to search through the papers within, coming at last to a gentleman's calling card which had lain for any number of years upon the bottom of the pile. The name of Mr. Jason Farley was inscribed upon it in bold black letters. Lady Farnsmoor stared at it pensively and then turned it over to read the lines written upon the back. "LOVE is constant," it said. "LOVE is ageless. Despite all things, LOVE abides." How many times, she wondered, have I stared at these lines in the past twenty years? How many times have I come crying to this room and tugged this card from beneath everything else and stared at these lines and known that Charles did not love me and I did not love him?

Jason Farley had wandered in and out of Mrs. Grimshaw's kitchen at least fifteen times and it was only nine o'clock in the morning. It was not that Hattie Grimshaw did not appreciate the parson's company, but she had never before worked for any gentleman who had put one foot into her kitchen. "Be ye waiting on someone, then, Mr. Farley?" she asked when once again he appeared and straddled one of the kitchen chairs.

"Yes, Mrs. Grimshaw. Am I disturbing you? I do not mean to do that. It is just that I cannot seem to alight anywhere. Lady Farnsmoor has promised me a mousetrap and—"

"A mousetrap?" Mrs. Grimshaw looked up from her mixing and fixed Mr. Farley with a puzzled gaze. "Do ye be planning to catch some other mouse, then, to keep our Andrew company?"

"No, it is to catch Andrew in."

"To catch Andrew?" Mrs. Grimshaw's flour-covered hands went to her hips as she stared at him. "Ye have been leaving crumbs and plying that mouse with cheese for four whole days and ye have got him to come and take them right from your fingers. Do not tell me you have not, for I watched you feed Andrew this very morning. Why do you need a trap to catch him, eh? Scoop him up and put him in your pocket, you might do, and him be pleased as punch at your doing of it, too. I never before seen nothing like it, and that's a fact."

"Yes, but that will not do, because—Is that a carriage I

hear, Mrs. Grimshaw? No, no, keep on with your mixing.
I shall get the door.''

The Reverend Mr. Farley dashed from the kitchen
toward the front door with such exuberance that Mrs.
Grimshaw could not help but laugh. Such an odd young
gentleman, she thought, smiling. Not a bit like old Reverend Mr. Gorsuch who had been dour and peevish and
only enthusiastic about his condemning of sinners. This
one, he be enthused about everything, even a carriage
making its way to the door. 'Tis most likely only Mr. Beam
come to see can he be of help with the gardening.

It was not Mr. Beam, however. Little Lord Farnsmoor
in a buff skeleton suit topped by a bright red jacket, his
reddish curls tumbling rakishly from beneath a most mili-
tary-looking forage cap, hopped down from the carriage
tugging a most unlikely looking animal behind him.
Directly upon his heels, Lady Farnsmoor descended with
the aid of a footman.

Mr. Farley inhaled deeply in the open doorway. She was
even more beautiful today than she had been yesterday.
In a gardening dress of sprigged muslin with a bleached
straw bonnet upon her head and a mere whisper of a shawl
floating about her shoulders, she was the very embodiment
of his dreams. It was all he could do to keep from running
to meet her. But he knew in the very depth of his soul
that if he did run to her he would frighten her away. He
had worried all night, in fact, that perhaps he had been
too forward yesterday, sending for her to see the mouse
and suggesting that they catch the thing for Charlie. And
he knew that he had been overly optimistic to think that
Meredith might actually deliver the trap herself. He had
tossed about on the edge of sleep, telling himself over and
over that she would send a footman with it, that any lady
would simply send a footman with it, that no one of any
stature, gentleman or lady, would personally deliver a

mousetrap into the hands of a mere parson. And yet there she came through the garden gate, Charlie bouncing excitedly before her and a footman holding an enormous mousetrap trailing in her wake. "Good morning to you," he called as she made her way up the cobbled path. "I did not expect anyone quite so early."

"Mr. Reveren' Farley! Mr. Reveren' Farley! I have brought my horse! Look! I have brought my horse to show you!" cried his little lordship, jumping up the two wide steps and launching himself into the parson's arms, unwittingly clunking the parson's head with the carved wooden head of the horse.

Lady Farnsmoor flinched at the sound of it and hurried up the steps to disarm her son with all haste. "I am so very sorry, Mr. Farley. Are you all right?"

"Fine, fine," murmured Mr. Farley, his lips twitching upward. "Lethal steed, that. What is his name, my lord?"

"He is named Dragon because he is fierce and ter'ble."

"I see. And I will bet you are the only person in all the world who can ride him, are you not? Because he trusts you and has taken you for his master?"

"Zactly!" crowed the earl, his chest puffing out as he settled upon Mr. Farley's arm. "I am the onliest one. Not even Mama can ride him. Only me."

Lady Farnsmoor could not take her gaze from Mr. Farley as he held her son in his arms. Truly, she thought, Jason Farley has grown into a most admirable gentleman in many ways. I have not seen Charlie so very excited and happy since before his papa died. One of her lace-gloved hands flitted to Mr. Farley's sleeve. "Are you certain you are not hurt? The horse is fashioned from oak."

"Solid oak, undoubtedly," grinned Mr. Farley, lowering his lordship to the tiny porch and patting the horse's wonderfully curly yarn mane. "A bit of blood and bone of which to be proud. You had best tie him up to that post, my lord, so he does not run off and lose himself. He has never been here before, you know."

"I am going to ride him around in your house," advised Lord Farnsmoor, the hand not holding his steed making into a fist and going to rest upon his hip. "I am going to take my mouse riding."

"I see. He will enjoy that I expect. But we have not yet caught the little beast," Mr. Farley added, leading the way into the rectory. "But we shall. We shall."

With great care and consideration on the part of both Mr. Farley and Evans, the footman, the trap was placed on the floor just beneath the mantel brace and Charlie was allowed to bait it with cheese from Mrs. Grimshaw's kitchen. "And now we must give him time to come into the parlor and sniff the cheese," declared Mr. Farley, taking Charlie's hand into his own and leading him toward the front door. "We shall go for a walk, shall we, so that he does not see us all waiting for him and run away?"

"Yes," nodded Charlie. "We will all go an' stroll about the grounds, willn't we, Mama? Me and Mr. Reveren' Farley an' you."

"And Evans will go and have some tea with Mrs. Grimshaw," added Mr. Farley, stooping down to whisper in his lordship's ear.

"An' Evans will go an' have teas with Mrs. Grimshaw," repeated his lordship dutifully. "An' John Coachman may have some too, mayn't he, Mr. Reveren' Farley?"

"Yes. John Coachman may definitely have some tea as well."

Lady Farnsmoor could not be certain whether it was the bright sunshine, the brilliant blue of the sky, or the sight of her son galloping happily about the parsonage garden on the back of his broomstick horse that filled her with happiness. "I never thought to feel so again," she murmured to herself.

"I beg your pardon?" asked Mr. Farley.

"Oh, I was muttering to myself, I'm afraid. Growing old."

"Never. In my eyes you can never grow old, Meredith, you merely grow more—"

"What? I grow more what? You were about to say something outrageous, were you not?"

"You might think it so."

"I have always thought you outrageous, Jason Farley. It is because I do not understand you. I did never understand you. Tell me what you were going to say. I promise I shall neither slap your face nor twist your finger."

"I was going to say that in my eyes you only grow more beautiful."

"Flummery."

"No, it is not. You *have* grown more beautiful. It is not merely your appearance of which I speak, Meredith. It is all of you—your heart and your soul. Look at that cherub cavorting amongst the grasses there and then think of Eloise. Are they not reflections of your heart and soul? And how beautiful they are! Their mother could be no less beautiful."

Lady Farnsmoor's heart fluttered in her breast. She could not think how to respond to him. "You are fond of children," she said after a long silence.

"Very."

"Why have you never married and produced a family of your own? You ought to have any number of children climbing upon your lap and tugging upon your coattails by this time. Yes, and you ought to be trapping a mouse for your own little boy."

"I expect because I did never fall in love with any other woman and I made up my mind long ago that I would not

marry without love. Marriage is very difficult; without love it
is near impossible to survive it. Which reminds me, Andrew
ought to be sniffing at that cheese by this time. We ought
to go see."

"Marriage reminds you of that mouse?" laughed Lady
Farnsmoor.

"No. It was a *non sequitor*. I am not quite as mad as that."

With one sharp whistle, Mr. Farley brought the intrepid
Lord Farnsmoor and Dragon galloping to his side and they
strolled back to the rectory. "Now, we must be very quiet,"
instructed Mr. Farley, dutifully tying his lordship's horse
to a rosebush beside the front porch. "We must sneak in,
so as not to disturb him if he has not yet entered the trap."

"Yes," whispered Charlie excitedly. "We willn't 'sturb
him. We will sneak very much, won't we, Mama?"

"On tippy toes," replied Lady Farnsmoor, smiling.

And with little Lord Farnsmoor in the lead, the three
quietly opened the door and slipped into the tiny hall.
Charlie was the first to peer into parlor and he hurried
back to his mama literally on tippy toes. "He is there,
Mama. He is inside the trap, but the little door did not
close."

"Uh-oh," mumbled Mr. Farley.

Lady Farnsmoor giggled at him.

"I expect we must attempt to close the door upon him
ourselves."

"How are we to do that? Surely he will see us and run."

"We shall need to crawl very quietly across the carpeting.
You shall tiptoe around and approach from the west and
Charlie will approach him from here and I shall come at
him head-on. On my signal, we will all approach at once,
and he will not know which way to run and will huddle
against the rear of the cage and I will shut the door and
we will have him!"

Lady Farnsmoor's first thought was to declare that *she*

was not going to crawl about on the floor in her skirts and make an utter fool of herself, but one look at little Charlie's eager face prevented *that* protestation. And a glance at Mr. Farley's sparkling green eyes prevented any other. Why, he is just as eager and excited as Charlie, she thought, a most warm and tender feeling spreading through her. Oh, I cannot possibly disappoint them both. And lifting her skirts, Lady Farnsmoor made her way silently into the parlor and around to the far side. She managed it so quietly that the mouse did not so much as look up from the cheese it contentedly gnawed upon.

Good boy, Andrew, thought Mr. Farley, with a fond gaze at the mouse. I knew you would not be afraid. He set Charlie in the doorway and then moved past the boy, around to the front of the trap. When he had reached the optimal position, he sunk to his hands and knees. "Now," he whispered to his companion hunters.

At once the parlor was alive with a giggling Charlie crawling madly across the carpeting and a laughing Lady Farnsmoor struggling with her skirts, but managing to crawl forward despite them, and the Reverend Mr. Farley scrambling on all fours toward the trap.

The mouse sat up on his haunches and looked confusedly from one to the other of them. Then, recognizing the rector, it squibbled about a bit and squeaked, wiggling its whiskers in anticipation of another treat to accompany the cheese.

"Oh!" gasped Lady Farnsmoor, tangling in her skirts and falling forward toward the trap.

"Got him!" cried Mr. Farley, launching himself forward at the same moment and tumbling right on top of Lady Farnsmoor, but managing to close the little door as he fell.

"Ooph!" giggled Lady Farnsmoor. "Jason Farley, you are as heavy as an ox!"

"No, am I?" asked Mr. Farley, rolling away and lying upon the carpeting laughing up at the ceiling.

"We have gots him!" shouted little Charlie, joyfully flinging himself upon Mr. Farley's stomach and bouncing up and down. "We have catched my mouse!"

Lady Farnsmoor raised herself upon her elbows and gazed at the two of them with the most loving light in her dark eyes. What a wonderful jumble of man and boy they made, and both of them in ecstasy over the capture of one little creature. For a long moment she contemplated the supreme impropriety of adding herself to the pile of laughing gentleman and joy-filled little boy, and then she did that very thing, eliciting a laughing groan from the rector and a scream of glee from her son as she toppled upon them.

Seven

The Reverend Mr. Farley waved them goodbye with only the merest whispering of guilt. Undoubtedly the footman knew that he had rigged the door of the mousetrap to remain open. He had even pointed out the mistake and suggested the necessity of adjusting the thing differently. But Evans surely would not speak of it to Lady Farnsmoor. Footmen did not converse on such a level with their employers. And if he did happen to mention it among the staff at Twilight Hill, they would merely shrug and think the new parson not particularly mechanically minded. And he had trapped his mouse! Not Andrew—he might have given Andrew to the boy simply by picking the creature up in his hand. No, he had trapped a much more delicate and beautiful mouse than Andrew—trapped her into laughter and playfulness and the sharing of joy.

Lady Farnsmoor watched Mr. Farley until he turned and disappeared into the rectory. In the barouche with the top folded down and the sun shining upon her, she experienced the oddest feeling of rebirth, as if a great shell had split up the middle and shattered, allowing a new and freer Meredith Cottesmore Hanforth to emerge into the glorious light of day. And then her great dark eyes shone down upon her son as he sat cradling the parson's mousetrap in his arms, and she smiled a most beguiling and enchanted smile, a smile that, if only the Reverend Mr. Farley had been privileged to see it, would have sent his heart directly to heaven.

The wedding guests began to arrive at Twilight Hill the following day and Lady Farnsmoor welcomed all of them with great propriety, saw them comfortably settled, and set about entertaining them as any good hostess might. And if she forgot that her brother Theo's wife, Aurelia, could not bear the sight of Great Uncle Spencer and placed the two beside each other at the dinner table, who could blame her? She was the mother of the bride-to-be after all. And when she, quite by accident, spilled a glass of wine into Bishop Mallory's lap and then, flustered, followed that with a buttered scone, how could the groom's uncle hold it against her? She was the mother of the bride-to-be. And if, in the midst of a rousing game of crambo, her gaze continually strayed to the drawing room windows and she offered "cherry" as a rhyme for "tree," who could do anything but smile and forgive her because she was the mother of the bride-to-be. But when she joined the dowager Duchess of Weyland in the privacy of the Twilight Hill study on Sunday afternoon and had the audacity to offer that formidable lady tea instead of her customary afternoon brandy, the dowager duchess did not smile and forgive her the oversight.

"Meredith Hanforth, what has gotten into you?" the

elder lady in a purple satin gown, who was busily removing a fuschia turban, asked peevishly. "Anyone would think you had sold your wits for wombats, gel!"

"Wh-what? Wits for—? Oh! I am so very sorry, Your Grace. You do not drink tea, do you?"

"Never since I married Weyland, nor do I intend to begin the frightful habit now. And I generally do not blink a blind eye upon a friend in need either," grumbled the mother of the groom.

"Blink a blind eye? A friend in need? But who is it that you perceive to be in need, Your Grace? Is it someone in this establishment? You must only tell me. I shall be more than pleased to offer them aid myself."

"Balderdash," muttered the dowager and she focused a most forceful stare upon Lady Farnsmoor and then looked her up and down with terrifying efficiency. "You, Meredith Hanforth, are the person I see to be in need," she stated after a long silence. "Since when have you become a complete peagoose?"

Lady Farnsmoor's eyes widened in surprise. "Me?"

"Indeed. Do you think I have not the least idea what is going on here?"

"A wedding is going on here," offered Lady Farnsmoor, removing the offending cup of tea and replacing it with a glass of cognac. "And I am quite sorry to have poured you tea, Your Grace. Indeed, I am at wits end. I cannot think what has come over me of late."

"Humbug! You know perfectly well what has come over you. Jason Farley has come over you, and if you are half the woman I think you are, you will admit it, too."

"Oh!" The pretty pink that tinged Lady Farnsmoor's cheeks put a most triumphant sparkle into the dowager's eyes.

"Thought no one would notice, eh? Well, you are wrong, m'dear. Your mind ain't on this wedding at all. It is on those madly flashing emeralds that all the Farleys have for eyes and on those curls the color of autumn leaves and on a pair of broad shoulders and slim hips. He is a devil of a handsome man, Jason Farley. Never thought to see the brat grow into such a paragon. And he is a devil of a preacher, too, ain't he? Came near to flabbergasting everyone this morning, did he not? Not a word about sinners and hellfire, not Jason Farley. Love. The man speaks of loving one's neighbor with the most incredible intensity. And I could see immediately, m'dear, which of his neighbors he intends to love with such intensity, too. And from the way you colored up every time he looked at you—I have not the least doubt why it is that you have been fluttering about like a woman with air for brains this entire week. Good heavens, gel! At long last you have discovered that you love the man. Admit it."

"I—I—" Lady Farnsmoor lowered herself into the nearest chair and began to fan her flaming face with a napkin. "I have just come to think of Mr. Farley as—It is too soon to think that—I thought once that I loved Farnsmoor and that he loved me. How on earth am I to trust that I know what love is?"

"Love is constant," declared the dowager in stentorian tones. "Love is ageless. Despite all things, Love abides. I told Jason that when he came to me, a boy without a mother or one sister to consult. But even I never dreamed that his love for you could abide without one significant sign of hope for some twenty years! If you cannot trust yourself, Meredith Hanforth, cannot you trust such a constant and fearlessly determined heart as his?"

* * *

The woman who came galloping up to the rectory on Monday morning, no groom in her wake, had no far off look in her eyes, no unsettling, lovelorn twist to her lips or wistfulness to her smile. She held her head high and her eyes blazed with determination. She called out his name and the Reverend Mr. Farley came running out into the sunshine as though summoned by the Almighty Himself.

"Help me down, do, Mr. Farley. I must have a word with you."

His arms lifted, his hands clasped about her waist and in an instant she was upon the ground beside him, tapping her whip against the skirt of her riding habit.

"To what do I owe this—"

"Hush, Jason, I am thinking exactly what to say."

Mr. Farley cocked an eyebrow at the use of his given name.

"I have thought about this all night and still I do not know where to begin."

"At the beginning perhaps," he suggested with a smile. "Will you not come inside and be seated?"

"No. I wish to wander with you among the weeds of the rectory rose garden," she said, slipping her arm through his and urging him toward the rear of the parsonage. "Jason Farley, do you vow you loved me all those years ago and were not merely set upon plaguing the life out of me?"

"What? Yes, of course I vow it. I loved you then with all my heart."

"Just so. And that is why you followed me all about London, and embarrassed me publicly at every opportunity."

"I was a boy, Meredith. I had no thought to embarrass you. I merely wished for you to understand that I loved you."

"You loved me when you doffed your coat and threw it over that puddle on Albemarle Street right in front of me and set all of society talking for three whole days?"

"I threw it there for you to walk upon so that your half-boots might not get wet. Do not look at me so. It seemed most romantic when Sir Walter Raleigh did it."

"You were not Sir Walter Raleigh."

"No, obviously not."

"And when you dressed up like a highwayman and stopped my coach on the way to Lady Redding's masked ball, and swore to steal all my jewels if I did not kiss you?"

"It was most uncircumspect of me," mumbled the parson.

"There were five coaches filled with ballgoers all pulled up to see what the ruckus was. You were nearly killed and it was the talk of the *ton* for weeks—you did that because you loved me?"

Mr. Farley nodded sadly and stared down at his shoes. "I loved you. I admit I was a veritable nodcock, Meredith. Must we go down the entire list of my villainies?"

"No. Only one more. When you accosted me upon the hill during the fireworks display at Vauxhall and literally dragged me off to your brother's coach, whatever was in your mind?"

Mr. Farley came to a dead halt. He turned to face the lady, his emerald eyes afire. "What was in my mind, Meredith," he said. "What was in my mind was that you were going to accept an offer from that rogue, Farnsmoor, who did not love you, who could not love you, who had never loved anyone but himself in all of his life. I could not bear it!"

"And?"

"I meant to carry you off with me to Gretna Green and to convince you along the way how much I loved you. I thought to make you wish to marry me. It had to be Gretna, you see, because I was only sixteen and my father would never have countenanced the marriage."

"Charles beat you to within an inch of your life when he came up with us that night."

"Yes," chuckled Mr. Farley, "I am well aware of that. And you thought him most heroic for saving you. Was there ever a more ill-fated lover than I, Meredith? Or a boy more inept at romance?"

"No," Lady Farnsmoor replied softly, one gloved hand going to caress his cheek, "never a more ill-fated lover in the entire history of England, nor a more misunderstood one."

"Meredith?" Mr. Farley's pulses thundered at the gentleness of her touch and his eyes widened considerably.

"Jason Farley, do you love me still?"

"Yes."

"I am thirty-eight years old and a dowager countess. You are a mere thirty-three and a country parson."

"It matters not."

"You would be the talk of the countryside. You would be marrying the mother of your benefactor. Society will label you a fortune hunter and worse to marry an older woman who is above your touch. Such things are not done, Jason."

Mr. Farley's heart shot up into his throat and came near to choking him. His eyes teared at the sudden intense pain of it. "D-do not," he gasped. "Do not turn me away again, Meredith. If you turn me away again, I will surely die. I will wait. Until your Charlie is of age. Until we are so very old that no one will take the least notice of our union. Anything. Any length of time. Because I do truly love you, Meredith Cottesmore. I have always loved you. And I will love you forever."

"Love is constant," whispered Lady Farnsmoor, dropping her whip and placing his arms around her waist. "Love is ageless and despite all things, love abides. And you, Jason Farley," she sighed as her arms went around his neck and she raised her face to his, inviting his lips to taste her own, "You truly *are* love, are you not?" And then she found she could say nothing more.

"Mama is goin' to be a bride," announced little Lord Farnsmoor the morning of Eloise's wedding, as he ran into the tiny antechamber of the church. "Ellie, Ellie, Mama is goin' to be a bride. Oooh, how pretty you look."

"Why, thank you, Lord Charles," grinned Eloise down at him. "You are dressed to the nines yourself, my lord."

"Yes, I have got on real gentleman's clothes, Ellie. Grown-up gentleman's clothes and I look dashing."

"You do? Who said that you look dashing?"

"Mr. Reveren' Farley. An' he looks dashing as well. An' Duke, too. The onliest gentleman who don't look dashing is Andrew, Mr. Farley says."

Eloise laughed as the mouse poked its head from her brother's pocket and wiggled his whiskers up at her. "You will make it clear to Andrew that he is to stay well hidden during the ceremony, will you not, Charlie? Because he may frighten some of the ladies, you know, if they should see him climbing about upon your shoulder."

"Yes, I already knows that. But Ellie, Mama is goin' to be a bride just like you."

"No, dearest. Mama is the mother of the bride."

"Uh-uh," corrected Lord Farnsmoor with a shake of his head.

"Uh-uh," echoed a deeper voice from the antechamber doorway.

"Uncle Theo, whatever is going on?"

"You are getting married, my dear. And I have come, all decked out in my finest morning clothes, to lead you down the aisle and hand you into the arms of that lucky devil, Weyland. Do not tell me you have forgotten," he teased.

"Uncle Theo, do be serious. What is it Charlie is saying about Mama? Oh! Do not tell me. Mr. Farley has stated his case and Mama has accepted his proposal. Oh, Uncle Theo!"

"And Bishop Mallory at Mr. Farley's request has brought a special license with him from London. Audacious brat, Farley! Planned on catching your mama from the very first. I always hoped that Meredith would come to her senses and marry that upstart. It has taken forever. But it is to be a secret for now, Eloise. No one but Charlie and I are to know until you and the duke are off on your wedding trip and the wedding guests packed and gone."

"But whyever not? It is the most romantic thing in all of history. Mr. Farley has waited for Mama for twenty years. And at last he has caught her. Everyone should know of it."

"But this is your day, Ellie, and your mama does not wish to detract from you in any way. She only told your Aunt Aurelia and I because she and Mr. Farley wish us to stand as witnesses for them. Charlie," he added with a wink at the little boy, "overheard."

"And a good thing, too," declared Eloise. "Where is David? Tell him I must see him at once, will you not, Uncle Theo? It is most important."

On Wednesday morning, June twenty-third, the Reverend Mr. Jason Farley, his eyes glowing with happiness, pronounced Lady Eloise Hanforth and David Adam Mallory, Duke of Weyland, man and wife before a small party of their relatives and friends in the church of St. Agnes of the Moors. "Well, and what are you waiting for?" he whispered as the two smiled up at him. "Kiss the girl, Duke, and lead her out of here. I have an entire flock of parishioners standing outside in the sunshine waiting to sing the two of you to your carriage."

"Is that so?" queried the duke, one eyebrow rising as he studied Mr. Farley appraisingly.

"Yes, that's so. Why are you staring at me with that particular look in your eye? Now where the devil is Mallory off to?" he asked as the bishop exited his pew and strolled toward the narthex.

"You will discover that quite shortly, Mr. Farley," grinned Eloise. "Do not move from that spot, will you. I shall return in a moment."

"Return in a moment?" Mr. Farley's brow furrowed as Eloise turned and, lifting the skirt of her gown, stepped down the three steps to the stone floor of the church that the duke had so recently scrubbed.

"Do not look so very flustered, Jay," offered the duke conversationally. "I shall kiss my bride eventually. I assure you of that. It is merely that there is something missing yet to this ceremony."

"No, there is not," protested the parson. "I have married any number of couples, Duke. I did not miss a thing. You are well and soundly hitched."

Uncle Theo whispered in Aunt Aurelia's ear and that lady giggled the tiniest bit as Eloise stepped into the very first pew and took one of her mama's hands.

Uncle Spencer's eyebrows rose and he cast a most confused glance at Miss Hortensia Parker as little Charlie took his mama's other hand and together the brother and sister led Lady Farnsmoor from her pew up to the altar.

"An excellent idea," laughed the dowager duchess quietly, poking an elbow into old General Dunleavy's ribs as he sat looking quite confused beside her.

The Duke of Weyland stepped up to his new mama-in-law as she arrived at the spot beside him and he placed a tender kiss upon her cheek. "We will not have you and Jay married without us to support you, you know," he whispered. "So now it is your turn, my lady, to take the leap."

"Lady Fransmoor, you will not mind that I marry you to my audacious relative now, in front of everyone, will you?" queried Bishop Mallory in a resonant voice that carried throughout the church, as he swished up the aisle in the robes of his office and caused any number of people to gasp and one or two of them, including the dowager, to cheer merrily. "Jason, step down, step down where David stands. And David, help him out of those robes. Man don't want to be married in cleric's robes."

With a wide grin, the bishop took Mr. Farley's place and announced in his most authoritative tone, "The Duke and Duchess of Weyland and Lord Farnsmore—oh, and Andrew—have proclaimed that there will be two brides sung from this church this morning and that one of them will belong to Mr. Farley."

"You will belong to Mr. Farley, will you not, Mama?" asked Eloise, giving Lady Farnsmoor a hug.

"Yes," smiled her mama, her black eyes alight with enchantment. "I will belong to him forever and ever."

"An' he will belong to us, too," pointed out little Lord Farnsmoor happily.

"Indeed I will," Mr. Farley agreed, his emerald eyes lighting more of the church than the morning sunshine as he took Lady Farnsmoor into his arms and kissed her soundly upon the lips.

"Not now," laughed the Duke of Weyland, scooping Charlie up and tugging Eloise to his side. "Not now, Jay.

You have got to wait for the kiss until after Uncle Adam marries you."

"Which reminds me," declared Eloise. "You, sir, have not kissed me as yet." And she rectified that situation quite nicely as the second ceremony began.

Bride of Enchantment

Marcy Stewart

"Of *course* I am happy." Beryl Carraday briefly closed her eyes against the breeze drifting across the heath. "How could you ask such a question, Charlie? You know I am soon to be wed."

"The very reason I inquire," said her companion, Charles Longstreet, who was fighting a strong urge to kiss the frown from her brow. "You don't appear the beaming bride."

"I think you can guess why," she said quietly. "Shall we walk? The morning is unusually fine, even for June. I vow I can smell the sea and hear it as well, cannot you?"

"What I hear is you changing the subject of our conversation," he replied dryly, but after a glance at their horses which remained docilely tied within the windshorn coppice bordering the moor, he offered his arm willingly enough. Instants later, he thought he *could* hear the waves breaking against the Devonshire cliffs, though they fell downward to the English Channel more than two miles from the Carraday estate. Probably only his imagination, he decided, prompted by the suggestion of his childhood friend, the fair lady at his side, who from the height of a seedling had planted enchantments in all of their heads: his own, her brother Brian's, and of course, Joshua's.

Joshua. After more than a year, the name still evoked a storm of feelings. And if Joshua Kent continued to affect him so fiercely, there was no accounting what spell the man's shade cast over *her*.

He tightened his hand over Beryl's to assist her past an uneven patch of ground. But it was he who stumbled and she who aided him, a thing that brought a flash of anger to his eyes, a single shake of his head, before he forced his expression back to what he hoped conveyed distant interest.

"When does your betrothed arrive?" he asked, determined not to let the subject die until he drew the answer he needed.

"Mrs. Garrison and Caroline will be here in a few days, but Patrick won't be able to leave town until the day before the ball. He has unfinished business—some estate he is settling, I believe."

Charles nodded, knowing Patrick Garrison to be an up-and-coming solicitor with his father's firm in London. He hesitated, then decided to plunge ahead. Of what use was a lifetime acquaintance, if one could not speak his mind?

"Are you certain this is what you want?"

"Of course it is not." She smiled lazily, her glance skimming across the wasteland on their left to the stretch of grassy meadow before them. "I wish Patrick might arrive with his family, since I have never met them. But we will get on, I hope, with Mother to help."

"That's not what I meant, and you know it."

"I know what you meant, Charlie."

He waited an instant. When she added nothing more,

he said with mock fury, "Do I receive an answer, or must I throttle it from you as I did when you were nine?"

Under heavy lids, her hazel eyes glimmered with humor. Good. He had not offended her; not when she drifted *that look* at him, the one they all coveted as boys. Even then, though years younger than them all, she projected a precocious sophistication and poise as she sent them on one quest after another like an adult playing at children's games.

Only Joshua slipped the reins from her control upon occasion, whenever the boys felt the need for a life-threatening adventure. And often as not, somehow she would become a part of those missions as well, carrying out her assignments without squeamishness did it require hands upon beetles or worms or expeditions into abandoned, crumbling cottages thick with cobwebs, dust and rats.

Though one or the other of the lads frequently complained at her gentle tyranny, Charles knew they loved her for it—despite her unprepossessing looks. How overlarge her eyes had appeared in her little-girl face; how plain a child she seemed to him all those years ago with her long, straight nose and wide mouth. But a transformation occurred, a magical, almost overnight change during her thirteenth year. She had grown into her face, a face that shouted beauty from every finely sculpted bone. During that same stretch of time, her slight body had lengthened, rounded, become queenly in grace. And now, instead of despising her unfashionable height, she apparently gloried in it; he had never seen a lady with finer posture or self-composure. He knew no person so willing to be oneself without excuse. Excepting, of course, Joshua.

But Joshua was gone, felled at the Peninsula after three years of heroic fighting during which he received not a scratch. The irony had shocked Charles almost as sharply as the death itself. Nothing bad ever happened to Joshua.

They had reached a stretch of ill-kept fencing, and Beryl paused to lean against one of the posts, fixing an earnest look up at him. "I'm a fortunate woman to be marrying Patrick. You know what kind of man he is; from the time Brian went to Eton, he spent most of his school holidays with us. He's one of my brother's closest friends, so they get on well together—"

"Certainly an excellent reason for marrying."

"I am not finished, Charles Longstreet, and I'll thank you to keep a civil tongue in your head. Patrick is kind, responsible, fine looking—" She appeared to be searching. "Personable—"

"Wealthy," he could not help adding, and immediately repented.

"That's unfair."

"You're right. My apologies, Beryl."

She turned and began to walk rapidly. He strained to keep up with her, his accursed leg threatening to throw him into every dip and clot of grass.

"You don't know what it's like, Charlie. Damara wants us away. No, I am not putting it strongly enough. She *craves*, she *pines* for my mother and me to leave. Oh, I suppose I can understand how a new bride would wish to be alone with her husband, and we try to stay out of their way as much as possible. Yet it isn't enough. At every meal together, every evening when we gather in the drawing room afterward—and I declare to you, Mother and I make those as short as possible; we withdraw upstairs as soon as Brian or our guests allow—I feel her eyes like daggers upon us, and especially myself, everytime I speak. And her speech! You cannot imagine how often she says such things as, 'When Brian and I have space to start a nursery,' or 'When Brian and I are alone, how he speaks to me about his dreams for a family!' as if it is Mother or myself keeping them from procreating! Oh, Charlie, I shouldn't be saying all of this, not even to you. Forgive me."

"I've heard her, child. She can't compete with you in conversation or looks, that's all. She's jealous, and justifiably so. When you leave, Brian will go mad with boredom."

Beryl laughed and impulsively kissed his cheek. "Oh, Charlie, you are the best of my friends, as close to my heart as my own brother. I don't know what I shall do without you. Promise you will visit us in London often."

He averted his face, finding sudden interest in the path of a grouse fluttering skyward. "On holiday perhaps," he said after a moment. "I can't often get away from the school."

"And yet you are here today with me. Thank you, dear Charlie. You knew I needed to talk with you. Somehow you can always sense it."

"I'll have to get back soon," he said in carefully light tones. "We've a new tutor who hasn't learned how to tame the boys yet, and even the girls are beginning to take advantage of him. Yesterday someone spilled honey beneath his desk, and he spent the rest of the afternoon sticking to the floor."

The sound of Beryl's laughter cut through the air like delicate bells. "You have done wondrously well with the school. When your father died, Brian and I thought you would finally fulfill your dreams for travel. But instead you have continued your sire's work in the village."

"Unfortunately, it requires funds to travel. I've tried living on poetry and dreams, but my stomach speaks another language."

"Yes," she said soberly, not rising to the jest in his voice. "Funds are necessary for everything."

"Which brings us back to your wedding."

She turned from him and braced her hands against the

fence railing. "Are you implying that I'm marrying Patrick for his fortune? Do you think so poorly of me?"

"I've never heard you mention love," he said gently. "Will the fabled wedding gown glow brilliantly for him?"

He saw he'd disturbed her and regretted it. Perhaps he shouldn't have mentioned the gown, the heirloom bridal costume that had a reputation for flaring to newness when the brides of her maternal line wed their true loves. But he'd heard her mother's stories about it from his childhood and had always been fascinated.

"Oh, as to love," she said. "I have a very great fondness for Patrick."

"A very great fondness. What precisely does that mean? I've heard you express a fondness for Brussels sprouts."

"You most decidedly have *not,*" she giggled, then grew more solemn. "It's barely been more than a year since Joshua . . . I loved him deeply, Charlie. To have lost him so cruelly, to never know how he died . . ."

"We know how he died, Beryl. His sergeant saw him fall. His end was as quick as any can be on the battlefield. You needn't torture yourself with conjectures."

"Yes, but not to have him here with us, to be able to place flowers on his grave . . . Even the most basic comfort has been denied us. He should have been brought home."

"You know the ways of war. It often happens."

She shook her head. "I think—I think if my heart could recover from his loss so quickly, it would be a cold one indeed, don't you?"

"Yet you are marrying Patrick."

She clenched her fists together, an uncharacteristic gesture, then released them. "You're very hard, my friend. Listening to you is like hearing my own conscience spoken aloud. But the situation at home grows intolerable."

"So intolerable that you're willing to risk your future happiness to relieve a temporary inconvenience?"

"What makes you think it's temporary? Is Damara going to change her attitude toward me? Shall a bequest fall from the sky to enable my mother and me to buy a cottage together? It's unlike you to be so unfeeling."

"Some females find employment when such situations arise. Something genteel, such as governessing. Or serving as a companion." Lighten, he counseled himself. You are going it too strong. Forcing mischief into his expression he added, "Or perhaps pickling radishes. Even better, *dressmaking.*"

Puzzlement clouded her features. "Charlie, be serious. I've known of no governesses or companions who were allowed to bring their mothers to their positions, have you? And you know how much I detest the needle."

He fingered a section of railing, snagging a splinter which provided a welcome diversion as he worked to pull it out. "If things are so bad, you might consider teaching at my school. There are faculty quarters above the dormitory—rooms spacious enough for you and Mrs. Carraday."

"Oh, Charlie." The rims of her eyes reddened. "Bless you. You thinking of me. You are always doing that, always putting the needs of others before your own. You're speaking of your personal living quarters, are you not?"

"I don't require so much space as I have." He clasped his hands behind his back, a gesture he'd seen his father do many times. Realizing it, he quickly loosened his fingers and commanded them to stillness. "I really only need one room, and there are several standing empty."

"Thank you, dearest. But can you imagine what my brother would say to that?"

"He would not be able to get past the villagers' gossip, I daresay." His face lengthened in mock solemnity as he intoned, "Master Carrady has cast his penniless sister and mother from their home to make their way in the cruel world. What an ogre!"

Beryl's lips quirked. "No, that would be Damara's concern. Brian would snatch us back in a trice and declare our home was with him."

"I suppose he would, and without one word of thanks to me. Which once more leads us back to the original solution, the only one which seems possible in your mind, though I think salting pickles would be more to my taste. Marriage to a man for whom you feel ... what was it, a *fondness?*"

"You make it seem as if I'm sacrificing myself like some maiden in an overwrought novel. I am eager to marry Patrick, I tell you. He is all that is wonderful, and I very much look forward to our future together."

He absorbed this for an instant, then said, "Excellent," in a voice too hearty for his own ears. "If that's what you feel, then I'm happy for you, Beryl."

"Thank you. Now promise you will stop worry—" She paused as a sharp sound of agony sliced the quiet. "What is that?"

Charles had already turned toward the noise, which seemed to come from the wood. "Sounds like a rabbit." Even as he said the words, he began running toward the trees. "Probably caught in a trap."

"The poor creature," Beryl murmured, trotting beside him. Despite the limiting circumference of her skirt, he sensed she held back, pacing herself so as not to outstrip his ungainly hobble. He silently railed at his leg, even as he prayed he would not tumble like a stone against the rough ground, the final humiliation.

They found the hare beneath a stunted oak, struggling inside a wire trap. The terrorized animal had caught one leg within one of the loops and was mangling it hopelessly in the effort for freedom. Moving awkwardly, Charles stooped to his work.

"I trust your brother wasn't hoping for rabbit at table tonight."

"This is a poacher's trap, not one of ours. Brian doesn't hold with using traps."

"I know. If you can't shoot it, leave it go." Charles sighed as the rabbit bounded away, its left leg dragging useless and bloody. "Hope I did it a favor."

He settled tiredly on the ground, his game leg extended. Joshua, he thought, looking at the aching limb, for a heartbeat his rage drowning out all thought.

Beryl sank to a stump, her eyes warm upon him and only for an instant flashing at his leg. "Your knee," she ventured. "It hurts you."

"No. I'm not used to exercise anymore. Not like the old days."

"Truly? I hope you aren't saying that just to be brave. You and I have always spoken truth to each other and always shall, will we not?"

He smiled. "In everything that matters." Everything, save one.

In her bedroom on a bright morning five days later, Beryl lifted her wedding gown from its tissue with dismay. The ancient satin with its overlay of lace looked even more yellowed than it had when she wore it for her fittings last year, if that were possible. And was there a trace of *mildew* on the sleeves? Perhaps the tears she shed while packing it away had festered.

"Is *that* it?" Fifteen-year-old Caroline Garrison inquired from her perch atop Beryl's bed pillows, her plumply attractive face for once looking serious. Pensively, she flicked her fingers across her bottom lip, making a wet popping noise. "That's the gown you're wearing to marry *my* brother? Oooh, he won't like that." Moving suddenly, she clapped her hands to her cheeks. "No, no, why can I never hold my tongue! Beryl, my pardon. He'll like it well enough if you're in it . . . and even more *after* the wedding, when you are removed from it! Oh! I make my ownself blush!"

Beryl steeled herself for the high-pitched laughter she had come to expect from her future sister-in-law. When it came, a sound Beryl could only liken to a horse being gelded, she forced her lips to respond. There was that about Caroline which compelled others—or at least she found herself to be so moved—to participate in her merriment, no matter how unamusing its origin.

"Really, Caroline," said Mrs. Garrison from one of the chairs flanking the fireplace.

Beryl fought a spasm of irritation. Mrs. Garrison was *always* saying, 'Really Caroline' in her stiff manner, as correctly formal as her daughter was informal, yet equaling her in dullness.

Placing the dress upon the bed, carefully avoiding Caroline's stocking-clad toes, she counseled herself to stop being so uncharitable. They were both kind to her in their individual ways, and that was the important thing. Even more encouraging, her own mother seemed to get along well with Mrs. Garrison. Surely they would make a congenial household, unlike her present one had come to be.

"The gown is over seventy-five years old," said Estelle Carraday, who sat in the wine-colored wing chair opposite Mrs. Garrison, "and was initially worn by Beryl's great-grandmother, then her grandmother and finally myself. The first daughter of each generation in my family traditionally wears it."

"I have heard of household economies," pronounced Caroline in the tones of one about to impart a high jest, "but this is going too far!" She held her sides as she laughed. "Stitch a new dress, I beg you!"

Damara Carraday, seated sideways upon the bench footing Beryl's bed, twisted slightly to face Miss Garrison. "Beryl doesn't want a new gown. She's waiting for *magic* to transform it."

Hearing the scorn in her sister-in-law's voice, Beryl gave her a telling look. Damara lifted her brows but otherwise remained unmoved.

"Magic?" breathed Caroline. "Is the gown magic?"

"I prefer to use the term *enchanted,*" Beryl said.

Damara waved a dismissive hand. "As if there is a difference."

"Magic or enchanted, tell me more!" pled Caroline.

"Mother relates it better than I." Beryl exchanged smiles with her parent. Obligingly, Mrs. Carraday folded her hands in her lap, palms upward, in the manner of one about to relate a story.

"There is a legend in our family about the gown," she began. "It was stitched by a gypsy seamstress in the mid-seventeen-thirties. This woman, whose name was Zella, camped with her family on my great-grandfather's land every spring. He willingly permitted their trespassing and never gave them trouble so long as they remained orderly and lawful. One spring Zella came alone, excepting for a small daughter. She begged my great-grandfather's kindness that year, saying the rest of her family had died due to a contagious illness, leaving her destitute. My great-grandfather took her and the child in, and for several years the woman earned her keep by making clothing for the family and servants.

"During this time, my grandmother Rosa became a young woman. She was beautiful; if her portrait does not prove it, the fact that she had two suitors begging her hand in marriage surely did. Great-grandfather was a good-natured man, or so I believe, for he left the decision making

to her. But she could not decide between the two gentlemen, and the distress of choosing made her ill.

"Zella, who loved Rosa as a daughter, came to her sick-
bed and told her she had secretly sewn a bridal gown. It
was no ordinary gown, Zella explained, for she had woven
enchantments into every thread. Rosa had only to try on
the dress and think of each suitor in turn. When she
thought of the man who would make her happiest, the
gown would shimmer into pristine whiteness.

"Naturally Rosa thought it all foolishness, but she rose
from her bed and attired herself in the gown. Standing
before the mirror, she closed her eyes, thought of one
beau's name, then opened them. Nothing changed in her
reflection. But when she repeated the process with the
second name, she opened her eyes to an almost blinding
glow. And that is how she came to select my grandfather."

"Marvelous!" cried Caroline, clapping her hands.
"Would that I had such a gown. Not that I have any hopes
of needing it, mind. Though one can always pray. Which
I do. Every day!"

While Beryl winced at the gales this sally brought, Damara stirred. "Don't be duped by that old tale. Any bride
in love looks radiant. Rosa obviously preferred the man
who became my husband's ancestor, so she imagined the
change in the gown."

"I was thinking the same, though I beg Estelle not to
be disappointed in me for it," Mrs. Garrison said. "I don't
mean to quarrel."

"No one could ever accuse you of quarreling, Mrs. Garrison," Beryl said, a trifle impatiently. "But that explanation
doesn't explain how the gown changed for my mother's
mother. When she wore it over forty years ago, the dress
had already begun to fade. But according to several
accounts, no one could believe it was not new on her

wedding day. And then, when my mother wore it—well, I should let her tell the story."

Estelle Carraday's attractive features grew even more pleasant as she remembered. "By the time I wore the gown, it was almost as yellow as you see it today. I knew this long before my wedding, because from the time I was ten I began taking it from its trunk in the attic and pulling it over my head while thinking of various boys I knew." An impish light glinted in her eyes. "My mother would have screamed had she known.

"By my twelfth year I discovered whom I should marry. Daniel was visiting the home of one of our neighbors when I first met him. I thought him very handsome and grown-up; he was eighteen, which seemed most mature to me then. After our meeting, I hurried to the attic at the quickest possible opportunity. When I thought of him, the dress brightened considerably, and I knew he was the one."

"Again, that can easily be explained by the wishes of a young girl's heart," Damara said loftily.

"But the proof would have been at her wedding, surely," Caroline disputed, warming Beryl to her. "Did everyone speak of the newness of your dress then, Mrs. Carraday?"

"I had nothing but compliments."

Damara laughed. "Naturally no one tells a bride her gown looks as if it belongs in a museum."

"Well, I think we should put it to the test," Caroline said, her face bright with eagerness. "You must try on the gown, Beryl, and we shall see what happens!"

Thus came the moment Beryl had been dreading, though she thought to endure it alone, not amongst so many women whose interest in the legend's truth magnified her own trepidations tenfold. She wanted to believe. She wanted to remain as childlike in such matters as her mother, for she could aspire to no finer lady's example.

Did not such innocent belief imply a sweetness of nature
that was attractive in a female?

Yet she suspected the legend was as false as Damara
asserted.

She had good reason to do so. On several occasions
during the previous year, Beryl had worn the gown for
her fittings in preparation for her wedding to Joshua, the
wedding which was never to be. Though she had chanted
his name from the first occasion she wore it, alone and
hopeful of a miracle, to the last fitting, when the dress-
maker begged her to stop, the yellowed lace had not
appeared one shade lighter, the satin not a whit more
crisp.

Beryl had never told anyone of her dismay at this, not
her mother, not even Charlie, with whom she shared everything. She wondered what he would think to know the
gown had not whitened even for Joshua. He would doubtless make a jest of it, make her feel better. He could always
make her laugh. She wished he was here to do so now.

Smoothing the dress with trembling fingers, playing for
time as the ladies in her bedroom observed her, Beryl felt
disappointed not so much in the legend's untruth as in
the dismal lack in herself. If indeed the tradition was false,
then her feminine progenitors had loved so deeply they
were able to deceive themselves into belief. She wanted to
think her ability to love was no less than theirs. Either she
was incapable of such depth, or . . . perhaps the story *was*
true, and she was meant for Patrick all along? Perhaps
when she attired herself in the gown for the first time in
a year, she would blaze like a snow-covered field in the
sunlight?

But such was impossible, surely. She did not feel one-
half the affection for Patrick that she'd known for her
childhood love.

The thought crushed her with its disloyalty. She recalled

her painful conversation with Charlie and felt more shame. No. She loved Patrick, she *did*. And the gown would prove it. If only there were not so many people here. She cast a desperate look at her mother.

Mrs. Carraday immediately stood. "Well, ladies. If we wish Beryl to try on her dress, she must do so alone, for that is how it's been done traditionally, you see. No one excepting the bride-to-be should gaze at her reflection the first time, or the effect might be ruined. Not even a maidservant should be present."

"I've never heard that part of the tale before," Damara complained.

"What, did I never tell you? How thoughtless of me. Come, come ladies! We must away so Beryl may have her privacy."

A rustling of muslins, silks and excited chattering from Caroline ensued as the women filed from the room. Mrs. Carraday was the last to leave, accepting Beryl's whispered thanks with a fond look.

"Good fortune, my darling," the older lady murmured. Almost as an afterthought she added, "And remember that beauty is always open to interpretation."

Beryl's eyes lit with suspicion. "What do you mean by that, Mother? Are you saying you—"

"I meant only that if Patrick is for you, you'll know." And with that remark, she closed the door, leaving Beryl to face her empty room and the bridal gown alone.

She approached the bed slowly. Even more slowly she undid the buttons at the back of her morning gown and stepped from it, then pulled the yellowed threads of the bridal dress toward her, closing her eyes as she tugged the garment over her head. She kept her lids tightly shut as she struggled with some of the more crucially placed hooks in back; there must be a hundred of them or more and she needn't fasten them all.

Well, one good thing; without looking she could determine that the dress still fit, and at least no further alterations would be necessary. Now all it needed was for her to stumble her way to the cheval mirror and look. Reluctantly she did so, feeling her path past the posters of her Queen Anne bed and stubbing her toe on the bench. When she judged herself to be in position, she commanded her lashes to open while whispering, "Patrick, Patrick, Patrick. Please."

For an undetermined passage of time, Beryl stared into the glass.

Almost a half-hour later, she bubbled into the parlor downstairs, joining the ladies who put aside their book-reading and needlepoint to hear the answer to Caroline's squealed question, "Well? *Well?* What did you see?"

"The gown is beautiful," Beryl gushed, her voice sounding thick. Carefully avoiding her mother's penetrating stare, she cleared her throat. "You cannot imagine how lovely it looked."

"When may we see?" demanded Caroline.

"Not until the wedding," Beryl said. "That's part of the tradition."

Damara snorted. "Why am I not surprised?"

The next week passed quickly, almost too quickly to accomplish the many details necessary to hold the largest ball Carraday House had seen in nearly two years, since Brian and Damara's wedding fete. For the convenience of nonlocal guests, the entertainment was to be held on the Thursday evening before the wedding on Saturday. Relatives and friends began arriving the Wednesday before, swelling the ivy-bricked rooms of Carraday House to the bursting point, stealing the maids' chambers but not the butler's, whose sensible presence was too valuable to misplace for a moment. It was Maddox who greeted each guest with formal hospitality and saw to their needs, and it was Maddox who on that Wednesday evening ushered Patrick Garrison into the grand parlor.

Caroline spied the bridegroom even before Beryl, who was earnestly trying to become interested in her great-aunt's litany of skin ailments. Though the large room hummed with conversation, Beryl heard Caroline's squeals and saw Patrick. Gladly excusing herself from her elderly relative, she joined Caroline and Mrs. Garrison near the door.

Patrick embraced his mother and sister briefly, but as Beryl moved to do the same, he pressed her hands warningly, his glance flickering at the crowd. Of course, she thought, annoyed. It would not be seemly for such a display since we are not wed yet. Patrick is always correct.

But seeing his wide smile brought guilt. She loved his sense of propriety, which was not, after all, overdone. It was one of the things she'd found refreshing about him. The boys she had grown up with were all notable for their lack of same. Even as she thought it, Brian came forward, then Damara and Mrs. Carraday, all welcoming Patrick graciously.

"You must introduce me to everyone, my dear," Patrick said after the initial greetings were over, tucking her arm within his. She proceeded to do so, walking from one group to another, the restfulness of her mother's ivory-and-celery color scheme for once not making its impact. For while her outward self spoke names and attended to Patrick's polite exchanges with each person presented, her inner mind raced with impressions.

It was astonishing she had never noted it, but she and Patrick were of such similar heights they could carry a bench on their heads without tilting it, should they so desire. He was almost a dwarf compared to Charlie and

Joshua and Brian. But that was all to the good, for her neck would never ache from looking up at him. He was much more sturdily built than any of them, too, which made him look healthy.

And how well he spoke with the guests. He always knew the correct thing to say to bring out the best in each of them. She saw old faces, young and middle ones, all turning upward with corresponding politenesses, even blooms of pleasure. There was a predictability about his speech and manner perhaps, a timing wherein she began to anticipate the way he would tilt his head next, or when would come his manly laugh, just so; but that in no wise reduced the performing of his social graces. These were qualities that bode well for his future. How well she admired him for it.

Though, after the first seven or eight guests they greeted, it was hard to resist the game of guessing what he might say. She would think: Now he will compliment my cousin's clothing; and Patrick would declare: "How lovely you look in that lavendar gown, Miss Dawson." They would move to the next person. Now a comment about Great-Aunt Hortense's age. "What?" declared Patrick to her relative, "You cannot mean you are Beryl's aunt! Do not pretend you have enough years in you for that."

When she had been successful four times in a row, her head began to pound. "Shall we take a turn in the garden?" she begged when they had finished their long circuit around the room. "I feel the need for fresh air."

He presented her with a delightfully private smile, making her weak with relief. "I suppose they will forgive us for stealing a few moments alone."

Once outside among the sensuous aroma of roses, peonies, and sweet williams, she relaxed. The evening air was cool, bringing with it the tang of the sea and the moor, both out of sight but familiar and beloved. A terrible thought struck her, and not for the first time. Reluctant to break the peacefulness, but needing to know, she spoke softly:

"Your family has never owned a house in the country, Patrick?"

The question seemed to trouble him. He narrowed his eyes, gazed into the distance, nodded abruptly, and led her to a bench bordering a cluster of wildflowers. "I am about to tell you something that may shock you, Beryl, but I believe the time has come."

Her interest was immediately piqued. "I don't mean to intrude," she said, and wrinkled her nose at the lie.

"No, no, my dear. I only hope this information will not distress you. Truth is, two generations ago, all we *did* own was a house in the country." He briefly caught his tongue between his lips. "Mayhaps *house* is too grand a word. The Garrisons were no more than farmers tilling a scant living from the ground."

He batted his lids fiercely, as though the story pained him. "Then my grandfather moved to London to see what he could make of himself. For years he set aside his earnings as a shipping clerk. He married late in life, having only one son before he died." A long pause. "That man was my father."

"So I had imagined," she said, commanding her lips not to smile as she visualized Charlie's amusement at Patrick's pretentious narrative. *Pretentious!* How disloyal could she be to her future husband? All merriment instantly vanished.

Patrick continued, "Consequently, my sire was able to obtain an excellent education and later establish his firm. I don't like to speak of those beginnings, but you will soon be family and must know."

"But there is nothing of shame there. We cannot help how we begin."

"I'm not ashamed, my dear." He blinked again, several times. Strange, she thought, I haven't noticed that mannerism before. Perhaps he's nervous because of the wedding. If so, he's not alone. "Some would look down on Garrison, Wheeler and Garrison for it, however. That's the reason I never speak of it."

"I understand." A small silence fell. "Do you think you will ever be interested in purchasing a place in the country one day? Perhaps a little estate, not so very far from London?"

"I beg your pardon?" he said, looking confused. "Why should I do that when we have a perfectly fine house in town?"

Beryl had never been inside his home, but he had described it often. Now she mentally walked through its tall, narrow rooms, the steep stairways, and outside to the sliver of grass in front and the high wall in back, surely no more than ten feet from the kitchen door. The house would undoubtedly be one of five thousand such tall, narrow houses on a narrow cobbled road in the heart of the city. And all around, traffic running unceasingly, like blood coursing through an artery.

"Don't you ever feel the need to get away from town? To . . . have a change of scenery, enjoy nature?"

"My dear, I'm far too busy for that. But if you desire such, you may feel free to visit your brother and his family; I shall not be the kind of husband who won't allow you some autonomy." When she made no response, he said quickly, "And mayhaps sometime in the future, when we have children of our own, I'll consider leasing a place for the summer months. Then I could join you occasionally. How does that sound to you?"

She stared at the wood edging the north side of Carraday House. It looked very dark in there. Dark and lonely.

"Would you like to kiss me, Patrick?" she asked suddenly.

"Would I—what?"

"You have never kissed me. We are to be wed in three days, and I thought you might like to."

He fingered his cravat as though to straighten it, but finding no fault, his hand fell. "Of course I'd like to kiss you, Beryl. What a thing to say." He uttered a few staccato chuckles. "The truth is, I dare not touch you until we are wed. My affection for you is so great that I don't trust myself to remain the gentleman."

Joshua was always stealing kisses. Pulling her behind trees, leading her into empty rooms, backing her into draperies.

Patrick rose, smiling affably, and offered his hand. With the briefest of glances, she took his assistance and permitted a small degree of malice to bloom. Now he will say, 'We had best go inside before someone misses us.'

"We'd better go inside before my mother sends someone to look for us," he said.

I shall be able to predict everything my husband says for the next fifty years without even trying, she thought desperately. I must speak with Charlie.

She did not see her old friend until the next night at the ball, which took place in their large conservatory at the back of the house. She had almost given him up when he finally made his appearance. The receiving line had fallen away, the dancing begun, when she spied him at the entrance dais.

Her relief was sharp; his absence would be the worst of three she especially hoped would not occur, especially when she had passed over the ivory gown she'd had made for the occasion in favor of another new one in cerulean blue, a color Charles professed to love.

The other two guests she longed to see were Joshua's parents, whom she had invited personally over a month

ago. Mayhaps they thought a year was too soon for her to
replace their son. She prayed her coming wedding would
not hurt them. At least not as much as it promised to hurt
herself.

Longstreet looked quite striking in his black evening
attire, she noted as Patrick led her through the steps of a
Haydn saraband. The white linen of Charlie's shirt and
cravat made a pleasing contrast with his brown hair which
was, as usual, a trace too long and shaggy for fashion. She
smiled at the sight of him. Though the slight bump in his
nose robbed him of masculine perfection, he truly cut a
romantic figure with his deep brown eyes and full lips.
And his ebony cane.

She was glad he'd brought it. She knew how much he
detested his infirmity, and nothing she had ever been able
to say could dissuade him from his self-contempt. She
might at this moment name a half-dozen young ladies who
would give their eyelashes for a stroll with him, limp or
no, but he seldom spared any of them more than a
moment's polite notice. In point of fact, one was making
her way toward him now: Sylvia Radmoore, looking soft
and lovely in a creme gown trimmed in pink.

At that instant, Charlie's gaze met Beryl's. She sent him
her warmest grin over her shoulder. He returned her greeting with a half-smile, his eyes passing flatteringly over her
ensemble, then was distracted by Miss Radmoore's
approach. Beryl stumbled slightly, causing Patrick to
chuckle and caution her to mind her steps. But she did
not. At every opportunity she threw glances in Charlie's
direction while wondering why the dance did not end.
He expected her to rescue him from Miss Radmoore's
machinations, she knew he did.

When the final chord sounded at last, she made her
away across the room, excusing herself from Patrick, apolo-
gizing to the young curate, Curtis Stone, who was intent

on claiming her next dance, cutting around and between couples indiscriminately. Unable to miss her approach, first Charles and then Miss Radmoore paused in their discourse, both looking somewhat startled. Their expressions made Beryl flush but did not stop her.

"Charles," she said pointedly, "how good to see you. I have saved this dance for you as requested."

He gave her an intent look, started to say something, but checked himself.

"Now don't start protesting that you can't dance, though you could if you wished," she scolded, laughing prettily, pushing him toward the threshold. "I haven't forgotten that you prefer not to, but has it slipped your memory that I always walk the um, second number with you? My goodness, how long has it been since your last ball? Please do excuse us, Miss Radmoore, it is merely one of those long-held customs of good friends; I'm sure you have them as well. Oh, look! I do believe the curate is coming to claim the quadrille with you."

Miss Radmoore, appearing none too pleased, had little choice but to step aside. Charles murmured an apology as Beryl hurried him from the room.

"Am I being kidnapped?" he demanded as she led him from one parlor to the next, hoping to find an empty chamber but discovering tables of card players and clutches of gossiping matrons instead.

"Hush, Charlie, we must find someplace quiet." She tightened her hold on his arm, liking the feel of strength beneath his sleeve. How reassuring he was. But how frustrating there was no private spot, not in the whole of Carraday House on this evening. Finally, in a fit of haste and without sparing more than a glance at Maddox's disapproving stare, she bullied Charles past the butler, out the front door and past the line of waiting carriages in the drive, ignoring the curious glances of drivers and lackeys as she pulled her escort toward the side of the house to the rose garden and the bench where she had twenty-four hours earlier sat with her fiancé.

"The quadrille must be halfway done by now," Charles observed, his voice flavored with irony. "We have just enough time to retrace our steps before the third set begins and Patrick misses you."

"I don't care a fig for the next dance," she said, adding with a little catch in her throat, "and I don't believe Patrick's depth of feeling extends to missing me."

Longstreet grew very still. "What's this, child?"

In spite of her best efforts, she felt tears gathering. "Oh, Charlie. I am about to marry a man who will never surprise me."

A flare of amusement died when he saw the depth of her distress. "Are surprises that important to you?"

"You don't understand. Patrick is the most polite gentleman I have ever met; he would rather die than do something impulsive or unexpected. Last night I found myself able to predict every word he would say next! Not only that, I can anticipate his every act at every moment! And I am certain he has each detail of our lives planned just as precisely—from the instant we walk from the church to the wording of the headstones on our graves. Oh, I am wicked for speaking so, I know that. He is a good man with a wonderful family. I'm ashamed of myself for feeling as I do."

Longstreet took one of her hands in his. "You're experiencing prenuptial jitters. It's quite common, or so I understand."

She shook her head. "That's not all that worries me. He is—or he seems, a cold man."

Charlie's eyes narrowed. "Cold?"

She squirmed, uncomfortable to speak of this even with

her closest friend, but he would never understand unless she did so. "Patrick is so different from Joshua," she began.

For a fraction of time, Charlie seemed in a far place. It made her curious, for he often acted strangely when his friend's name was mentioned, but it was doubtless caused by his continuing grief.

"That doesn't surprise me," he said finally.

"Joshua"—her cheeks grew warm—"often kissed me."

"That doesn't surprise me, either."

Her lips curved upward at his flattering tone, even though she knew he was only teasing. "But Patrick has never touched me, other than to offer his arm."

"Are you saying he has never kissed you?"

"Never, not even when I asked him to."

"Now I am shocked. No matter what his sense of propriety, what man in his right mind would refuse such an opportunity?"

She laughed. "I knew you would make me feel better. Although, now that you mention it, *you* have never done so." The words stunned her as soon as she heard them.

"I once tried to kiss you," he said a heartbeat later. "But you told me you belonged only to Joshua."

"Did I? That was so long ago I hardly remember. I was little more than a child. Children can be cruel."

"Yes, I know," he said. She searched his face, drawn by the intensity of his words. "I'm the headmaster of a school, in case you've forgotten."

Beryl nodded, then looked away, pretending interest in a pair of older ladies taking a turn in the night air. She was relieved the evening was so young. A little later, after a few more dances, couples would begin wandering outside to cool themselves. Or perhaps to seek the warmth of stolen embraces, as she once had done with Joshua. But for the time being, she and Charlie were alone, and she reveled in the gift. He gave her strength, heartened her. He always had. Even if his memories did disturb her.

She tried to recall the incident Charlie mentioned. It seemed absurd she would refuse such an innocent request. Perhaps she'd done so because he was as close—no, closer to her heart than her brother. Charlie had always been there, her first playmate when she entered his father's school, the first to see her potential as a participant in the boys' adventures. He had gradually caused Brian, who thought of her only as an annoying little sister, to look at her in a different way. He convinced Joshua, too. Joshua had come into their lives later, when his family inherited his grandfather's estate, which bordered Carraday House. And once Joshua entered, he took over.

Beneath the cover of her lashes, she studied Charlie's dear profile, the noble chin tilted slightly upward. A healthy breeze was ruffling the treetops, but it was not that which caused her heartbeat to accelerate.

"I beg your forgiveness for my refusal," she said in a soft voice.

His smile was so sadly sweet, his eyes so warm that she ached. "It was a long time ago. Surely you don't dream I would hold that against you."

"I can't imagine you holding anything against anyone, Charlie."

Something moved in the depths of his eyes. "I'm not a saint."

"Yes, you are. And if—if you truly don't hold a grudge, then I would like to give you that kiss before I become a married lady and mustn't do such things."

She thought she saw a look of pain enter his eyes, but it changed so quickly to devilment that she decided her imagination was overwrought. "What are you speaking of? You're constantly bussing my cheeks as though I were your prize uncle."

"But not like this," she said, touching his hair lightly, guiding his mouth to hers, made bold by the certainty that nothing could matter now; her life was on the precipice of ruin, she was about to be bored to death.

Charlie allowed their lips to touch only an instant before he drew back, the teasing light in his eyes completely overtaken by something fierce. "Don't dally with me, Beryl. It's beneath you."

Her chin began to tremble. "Do you think I am playing, Charlie?"

His dark glance swept across her face. And then he crushed her to him, his mouth claiming hers in a long kiss that shot threads of pleasure down to her toes. She could not think beyond the joy his nearness brought her. But eventually she forced herself to pull away and, briefly pressing her hand to her heart, stood and walked a few steps from the bench.

"Oh . . . my," was all she could think to say.

"I'm sorry, Beryl, I didn't mean to take advantage of you." He also rose, making a great fuss over finding his cane and straightening his cravat, all the while mumbling about moonlight and lovely young girls and spring.

Beryl suddenly found herself angry. Her previous distress, so sweetly detoured, now returned in force. "Oh, stop it, Charlie, I'm not going to call an alarum over a kiss from my closest friend, especially when I asked for it. But you must tell me: how can I go through with marrying Patrick now? In one instant you have made me feel more—more—*more* than he has in ten months!"

He was quiet for the space of several breaths. "Have I?"

"Stop looking so pleased. I suppose now you will consider yourself a ladies' man. But at least you have helped me realize I don't love him and am likely never to. I should cry off, shouldn't I?" She walked a few paces, wringing her hands, then reversed direction. "Yet how can I not go

through with the wedding with all of these people here
and after my brother has spent so generously? Oh, the
shame of it." She stopped, opening her hands skyward.
"But I have made a great mistake; even the bridal gown
declares it."

And then she must explain to Charlie what had happened when she wore the dress. She was surprised at how
seriously he took the failure of the gown to transform itself
and said so.

"But you believe the legend," he said. "Why shouldn't
I?"

"I can't countenance that you set any credence in the
tale, even if you always did have a vivid imagination.
Besides, I'm not so certain I do believe it." Reluctantly,
she added, "It didn't change for Joshua when I tried it on
last year, either."

He stared at her for a few seconds before continuing.
"Why mention it then? Do you feel the need for more
excuses to call off this misguided wedding?"

"Then you agree with me, Charlie? I *should* cancel it?
But the scandal. And I don't wish to hurt him."

"He'll get over it. Better a brief illness than a chronic
disease."

She pulled a face. "How flatteringly you put it." Now
that the decision had been made, though a part of her
was filled with dread, she could scarce contain her buoyancy. "Oh! Here he comes now. I can't face him. I must
avoid him as much as possible tonight. After the ball, I
shall tell him. Or maybe in the morning. Hurry, Charlie,
before he sees us."

Longstreet guided her toward the corner of the house,
where she could follow the lighted pathways to the doors
of the conservatory. "You go on. I'll distract him."

"Thank you, Charlie. You've saved my life."

Looking almost as happy as she felt, he motioned her

forward. She scurried along obediently. Before she made the turn that would hide him from view, she glanced back. Charlie and Patrick were now walking in the opposite direction toward the front. How good Charles was to her, had always been. And how delicious his kiss. Charlie . . .

Sudden possibilities began to play within her mind, things she had never contemplated in relation to him. But considering Charlie as a mate was as ludicrous as trying to wed Carraday House: both were part of her natural landscape. He was not the stuff of which husbands were made; at least not for her. She needed a man dashing and adventurous, bold and impulsive, as her one true love had been. A pity she'd not realized it before trying to shackle herself to Patrick, bless him.

But at least she understood herself now, before she embarrassed herself and Charlie by saying something foolish that would make him think she was attracted to him. Horrors! How he would laugh to know the direction of her thoughts instants ago. Desperation was making her foolish. Should she keep on, she would end up trying to wed half the men in the village.

The thought stopped her cold. "What shall Mother and I do?" she whispered. How long could they bear Damara's complaints?

The next hours passed slowly. She was certain the musicians played three and four repeats of every selection instead of two, and at half-tempo. She moved through the dance steps like a slug through water. She felt glad of Charlie's presence, for he had stationed himself near the dowager's corner and kept busy bringing them glasses of ratafia and punch. Now and then she caught his glance upon her and felt a rush of warmth every time their eyes met.

No one understood her like Charlie. This had long been true, even before tonight. But now they had a special connection. Of all the people beneath this roof, he alone knew of her coming dread conversation with Patrick. Her need to speak with Charlie again, to hear his reassurances, became agonizing.

As the evening crawled on, she could not avoid waltzing with Patrick, nor going in with him at supper. But afterward, while he danced with Caroline, she made her way back to Charles.

He was listening attentively to the vicar's elderly wife, who was making elegant gestures with every word. Beryl did not interrupt but tilted her head toward the entrance as she passed by. Within a moment Longstreet joined her.

"Have I been summoned again?"

"Yes. I need your support once more, if you are willing to give it. As the time draws near for me to speak with Patrick, I find my courage deserting me."

"I can well imagine." He regarded her closely. "You don't expect *me* to tell him, I hope."

"I wish you could, but I have made this stew and must . . ." She paused as three gentlemen passed through the hall.

"Take the pot from the fire?" Charlie supplied helpfully.

She cast him an amused glance and smiled a greeting at the gentlemen. When they disappeared into the grand parlor, she continued, "I—I suppose I want you to say I'm not a bad person for doing this."

In the gentlest voice imaginable, he echoed, "You are not a bad person for doing this. A little indecisive, perhaps."

She was torn between laughter and tenderness. The moment stretched, filled with undercurrents she scarcely understood. Such tension must be lightened, and she struggled to think of a way.

"Listen." She smiled at the overly intense look that crossed his face. "The orchestra is playing 'Margaret's

Waltz.' Would you think me dreadfully bold if I asked you to dance it with me?"

"Beryl, you know I cannot."

"Oh, stuff. Put down your cane and waltz. We are in the hall and in no one's way; almost everyone who is not dancing is either still at supper or walking in the garden. Who is to mind?"

"Well, for one, Maddox standing there."

"He doesn't disapprove; that's his natural expression. Now do you dance with me, or shall I retire to the bench in humiliation?"

"You are much too bold, miss," said Charlie, but he lay his cane on the bench, slowly took her in his arms and began the steps of the waltz. They did not whirl in great, graceful arcs but in short, halting ones. She could feel him laboring to keep in time with the music, but it was impossible. All at once he stopped, dropping his arms.

"I can't do this."

"You *can*," she said, fixing him with a hard stare. "You're having difficulties because it's been so long since you danced, that is all. You will improve with practice, just as everyone does."

"I can't think you'd want to be seen with so awkward a partner."

She pressed closely to him, forcing him to clasp her in his arms again. "There's no place I'd rather be."

It was true, she realized suddenly. She felt safe within his embrace, but there was more to it than that. She closed her eyes, then opened them with irritation. Someone was beating the knocker forcefully. Why would anyone try to join their fete so late? From the corner of her eye she saw Maddox open the door, then heard him give a great cry.

Both she and Charles stopped at the same time. Maddox *never* cried out. Something must be terribly wrong.

And then Joshua Kent burst into the hall looking elegant

in a charcoal waistcoat and ivory pantaloons, his perfect white teeth gleaming in an enormous smile, his dark hair curling over his forehead just as she remembered. He opened his arms wide and strode toward them.

"Beryl, my love! Charles! I am returned from the dead!"

The hall's crimson wallpaper faded to black. Without uttering a sound, Beryl sank mindlessly into Charlie's arms.

Brushing aside Joshua's and Maddox's offers to help, Longstreet carried Beryl to the chaise lounge in the drawing room. Beads of effort dampened his brow, but he did not stumble once. As soon as Charles released Beryl, Kent pulled a chair next to her.

The flurry of activity drew a number of curious observers, many of whom shrieked or exclaimed when they recognized the visitor. Joshua laughingly brushed aside their questions, declared he was not a phantom, promised to explain all but begged they allow Miss Carraday's recovery first.

The word of Joshua's amazing return spread through the house like fire. Charlie had time to utter no more than a choked greeting before Mrs. Carraday hastened into the room, embraced Joshua with a gladsome cry, and then, seeing the state of her daughter, began waving her fan near Beryl's face. An instant later, Brian entered to seize his old friend's hand, then Damara, who looked less enthusiastic than her husband but welcomed the prodigal politely enough. Behind her, the threshold thickened with ogling guests.

"Close the door for pity's sake!" Brian ordered Maddox. "My sister won't thank us for this large attendance at her collapse."

As the door clicked shut, Beryl opened her eyes, her

gaze immediately locking with Kent's. She gave a little gasp.

"I didn't dream you, then? You are truly here?"

"In the flesh," Joshua said, laughing, and enclosed her in his arms.

Averting his eyes from the embrace, Charlie looked to the door, which snapped open to admit Patrick Garrison. Patrick's face took on a gray color as he surveyed the scene. "So it's true. You've returned."

Joshua's expression became sardonic. "You don't look happy to see me, Garrison. Now why is that, I wonder?" One dark brow arched. "Could it be you were a little hasty in trying to snatch my bride?"

"We thought you were dead," Patrick whispered.

"Yes, so I understand. My parents filled in the blank places for me when I arrived this afternoon. When they said Beryl was to be married on Saturday, I couldn't heed their wishes and wait 'til tomorrow to come. You and I have a few things to discuss, old man, and the sooner the better."

Charlie watched as Beryl's wide-eyed stare moved from Patrick, to Joshua, to himself, and back to Kent again. "What *happened,* Joshua?" she begged, her voice so tremulous that Charlie's fingers curled into fists. "Your sergeant wrote a letter telling us about the battle at Badajoz. He described in great detail how you were—were—"

"Slain as valiantly as I lived, I'll warrant, knowing how Henderson enjoys waxing on," Kent chuckled. "Wish I could tell you what happened exactly, but some things are still vague. Guess they always will be. I do recall being winged in the shoulder, which made me fall off my horse. Then I saw a Frenchie coming toward me. Suppose he didn't want to waste gunpowder. The last thing I remember was his musket butt descending.

"The blow to my head drove everything from my brain,

and I do mean *everything*. Didn't know who or what I was for the longest while. Didn't know my own name or even that I was an Englishman. Reckoned I was a simpleton when I woke because I didn't understand a word of their Spanish chatter." He grinned at Beryl and began to chafe her hands. "How are you doing, old girl? Thought you'd seen a ghost, didn't you?"

Beryl, her eyes shining with wonder and tears, shook her head, too overwhelmed to speak. Charlie gave her his handkerchief, causing her to release one of Joshua's hands, and asked hoarsely, "Where were you all this time?"

"On a farm near Badajoz. Many of the residents nursed wounded soldiers after battles, I found out later."

"Why did your hosts not contact someone about you?"

Joshua chuckled. "I wondered that myself when my memories first started coming back. By then it was about a month after Wellington retook the city. Understand that my uniform had been stolen while I lay senseless on the battlefield, so the Navarro family really didn't know what to do with me. They found out I was English soon enough, but I could have been a deserter, a spy, anyone. View it one way, they were protecting me. Looked at another way, and much more useful to them, they were getting a free pair of hands." He lifted his palms demonstrably. "See these calluses and scars? Imagine me wielding a plow and scythe."

"Oh, Joshua," Beryl said, pressing the handkerchief to her eyes. "I cannot believe such a thing happened to you."

"Try harder. It's what I did for nearly a year. Little by little my memories returned to me. A flash here, a flash there. One of my first recollections was of you as a child, Beryl. Remember the day you made us pick bluebells to deliver to the elderly residents on our estates? By the time we'd made our bouquets, the flowers were brown as dirt."

He directed a glance at the others. "This elf forced us to take them anyway."

"I remember that," Brian said with a fond look for his friend.

Smiles passed among the observers, smiles born of warmth for this miraculous homecoming. Charlie's lips felt tight from holding his, and he cursed himself for it.

"Everyone declared they loved the bluebells," Beryl said.

Kent gave a bark of laughter. Charles thought: I'd forgotten how much Joshua laughs.

"Too afraid of your tears not to," Kent rumbled. "Anyhow, my memories came back faster as the year went on. About four months ago, I recollected my name. After that, everything, or almost everything, returned quickly. I started spending every waking hour planning my escape. Finally, I took my chance and left. You wouldn't have known me when I walked into the general's headquarters: bearded, ragged, scrawny, a total eyesore. And here I am!"

"You had to escape?" Beryl asked. "How terrible!"

A strange expression crossed Joshua's face. "Don't want you thinking it was a prison on the farm. They were kind to me in their way. Thought it better to leave quietly, though—easier all around."

Charlie sensed a reservation; Joshua was hiding something. But Beryl didn't know it, not by the way she shook her head in sympathy and squeezed his hands. She had never been able to judge truth plainly, not with Kent. She saw what she chose to see.

"How good it is to have you home," Beryl said, and burst into tears.

The door to the chamber again opened and shut, this time permitting Caroline Garrison to gain entrance. Seconds later, her mother followed.

"Is there a real ghost here?" Caroline went to stand beside her brother and was introduced to Joshua. "I know all about you. Patrick spoke of you many times after his visits to Brian from school. Heard you almost married Beryl before you got killed. Or didn't get killed. I hope you're not here to claim her again."

"Really, Caroline," said Mrs. Garrison. "Do not be so forward."

"But I want her to marry Patrick, Mama! I have always wished for a sister like Beryl, who will tell me what to wear so I don't look fat as bacon in my clothes!"

"Hate to disappoint you, Miss Garrison," Joshua said with a charming expression. "That's why I came running as soon as I found out. It boggles me to think what might have happened had I arrived two days later."

Patrick looked ill, Charlie noticed. "I'm sorry for your misfortune," Garrison said in slow, measured beats. "But you cannot think that after the absence of a year Beryl's feelings will be the same toward you."

"Sorry old man, but I do."

"Ridiculous!" Patrick's gaze flickered. In a calmer voice he added, "If you'll pardon my saying so."

"Well, I don't pardon you, Garrison. And I especially don't pardon how quickly you made a march on my bride."

"I've already said we thought you were—"

Joshua held up a restraining hand, his cheeks reddening. "While I was serving my country, what were you doing? Arguing boundary lines in a powdered wig and collecting inflated fees from the gullible! And now you expect to proceed in wedding *my* fiancée and call *me* ridiculous. Hah!"

"Oh, this will never happen to me!" cried Caroline. "Two handsome gentlemen arguing for my hand! Beryl, you're so fortunate. Why don't you say something? Shouldn't you be the one to choose?"

As all eyes turned to Beryl, Caroline folded her hands

prayerlike, squeezed her lids tight, and whispered repeatedly, "Please choose Patrick, choose Patrick!"

Charlie crossed his arms against his chest and watched Beryl's confusion. Her gaze wandered from one to the other of them and back again. Rattled she was; shaken to the core. He knew the battle that warred behind her eyes. She had already rejected Garrison, but could hardly tell him so now.

And of the battle within himself? A quarter-hour ago, he had been fool enough to think her free. But she had been unencumbered before, and he'd done nothing. He could do nothing now, save relieve her suffering for the moment.

"This isn't the time," he said firmly.

Joshua sent him an appraising look. "Well, well. Always the champion, Charles. You haven't changed."

"If this isn't the time, when is?" Patrick inquired in reasoning tones. "Our wedding is less than forty-eight hours away."

"I've already told you that's off," Joshua said.

"You don't have the authority to cancel *my* wedding," Patrick blustered.

Charlie stepped closer to the divan. "Both of you are behaving like fools in a play," he said bitingly. "How's this: I give you dueling pistols and the pair of you have it out in the drawing room. Last man standing takes all. If that fails to appeal, then perhaps you'll stop flapping your jaws and give Beryl time to think."

"I've had my fill of weaponry," Joshua said with a dangerous smile. "Fisticuffs is much more to my liking. What say you, Gar—"

"Stop it, all of you!" cried Beryl, pressing her hands over her ears. "I mean—I—I do need time." The room fell silent. After taking several deep breaths, she said, "Under the circumstances, I believe our guests will pardon a postponement. Patrick, I beg you to forgive me, but you must understand I can't go through with the wedding now.''

Garrison's glance encompassed the inhabitants of the room. Charlie felt unexpected sympathy for the man, who seemed to spend a great portion of his life worrying about what people thought. Aside from the potential loss of Beryl, this dilemma must spell torture for him.

At last Patrick spoke, his voice scarcely audible. ''Do you mean you can't go through with the wedding in two days' time, or you can't go through with it at all?''

''I—I can't say now,'' she whispered.

He seemed encouraged by this. ''You are not sure which way your heart lies. Very well; I can wait. But not for long. I've important business in the City.''

''Halt!'' Damara cried. ''You cannot mean to cancel the wedding! Do you have any idea of the expense my husband has entailed, or how much I have worked?''

Several voices sounded next: Beryl's, sniffing apologies; Mrs. Carraday's soothing; and Bryan's, who cut above everyone else. ''It's all right, Damara. We'll not starve, and the servants have done the work. There's still time to inform our guests of the change in plans. You write notes to everyone tomorrow and I'll send Maddox with them. They'll understand.''

Damara looked ready to ignite, but she said nothing more.

Joshua said, ''Enough domestic talk. I'd like to take my betrothed for a drive. Are you willing, my love?''

Darting a glance at her mother, who nodded permission, Beryl struggled upright. ''Of course.''

''Now hold just a moment,'' Patrick protested. ''She is still affianced to me.''

''Listen, old boy. As I recall, she was my betrothed first;

a betrothal that was never broken. Your engagement wasn't real in the beginning."

"Wait! That cannot be right. Your death canceled the engagement. Or rather, the report of it."

"But obviously I'm not dead. The report was beyond my control. Therefore, I propose to take my fiancée for a ride."

"But it's nighttime!" protested Caroline.

"The horses will be able to see. We won't go far or get lost. I haven't forgotten any of these old lanes."

"How fortunate that you haven't," Charlie said quietly, "when you have forgotten so much else."

Kent gave him a quizzical glance. Charlie met his stare unwaveringly until he felt Beryl's attention on him. When he saw the joy in her eyes, he smiled faintly and looked away.

"Promise you won't go further than the end of Hornburg Road," Mrs. Carraday said, her smile softening the entreaty. "Our guests have enough to gossip about tonight as it stands."

"I promise, ma'am. We'll return before most of them find their coaches."

Joshua pulled Beryl to her feet and walked her to the French doors that led outside, his arm protectively circling her waist. Charlie watched them leave. Beryl didn't spare him so much as a backward glance. The instant they were gone, everyone began talking at once. He pretended to listen a moment, then slowly walked from the room.

Beryl shuddered slightly as she climbed in Joshua's phaeton. His vehicle and pair were dark as the night around them, and, less than an hour ago, she had believed her companion dead. Thoughts of ghostly midnight rides spooked her imagination. She bid them flee. Joshua was alive, *alive!* There could be no happier news.

The circular drive was not wide enough to allow him to turn the horses, so Joshua clicked them forward and carefully drove past the coaches. When he turned onto the road, he snapped the whip, and his blacks clipped forward smartly.

He grinned. "You're very quiet, Beryl. Hope the shock hasn't made you ill. Are you glad to see me?"

She stirred to life. "Glad? That does not begin to tell it. Oh, we have so much to speak about. I want to know everything. What was it like, living in Spain? Was your return dangerous?"

"Wait, wait, my love. There will be time aplenty for that." His blue eyes looked black in the dimness, and in spite of her chill, she warmed to the desire she saw within them. When they were out of sight of the house, he allowed the reins to slacken, and the horses slowed to a walk. Seconds later, he pulled her into his arms. "You don't know how long I've dreamed of doing this again."

Beryl blinked. It took all her control to avoid leaning back, and she could not imagine why unless it was the length of time that had elapsed since she last saw him. Surely her shyness was not caused by superstition; he most definitely was *not* a specter. She spoke lightly to mask her confusion. "It cannot be so long as all that. You forgot me for almost a year."

"Ah, you're teasing, Lady Bear. Come here."

Obediently, she moved closer for his kiss. The taste of his lips was sweet, but as the kiss became two, then three, she pulled back, gasping for breath, recalling another mouth that had touched hers tonight.

Two days before her wedding date, and she was becoming a loose woman. Precisely how many gentlemen *could* a lady kiss in one evening without being considered wanton?

"I thought we were going for a drive," she admonished, smiling so she would not seem harsh. "Now I see why you wanted to bring me out here all alone. You may have lost your memory for awhile, but you are no different than always."

"Don't pretend you don't like our kisses, minx. That's one thing I'll *never* forget about you. But becoming reacquainted was not my only reason for getting you away from everyone. I wanted to ask you something." He fingered a tendril of her hair, making her shiver. "I wondered if you would marry me on Saturday."

"Marry *you* on Saturday?" she squeaked.

"Think about it, Lady Bear. The guests are here. Our banns were read last year, so they should be still in effect. What could be more practical?"

"But—but—it doesn't seem fair to Patrick."

"I don't give a horse's droppings for Patrick's feelings."

"Well, you should. None of this has been his fault. And I don't see any cause for hurry." She recalled Damara's bitter eyes. "Or to hurry overmuch. We need time to get to know one another again."

"I already know you better than I do myself, and you should feel the same about me. Are you going to pretend you're still contemplating marriage with Garrison?"

She could not lie to him. "No. I don't love Patrick, though I thought I did."

He nodded. "Good. Don't make him wait to hear it. You'll not do him a kindness."

Joshua could, she thought, do her the courtesy of acting more surprised that she cared so little for her fiancé. Did he feel that only *he* could snare her affection?

But that was so, wasn't it?

"I suppose I should tell him in the morning, when we're alone." She had intended to tell him tonight, but she no longer had it in her.

"A superlative plan. Then there'll be nothing to stop us tying the knot on Saturday." When she started to protest, he gentled her lips, then stroked her cheek with the back of one fingernail, and she was helpless to do more than close her eyes. "Beryl, we've missed an entire year of our lives together. I've sold out. I'm ready to stay home and start a family. Let's not waste any more of our future. If there's one thing my experience has taught me, it's that we don't know how long we have. Not any of us."

What he said was true, she knew it was. "I'll consider it," she said.

"You'll consider it. Oh, I know what that means. You plan to ask your mother, don't you? When is my girl going to grow up and make her own decisions?"

"I don't believe asking for advice is childish," she said, miffed. "Yes, I'll discuss it with Mother, but not only her. I have other sources."

"Who? Your brother, I suppose. Surely not Damara, I know you two never got on." When she failed to answer, he crowed, "Oh, never say it's Long Charlie you run to for opinions."

"And if it is?"

"You won't get an unprejudiced answer from him, Miss Pert. I saw him loitering around you like a lovesick fly tonight. T'say truth, when my parents told me you were to be wed, I was surprised to find your fiancé was Patrick and not him."

"Don't be absurd!" she cried. "Your brain must still be bruised, Joshua!"

"Mark my words. Charles will tell you to avoid me because he's always wanted you for himself. Poor old Charlie. His thinking is as shaky as his legs."

Hours earlier, could she have pictured a reunion with Joshua, Beryl would not have imagined she could feel such wrath toward him. "Please take me home," she said in a controlled voice. "The guests will soon be passing us."

"I'll do as you ask, but it will cost you another kiss."

She knew him for a stubborn man, so there seemed only one thing to be done; she closed her lids and offered her lips woodenly. For a long moment, nothing happened; then Joshua turned the horses about. As the phaeton lurched, Beryl opened her eyes and looked at him curiously.

"I don't kiss marionettes," he said grumpily. "Thought you were glad I was alive."

Her anger melted at once. "Oh, Joshua," she said, and, despite the jarring springs of the carriage that bounced them up and down like butter in a churm, she pressed her lips to his.

One more time the fool, Charlie told himself, then never again. He stood before the wide windows of the grand parlor, watching the guests enter their coaches, nodding now and then to neighbors when they called farewells to him from the hall.

"I'm glad you're not rushing away," said a voice at his ear.

He turned and saw Estelle Carraday, the lines of her sweet face arcing upward in a smile. She was wearing a sienna-colored gown; the matching turban did not entirely hide her silver hair. He found the contrast striking and told her so.

"You always say the kindest things, Charles." She inclined her head toward the window. "Has this not been the most amazing night! Our friends will have much to discuss on their way home."

"They will. I hope you don't mind my staying past the

bounds of politeness. I desire a few words with Joshua before I leave."

"Of course you do! I'd be shocked if it were otherwise. Stay as long as you please; you are family to us."

"That was always my hope," he mumbled, then wished he could call back the words.

Her alert eyes fixed upon his. *"Was* it, Charles? Why, then, have you never said?"

Unsure of how to respond, he smiled awkwardly. In the next instant, he forgot all else, his attention focusing on the scene outside the window. At the far end of the drive, Joshua's phaeton was pulling into view. Charlie watched as Kent called to a lackey and threw the reins down, jumped nimbly, so very nimbly, from the conveyance, then reached upward to swish Beryl to the earth. She laughed at something he said, her cheeks looking flushed even at this distance.

Charlie didn't realize how tense he'd become until he felt Mrs. Carraday's hand on his arm. He turned to her mindlessly, a small part of him registering the sympathy in her eyes as she murmured about attending to her guests. He hardly knew when she left him.

Outside, Joshua had been caught by a clutch of well-wishers and was boisterously responding. Beryl hovered at his side, looking uncertain as to her role. And then her eyes found Charlie's through the glass, her expression lighting. She whispered something to Joshua, who hardly appeared to hear, and walked briskly toward the house, toward him.

Charlie steeled himself to wait.

She entered the hall, brushed past a knot of guests with breathless goodbyes, and swept to his side. The eagerness in her face filled him with loss.

"Oh, Charlie, you must tell me what to do!" she said in an urgent whisper.

How many times have I heard those words, he thought. With effort, he kept his expression neutral as she hastened him to a pair of armchairs in the corner.

"Joshua wishes me to marry him on Saturday, while all of my family is here," she said without preamble. "Don't you think it would be . . . disrespectful to Patrick if I did so?"

"Poor Patrick. Worse and worse."

"Don't be glib, Charlie; this is serious!"

He felt himself grow cold. "Why ask me? Who am I to be giving you advice? Only a neighbor, a childhood companion."

She drew back, her forehead puckering. "But you are so much more than that!"

"Am I?" He regarded her with detachment. "I would be happy to know just what I am. In your eyes."

Several expressions crossed her countenance, not the lest of which was distress. After long seconds of this, he took to his feet. "As I thought, Beryl. Excuse me."

Later, he would not be able to recall his exit from the house. But when he saw Joshua, who was still holding court in the center of a group of jocular neighbors, Charlie's senses returned in force.

He went to stand just beyond the half-circle, his stare at last drawing Joshua's eyes. Kent appeared to ignore him, continuing with his discourse, but Charlie recognized his air of covert attention. Before long, the prodigal shook hands with his well-wishers and made his way to him, clapping him on the back.

"Well, Charles, I recall that look. You've something to say to me, and you'll choke on it if you don't get it out. What's wrong? Ain't you glad to see me?"

"I'm happy you're not dead."

"But you'd as soon I were still across the ocean, eh? See,

I recall your tricky way of speaking, or not speaking. Say what you mean, old friend."

"I intend to." Charlie's eyes lifted to the front door, which was opening to expel more guests heading for carriages. "Come where we can have some privacy."

"Mysterious as ever," said Joshua, but he followed his companion's halting lead to the terrace, which opened off the drawing room on the east side of the house. On the brick pavement were several small wrought-iron tables and chairs scattered about, and the gentlemen walked to a table near the darkest corner and seated themselves.

The doors to the drawing room stood wide to admit the air. Longstreet glanced within, saw no one, and stretched his legs. "Tell me what really happened at the Peninsula," he said.

Joshua snorted. "Don't mince words, Long Charlie. Never mind the small chat, the inquiries as to my health and disposition after being lost forever."

"You told me to speak plainly, and that's what I'm doing."

"That's right, Lord Scholar, turn my words back on me; you always were a good one for that. Well. I've told you what happened, and it's God's own truth. I'm not going to share every little detail; I've no desire to bore you to suicide. Have I asked *you* to explain everything that happened during the past year? Do I want to hear about your truants, your favorite little apple-polishers, the fathers who won't pay their brats' bills? No! Do *not* tell me, I beg you!" Deep chuckles boomed into the night.

Charlie refused to be distracted. "You're hiding something. Something you don't want Beryl to know." He leaned one forearm on the table and pointed an accusatory finger. "I want you to tell me what it is."

Joshua lunged to plant both elbows on the table, his

chin jutting forward. "I've said all that needs to be said to anyone, and that includes you, old chum."

Longstreet eyed him a moment. "Very well. But be certain you don't do anything to hurt Beryl. For some unimaginable reason, she loves you—"

"How well I know it," Joshua said, placing his hand over his heart, his eyes turning heavenward and his smile beatific.

"—but if you do *anything*—even after you're wed—that remotely causes her pain, you'll have me to answer for it."

"Charlie, you frighten me. And crush me! Why would I hurt my sweet love? I've always cherished her, even when she led us into Burnworthy's pasture and flagged that bull after me!"

Longstreet turned aside, fighting the pull of Kent's charm. Too often his friend's magnetism had led him to forgive behavior he'd never have accepted in anyone else. Beryl, Brian, everyone in Joshua's path fell under that same power. But not tonight.

"You have a debt to pay me, Joshua," he said quietly.

A silence fell as Kent's gaze lowered to Charlie's leg.

"I didn't mean for it to happen; God knows I didn't.'

"But it did. And while you were able to serve your country, I could not."

Joshua winced. "Come, come, Long Charlie. Could I conjecture you'd go up those stairs looking for Beryl? How old were you—eighteen, nineteen? Man enough to figure no young lass would hide herself in a haunted house at midnight!"

"Beryl might have."

Kent gave him a lop-sided grin. "She might've at that. Still, I couldn't guess the landing would give way—you can't blame me."

Charlie closed his eyes briefly, the memory of that night bursting over him as if it were happening now: the eager search for Beryl and growing disappointment when she couldn't be found; his terror as the rotted wood gave way, plunging him down, down, to lie broken, alone, and in such agony he was half-crazed when Kent, worried at last, discovered him the next afternoon. And then the long months of recovery, the scalding realization that his leg and knee had not set properly and would never be right again.

"I can't blame you?" Charlie asked coldly. "Who wrote the note?"

"It was a prank," explained his companion, emphasizing each word, opening his palms outward as if to say, *I've told you this a hundred times: will you never understand?*

"A very cruel one."

"Aw, when are the young not cruel? Soon as I found you were soft on Beryl, I couldn't resist. After all, she was *mine!* Thought you deserved a night sniffing through the dark looking for her. 'Specially if you was such a ninny to think she'd ask you for a midnight tryst—gad, what a cabbage you were!"

Longstreet waited, saying nothing.

Kent shifted his weight in the chair and braced his fist on his thighs, his posture entreating. "Charlie, I've *told* you—if I could take it back, I would. Listen, old friend. I'm older now and better able to guess what you're feeling, what you've gone through, and I'm sorry for it. Since I was felled, I've learned something about pain. My head ached for *weeks;* my arm, too."

"But how well you've mended."

"Aw, 'tis only because my skull is harder than your knee." He gave a rascally smile, his eyes pleading forgiveness.

"That I believe," Charlie said after a moment.

"Hah! *There's* the droll old boy I remember! Enough

gloomy yammering. I've a fiancée to woo, though her kisses tell me I've finished the task already!''

Charlie's face went blank. ''Remember what I've said. Do nothing to hurt her.''

''Yes, yes, yes. You're like a horn with only one note.'' Kent's eyes narrowed. ''And just who appointed *you* her protector, may I ask?''

''I did. And it would grieve me to tell her how I got this limp.''

''Ho, are you threatening *me*? Wasn't it you who begged me to keep quiet? You never wanted Beryl to know you were idiot enough to think she'd gone to meet you, recollect it? Seems you've as much to lose as I.''

''Not any longer,'' Charlie replied with a frigid smile. ''I have only my pride to forfeit. You, on the other hand—''

''Bah,'' growled Kent, rising, striding away. ''Keep your secret and I'll keep mine. I've no intention of harming Miss Carraday. Satisfied?''

''No,'' Charlie whispered, watching until Joshua was out of sight, then slowly standing, working the stiffness from his leg. Perhaps talking about his knee made it hurt the more. He paused, a rustling sound drawing his attention to the house. The drapes were billowing inward with the wind. He stared into the empty room a moment, then began walking toward the stables.

Beryl closed the door to her bedroom and leaned against it, exhausted in mind and body. At last the carriages were all gone, the overnight guests tucked away, and Joshua home, asleep in his bed. Or so she prayed. It had taken all her powers of persuasion and self-control to break away from his kisses, his entreaties that they marry on Saturday, his declarations of undying love. It was more, much more, than she could endure, for every time he touched her, she saw Charlie's face, felt *his* lips, heard *his* softly spoken, "I would be happy to know what I am in your eyes."

Her lids closed, scenes from the past fluttering through her mind. Scenes of Charlie's thousand kindnesses, his championing of her, the many times he'd listened to her problems, her dreams, her silly childish stories. None of the others had treated her with such tender regard, but she had taken him for granted, never imagining what his attentions might mean. He had always been dear, funny Charlie, eclipsed as they all were by Joshua's exuberance, his brash leadership, his assumption that she belonged to him. Now she was not so sure.

She sighed and dashed tears from her eyes. "I am in love with two gentlemen," she told her fourposter, "and neither one is my bridegroom."

A sudden hope drove her to the wardrobe, from which she wrested her ancient bridal dress. She tore at the buttons of her ballgown, twisting, wriggling until she was free, and threw it in a heap on the carpet. Then, with a deep breath, she stepped into the mass of yellowed froth, sliding the sleeves on her arms but not bothering with hooks, closed her eyes, and turned in the direction of her mirror.

"Charlie?" she whispered, and looked.

The unfastened bodice dangled comically, and the loose waistline made her appear plump. She could laugh, were any small portion of the gown *white*. There was not so much as a pinprick of brightness.

"No," she moaned, pressing her palms to her eyes.

But . . . there was one other name to try, for perhaps last year's failure simply meant the *timing* was all wrong, not the groom. She swallowed and lowered her lashes.

"Joshua?" she croaked.

The gown stubbornly refused to lighten from the color of old teeth. Her shoulders sagged. Gone was her last hope for guidance. Disillusionment turned to bitterness.

"Count Otranto," she flung at her image. "Ivanhoe. Lord Byron. The Prince."

A knocking sounded at the door.

"Oh, the devil!" she cried, and then, clapping a hand over her mouth, gasped in relief when the gown did not spring white at this last, unintentional suggestion.

"It's Damara," came a heavy whisper through the wood. "Let me in, will you?"

The mirror reflected Beryl's dismay. "Just a moment." She tugged off the gown and stuffed it into the wardrobe, then hurriedly donned a robe over her undergarments.

When Beryl admitted Damara into the bedchamber, her sister-in-law's expression conveyed impatience. She wore an apricot pegnoir, her brown, wavy hair loose across her shoulders. Beryl thought it easy to imagine why Brian had become so enamored with the woman; with her large amber eyes, an upturned nose and full lips, Damara was lovely. But why hadn't Brian seen the harshness that had already etched a thin line on each side of her mouth?

"What were you doing—hiding someone?"

"Merely straightening the room; I told the maid not to wait up for me, so I had to do everything myself. Will you sit?"

"No. What I have to say won't take long."

It will be the first time, Beryl thought, but said, "Fine. I mean, I'm always happy to speak with you, but I can't deny I'm bone tired after everything that has happened tonight."

"That's good; perhaps then you can understand how I feel. Beryl, you've done some odd things in the past, but I never dreamed you'd postpone your own wedding. Just imagine what everyone will say! No, no, don't interrupt, allow me to finish, please! I know it was wonderful to see Joshua again; I'm as happy as anyone that he's well, but that's no reason to delay marrying Patrick. And to what purpose? The Hilde-Forsythes came all the way from Scotland—you know that, just as you know many of our other guests have come great distances. How many of them do you imagine can travel all that way again, for the same cause? I will tell you: none! Or I shouldn't imagine any would. So why not go ahead with the wedding now? Consider other people's feelings above your own for once, why don't you? Before I have to write all those dashed notes."

When Damara paused for breath, Beryl seized her chance.

"I'm not going to marry Patrick. I don't love him."

"What?" Her delicate features became frenzied. "Oh, no; you cannot be thinking. Love—love—you don't know anything about it. When you're wed, you will. You've allowed your memories of Joshua to confuse your mind."

"Are you trying to tell me you didn't love my brother when you married him?"

Damara paused. "I loved him then and always will."

Beryl nodded sagely, one brow lifting. This she did believe, for Damara, who had her pick of suitors since her father possessed a knighthood and was Crestinley Rock's one claim to nobility, had pursued Brian for years.

"Then you'll recognize why I wish the same for myself."

"But—but Patrick has over ten thousand a year! You and your mother will be much more comfortable than you are now!"

"Oh, don't be so torn up, Damara; you'll be rid of me yet. Joshua still wants to marry me."

"Yes, so I gathered this evening, but—but *when?* How long now must we wait? I mean, how long will *you* have to wait? You must be anxious to get on with your life."

"Not so anxious as you are, apparently. If it consoles you, Joshua wishes me to marry him on Saturday."

Damara absorbed this. *"Does* he? Well, that might be a solution. You would be living next door, but at least—um, yes. Indeed, why not?" Her voice grew brighter. "Yes, Beryl, do! Be true to your heart and marry Joshua."

"And you don't think that would be unfair to Patrick to wed so quickly?" She watched her sister-in-law carefully. Damara had a firm grip on the proper way of doing things.

Now her expression changed not a whit. "Unfair? I cannot see why he'd be so selfish as to begrudge you marrying someone else at his wedding. Our people are all here; it only makes sense to go onward."

Beryl gnawed her lower lip and pictured Charlie's face. *What am I in your eyes?* "I'm not sure I want to go onward. I haven't decided what I should do."

Damara plunged her fingers into her hair. "I vow you will drive me mad, Beryl! I'll listen to no more of this. I'm to bed, and I'll not send a note to anyone. If we don't have that ceremony on Saturday, you can run to Gretna with the stableboy for all I care!"

Although he'd not gone to sleep before three, Charlie awoke at daybreak on Friday morning, consumed a light breakfast, and took his usual morning stroll around the school's grounds. Long Meadows Academy consisted of his ancestral home, a wide, yellow-bricked structure having more spaciousness than charm; a stable; two sheds holding grounds equipment and school supplies; and several cottages for married workers. Slightly more than a hundred acres, much of it wooded, formed the setting for the school. A crushed shell road skirted the property, and it was upon this he walked, his cane making little holes in the surface.

In more prosperous days, before economic necessity forced his father to devise a means of supporting his family, Long Meadows had been a thriving estate. Charlie knew little of those times, having lived most of his life in his family's quarters in the attic, one floor above the boys' dormitory, two floors above the receiving rooms which had been converted to classrooms, and three floors above the kitchens, dining hall and the billiards room, favorite haunt of the boys after study hours.

From toddlerhood, he'd gone to sleep with the sounds of stifled laughter, startling cries of young rage, and mysterious thumps and crashes that never were explained. From forever, he'd awakened to the clang of the breakfast chime and dozens of feet clattering up and down the stairs. And from his attic window every morning for always, he'd watched the day students arrive, boys and girls from the village, their voices mingling with the call of seagulls and pipits and crows, their bodies pulsing the scent of peat fires and long days without baths.

Hardly a place to bring a bride. He'd always known that. Just as he'd known for the past five years that he was hardly a man to be a groom.

When he reached the top of a little rise, he paused, planted his cane in the gravel and leaned his weight against it. Fruitlessly he tried to view the buildings and grounds with an objective eye. He could only feel a mixture of love and hate.

His home breathed life. It was a good thing his father had done, establishing the school. While the boarders were prosperous enough to gain an education anywhere, the village children could not.

Unlike what Beryl thought, it was no sacrifice for him to stay when his father died. He loved teaching the children, appreciated the mix of personalities, even tolerated the administrative aspects of his post.

Besides, leaving Crestinley Rock would have meant leaving her.

But the place was beginning to drag at him. There was no reason to stay. He could endure being thought *closer than a brother* while Beryl remained single. But watching her nest with Joshua for the next few decades was more than he could bear.

The lure of his old dreams was beckoning. To travel, to see the world he'd only read about . . . *this* would satisfy him, surely. But he'd have to sell the academy. What would happen to the children then? Who would buy a school? To reconvert the house to a residence required more shot than he owned.

He remained awhile, frowning as he thought, then began to walk back. Before he had gone many steps, a scuffling noise signaled the approach of one of his students. He stopped, suspended by the urgency of the footfalls, and waited until a young boy appeared over the hill. The child was Lester Bainbridge, one of five offspring of the village smith, his ragged clothing more unkempt than usual, his mud-colored hair tangled into knots.

"Mr. Longstreet, sir, sir!"

Lester was normally a quiet boy, and his wild grey eyes alarmed Charlie. He immediately asked what was wrong.

"It's Jess, sir! Papa's done whupped him fierce, and he's run off!"

"Do you know where?"

"To the moors, sir!"

Charlie regarded him in astonishment. "Why? What's out there for him except to get lost?"

"That's wot I said to him!" Lester exclaimed with the air of an old man weary of the ways of the young. "Jess said he was climbin' down the cliffs to the sea and swimmin' out to a ship. *I* says why din't he just walk to a harbor, and he told me to shut my trap! Jess has puddin' for brains, Mr. Longstreet. That's wot Papa said to him this mornin'. See, Jess climbed on the roof to fetch a hawk's feather, and the thatch fell onto Papa and Mama's bed. Papa yelled, 'Puddin' brain!' and went for Jess, which is why Jess threw a cup at him, which is why Papa got the strap!"

"Have you told your father where he's gone?"

"I tried to tell 'im, but he don't listen."

Charlie could imagine. Lucius Bainbridge was a giant of a man, his muscles primed by hammer and bellows and fire, with a mouth full of thunder. Excepting Lester, all the Bainbridges had short fuses. He placed a comforting hand on the boy's shoulder and stifled a sigh.

"Tell me where you saw him last. I'd best go look for him."

"You're making a grave error, one that I beg you to reconsider." A single line furrowed Patrick's forehead. His round cheeks, normally shiny and pink, went a pasty color.

Beryl lowered her lashes. The interview with Patrick was not going well. They were seated in a corner of the grand parlor, well away from her mother, Aunt Aurelia, Felicia Burnbright, Beryl's cousin, and Caroline, all of whom were discussing the fashion plates in *Lady's Monthly Museum.*

Beryl had done her best to prepare for this dreaded meeting. After a lengthy stand in front of her wardrobe that morning—precisely how did one dress to cut off an engagement? It was not a question she'd ever wished to pose herself—she had selected her best day dress, the ivory embroidered in spring flowers at the hem, and allowed Marianne, the maid whose services she shared with her mother, to arrange a green bandeau around Beryl's short, dark curls.

Afterward, she'd gone to Mrs. Carrady's bedchamber and, over cups of hot chocolate, sought her mother's advice on breaking her engagement to Patrick and the suitability of wedding Joshua in his place. She did not mention Charlie at all, for though she believed he loved her, he'd never said anything to indicate it before last night; and those feelings were too new, too tender, to speak about.

She was also embarrassed to mention him. Beryl and her mother highly respected one another; the young lady was fearful of losing her parent's regard, for being thought heartless and frippery-headed in believing she had *three* gentlemen interested in her. Who was she to have such a problem? Many young ladies might long for a similar dilemma, but Beryl found the reality of it horrible.

As she suspected would happen, her mother declared her willingness to support any decision Beryl made concerning her future mate. As to wedding Joshua on Saturday, her parent was less enthusiastic.

"I'm more worried about your marrying Joshua so soon after his return than I am with Patrick's disappointment, though we must consider him as well," she said, setting her cup on the beside table and pushing backs her bedcovers. Beryl moved to assist her mother down the steps from her bed. "Thank you, darling." Mrs. Carraday adjusted her cap and walked to her wardrobe. "What can be the harm in waiting until you feel comfortable with one another again?"

Beryl settled back in her mother's overstuffed armchair. "Damara doesn't wish to send cancellations, for one thing."

"Doesn't she? Well, she needn't. It's been two years since our family has gathered; time enough for a grand visit, wedding or no."

Taking encouragement, if not firm answers, from her mother's words, Beryl had gone downstairs. After a breakfast of dry toast—she felt she didn't deserve any of their kitchen's delightful plum or peach jellies, not with the distasteful task set before her—she'd begged Patrick to accompany her on a walk. He'd refused, declaring the ground to be too wet, but she sensed he didn't want to be alone with her, whether for reasons of propriety or fear. So they had ensconced themselves in this public place, Patrick's choice.

Most of the ladies were granting them a measure of privacy; other than a brief smile, Mrs. Carraday very carefully did not look their way, and Beryl's cousin and aunt truly seemed absorbed in the latest fashions. But Caroline was not subtle; Beryl couldn't fail to notice how often she observed them.

"Patrick, you're a wonderful person," Beryl said now, her voice earnest. "I am so very, very sorry to distress you."

And he was distressed, she saw that; he no longer tried to hide it behind a polished veneer, but swiped his face with his handkerchief, his hands trembling. The sight made her feel low as a worm. All at once she knew she could *not* wed Joshua on the morrow; it would be too unkind, for Patrick had relatives coming as well, and she could not ask him such a thing. Relief flooded her at the thought.

Patrick coughed pitifully and blinked. "I wonder if you've contemplated what life will be with Mr. Kent. Are his prospects good? I know he has an estate, but does he have a house in town?"

"I have not said that I'm going to marry Joshua, but a house in town was never something I wanted. I love the ocean, and the countryside is—"

She stopped, drawn by Caroline's hurried approach. "You cannot mean to marry Mr. Kent," the girl said in a heavy whisper. "Don't dash my brother's hope and mine for him; the man's a bounder."

"Caroline, really," Patrick mumbled. "You're not helping."

"No, listen!" she hissed, pulling a chair closely to them. Seating herself, she stared pointedly at the ladies across the room until they returned to their fashion plates, then leaned forward with a conspirator's air. "I know something that will change your mind about Mr. Kent. What he did to Mr. Longstreet was horrible!''

Patrick lifted his hand. "Caroline—"

"No, let her continue," Beryl commanded.

Caroline's eyes gleamed with righteous zeal. "Last evening, I heard them both talking on the terrace. I was hidden behind the drapes. Don't scold, Patrick! If I hadn't, I wouldn't know what I'm going to tell you, so please don't frown!'' She patted her curls importantly. "As I was saying, it was Mr. Kent who caused Mr. Longstreet to fall and hurt his leg all those years ago, so he couldn't go for a soldier!''

Beryl shook her head. "No, that can't be. Charlie—Mr. Longstreet was exploring an old house when he fell. We'd heard stories about a ghost—a sighing woman who died while waiting for her husband to return from the sea. Mr. Longstreet decided to spend the night there to see if it was true. The next day, Mr. Kent discovered him—rescued him, actually.''

Caroline gave a peal of laughter that pierced Beryl's ears. "That's what he *said*. But truth was, Mr. Kent had written Mr. Longstreet a note saying *you* wanted to meet him there, which was an awful thing, for Mr. Longstreet had a *tendre* for you and Mr. Kent knew it, so he did it for spite. And when Mr. Longstreet's leg was all broken, he begged Mr. Kent never to say why he was at the house, because he was ashamed he'd been such a dupe as to think you liked him. And of course Mr. Kent didn't, because he wouldn't want anybody to know what a rotten, terrible man he was for sending the note at the beginning! So you see— you cannot marry such a person. Even *I* wouldn't!''

As Caroline's speech progressed, a roaring had begun to sound in Beryl's ears. Now her body felt as foreign, as numb to her senses as a stranger's. She realized suddenly that she was standing, that Patrick spoke her name softly while Caroline regarded her in surprise. She did not care;

their attentions could not move her. Her thoughts were
for Charlie alone; Charlie, whose life had been altered,
stricken forever for the worse, because of his love for her.
How bravely he'd borne his affliction; all those days and
years afterward never treating Joshua with the contempt
she would have, had he done such a thing to her.

And all the time she'd prepared to wed the man who
caused the accident, the man who'd seen the love she had
failed to recognize, what pain had *she* caused Charlie? How
many hundreds, nay, *thousands* of times had she sought
his advice on such inconsequential matters as the best
flowers to select for the nave, or whether to serve lobster
or salmon at the wedding dinner? She wanted to weep, to
tear her clothing with sorrow as the Israelites had done in
the Bible, for Charlie in his silence, for Charlie in his love.

How could Joshua have been so unkind to his friend—
to both of them? How well he had kept his hideous secret!
He was protecting himself, not Charlie; of that she was
convinced. What other things did he hide? Had he truly
lost his memory, or was that a lie, too?

With the thought came tears. She swept them away. The
time for weeping was past. This was the moment—was long
past the moment—for action. She dashed across the room,
paying no heed to her mother's startled eyes nor the que-
ries of her cousin. Flinging a cry for Maddox to order the
trap, she flew up the stairs for her bonnet, reticule, and
gloves.

Less than an hour later, Beryl entered the narrow hallway
of Long Meadows Academy and followed Mr. Merriweather, the school clerk, into the front parlor, the one
room in the house kept quiet and clean for visitors. While
he led her to a settee near the hearth, he apologized

for the dampness of the chamber and explained that Mr. Longstreet was away.

"But where has he gone?" she cried.

The clerk, a thin young man wearing spectacles, turned his lively eyes to the hearth. "I can't say, miss. It has to do with school matters, and I believe those must remain private. Do you wish to stay or shall I ask him to call on you later? It could be a long wait."

She clenched her hands together, then sat. "Why won't you tell me where he is?"

The clerk nodded, his friendly face resigned. "I suppose you're staying. I'll start a fire." He crouched before the hearth, his back to her. "Once or twice I've spoken about the private matters of students with folks not connected to them. Mr. Longstreet has kindly given me to understand that's not proper."

She glared at the faded wallpaper, a golden fleur-de-lis pattern on creme, and prayed for patience. Aside from the small settee upon which she sat, gold armchairs and scratched tables were the only furnishings in the parlor. Distantly she heard the murmur of teachers' voices, an occasional childish one, the sound of someone walking on the stairs, the clatter of dishes. Her attention returned to the room, which was austere, but projecting the cold of neglect, not emotional aloofness; the velvet on the chairs was too worn, too well-used, for that. She had rarely stepped into this parlor, had seldom visited Charlie's home. It seemed a further omission on her part.

If ever there was a chamber needing a woman's touch, this was it. Thinking so, a lightness entered her breast, but she could not smile. Perhaps it was too late. Perhaps love could withstand indifference only so long before it withered.

"If you do not tell me where he is," she said slowly, her

voice charged with tension, "I shall scream until someone does."

At this threat, Mr. Merriweather blanched. He stared wordlessly for a moment, then rose, brushing dust from his hands. "I can't tell you," he said. "But I know of someone who might." He strode from the room, not looking at her again.

When he returned less than five minutes later, he guided a young boy across the threshold. Introducing Miss Carraday to Lester Bainbridge, he asked the child if he would explain what happened that morning. At first Beryl feared the lad would be too shy, for his eyes had rounded to circles when he first saw her. But after a faltering beginning, he related his story well enough for her to understand. She watched his plain little face, the smudge of butter on his chin moving up and down at every word, with intense concentration.

"I should go!" she declared when he'd finished. "I must help Char—Mr. Longstreet. His leg—he could be in trouble."

Mr. Merriweather looked at her in surprise. "I shouldn't think that would be necessary, miss. Mr. Longstreet is quite capable. Besides, where would you begin?"

He presented a valid argument. It seemed there was nothing to do but wait and worry. Anxious to distract herself, her glance fell again upon the boy. "Does your father often beat you?" she asked in dread. Her own dear departed father, bless him, and never touched Brian or herself in anger.

"Not me so much," Lester said. "Mostly Jester. And Chester, before he got too big." The boy added proudly, "Chester works with Papa now in the smithy. He's even bigger than Papa. Ever seen him?"

"No," she said, bemused. "We have our own smith at

Carraday House. Lester, you—your brothers are named Jester and Chester?"

"Yes, Miss Carraday. Papa likes rhymes. He makes up songs, too, and sings fair 'nuff for the Prince to hear, Mama says. If the next one's a boy, it's to be Nestor."

Beryl's glance flew to the clerk, who struggled to subdue amusement at her expression. "He has a sister named Hester as well." He coughed into his fist. "We are fortunate to have avoided Fester thus far."

She forgot herself enough to smile. Her relief died, however, at the sound of the front doors flinging wide enough to strike the walls.

"Where's my boy!" rumbled a deeply masculine voice. "And where's that connivin' teacher! He's behind all no doubt!"

"Mr. Bainbridge!" whispered the clerk in horrified tones, rising to his feet. Alarmed, Beryl also stood, while Lester shifted his weight from one foot to the other, his gaze darting left and right as if he intended to escape. But there was no time to hide. The blacksmith, a very tall, bearded man attired in homespun, his white shirt buttoned low to display a plump chest, barreled into the room breathing heavily.

After a brief, furious glance at each of them, Bainbridge's eyes fell to his son. "Where's Jess? Better not claim you dunno. Hester heard you two plottin'."

"No, we didna," cried Lester.

Bainbridge reached for his son's ear with a hand that seemed big as a shovel and twisted, holding on. "Tell me!"

"To the moor! He's run off to the moor!" Lester cried. "Lemme go, Papa!"

"Wot a rattle-head!" he wheezed, eyeing the chairs with longing.

Much to Beryl's relief, Bainbridge released him. She'd

longed to peel his fingers away like an onion but hadn't
dared.

"I'm certain Mr. Longstreet could use your help in looking for him," she suggested. She could not stop thinking
of Charlie. How could he walk across the moors with his
cane? What if he fell into a bog?

"When I catch my breath, miss. I run all the way here."
He gave her an appraising look. "Don't mean to be talkin'
out o' place, but ain't you Miss Carraway?" When Beryl
nodded, he stated, "You're the one wot's gettin' married."

"Yes," she said without thinking, then: "I mean, I was;
that is, I . . . I don't know."

This reply had the result of drawing everyone's eyes to
her. She raised her chin and added nothing further.

"Well, beggin' you pardon, miss, but I'm sittin'." To
Mr. Merriweather's evident dismay, the smith lowered his
sweating hulk into one of the delicate velvet chairs.

The clerk's fretting gaze rambled to the boy. "You
should go back to class, Lester."

"Don't want to," the child protested. "Want to see wot's
wot with Jess." He sat on the floor beside his father.

Apparently they were all going to stay. Beryl drifted back
to the settee and folded her hands in her lap. Mr. Merriweather settled tentatively on the hearth. A few awkward
moments of silence passed, then the blacksmith began to
hum. The hum grew into a song softly sung, the melody
sweet, though the singer stopped frequently to exchange
one word for another, obviously composing as he sang, or
to draw in gasping breaths. Beryl almost forgave him for
his rough manner with his boys. He must love them, or
he would not be here.

From outside the open doors came the sound of a horse
galloping into the drive. Eagerly, Beryl hastened to the
windows. "Oh, no," she said in a deadened voice. The
very last person she wanted to see.

"It's my boy," intoned the smith, burying his face in his hands after viewing her dejected posture. "He's dead, ain't he? I knew it. My boy's gone. Oh, gawd have mercy. Oh, Jess, Jess, my lad, my favorite lad!"

"No, no," she said hurriedly. "It's Joshua Kent."

"Joshua Kent?" inflected Bainbridge in brighter tones. "Thought he got his head shot off in the war. Wasn't you and him goin' to wed long ago?"

"Jester's yer favorite?" Lester interjected pensively.

"Only if he was dead," the smith assured him.

Joshua strode into the room. Beryl caught a glimpse of his haggard face before she turned away.

"Thank God you're still here," he said, ignoring the blacksmith's hail and joining her by the window. "Maddox told me where you'd headed. I—I must speak with you." He threw a glance at the others. "Walk outside with me? Please, old girl?"

"I have nothing to say to you, Joshua."

He laughed weakly. "I was afraid of that. Patrick's sister nearly assaulted me at the doors of Carraday House when I arrived this morning. Said she'd heard everything Charlie and I talked about last night."

Softly, Mr. Bainbridge began to sing again. *"He came home from the battle, though the world done thought him dead,"* he crooned. *"He'd come again*—no, no; *he'd come back for his darlin'* . . . ah, let's see . . . *though the Frenchies took his head.* That's good, ain't it, boy?"

Joshua offered him an incredulous frown. "Beryl, why are you in this room with all of these people? Come, let me drive you home in the trap."

"I'm not going anywhere with you. Charlie is on the moor looking for one of his students, and I'm waiting here until he gets back safely." Pray God it would be soon.

"On the moor," he echoed. "Indeed, why not? Probably

bogged up to his neck in the mire. Would be just like him.''

She pressed her hands to her cheeks. ''Don't say such a thing! Why don't you—why don't you go away? You could search for him, if you wish to make yourself useful.''

Mr. Bainbridge, who had been quietly humming during this interchange, broke into words: *''But the girl had found another, and told him. 'go away!' ''* He paused, waiting for further inspiration.

''Is that what you want me to do? I'll do it. Anything you say. Just don't look at me like that.''

''How do you expect me to look after what you did to Charlie?''

''Beryl, it was an accident. I'm no prophet to guess what would happen that night.''

The strain in his voice steadied her emotions. ''I don't dream you intended it,'' she said in gentler tones. ''But even if Charlie hadn't fallen and hurt himself so badly, how could you play such a low jest—trampling on his affection for me? Such is beneath you, Joshua.'' She turned back to the window. ''And then to lie about it all this time.''

He tugged at the draperies in mindless exasperation. ''He's the one who gave birth to the lie!''

''And you the one who nourished it,'' she whispered.

From the velvet chair, the blacksmith sprang into melody: *''He said, 'I'll find yer sweetheart, and then I'll make him pay.'* No, too common. *'I'll dump him in the hay.'* No. *'I'll throw him in the bay.'* Wot you like best, Lester?''

Joshua pivoted toward him. ''Will you be quiet?'' he shouted.

Immediately Mr. Bainbridge began an intense study of his boots, while Mr. Merriweather squirmed. Lester looked bored. Kent clasped Beryl's elbow and tugged; she resisted at first, but then allowed herself to be led into the hall.

"Don't be angry, old girl." Almost timidly, he ventured, "That's no way for us to start our married life."

Beryl did not hurry her answer; she scanned his face, remembering. Almost a lifetime she had loved him: his brashness, his adventurous spirit and fondness for novelty. He was half rogue and half gentleman, and, aside from the weakness she'd discovered in his character, totally appealing. But not as a husband; not any longer.

She spoke slowly, her heart in her eyes. "I'm beyond happiness that you're still alive and part of my life. But I can't marry you, Joshua."

He replied so quickly she suspected he'd known what her answer would be. "You're trying to punish me."

She gave him an offended look and shook her head.

"What will you do then? Go back to Patrick?" His eyes widened. "Oh, no. Not Charlie!"

"If he'll have me." If he hasn't perished on the heath. Dear God, where *is* he?"

"That's pity talking, Lady Bear! Why don't you sprinkle some of that my way? I'm the one who nearly lost everything."

"But you didn't."

"I will if I lose you," he said sadly.

She felt tears pricking the back of her eyes. Could she do nothing but hurt people? Exchanging a long, sorrowing look with Joshua, she hardly noticed the sound of pounding hooves until Mr. Bainbridge pushed her aside in his effort to gain the entrance door, which still stood open.

"My boy, my boy—no it ain't. A pile of strangers in a carriage. One fellow on horseback, don't know him."

Bainbridge made as if to return to the parlor, then paused, his interest obviously caught by the visitors. Instants later, Patrick Garrison, closely followed by a woman and three men, stalked into the building. The men were dressed in dark, close-fitting clothes; the woman, too, wore black, though red embroidery enlivened the border of her gown. Beneath her mantilla, long, raven hair framed exquisite features.

Upon their entrance, Joshua stepped backward, his face ashen. The three men, their faces suffused with anger, moved forward. The young woman, petite as she was, spread her arms wide and cried, "No!"

The men stopped, though Beryl could see they only restrained themselves with great difficulty. In bewilderment, she looked from them to Patrick to Joshua, who appeared to be gauging the wisdom of a bolt upstairs. In the taut silence, the sound of the woman's slippers as she glided toward Kent mimicked Beryl's heartbeat.

The visitor did not stop until she stood a handspan's distance from him. Joshua could decently retreat no farther; he stared down at her with the look of a man facing the guillotine.

"*¿Por qué*, Joshua?" she asked in a trembling voice. *¿Por qué?*"

"Luisa." He swallowed. "What—what a surprise. How did you—" He dashed a look at her companions and seemed unable to continue.

"Don't pretend you didn't know they were following you, Kent," Patrick said in scornful tones.

Beryl gathered composure enough to speak. "Joshua?"

Luisa's soft black eyes swept her from head to toe, then returned to him. "*Esto no está bien, amada mía.* Is very bad."

Kent's lips formed a ghastly smile that swiftly died. His mouth worked. Nothing came out.

Patrick stepped forward, his eyes shining with vindication. "If you won't explain, I will. Beryl, these are some very weary travelers. They have come all the way from Badajos. And this morning alone, they've covered a good deal of ground. First the Kents' house, where they just missed Joshua; then your home, where they just missed

Joshua. And now that they've been successful at last in finding him, I'd like to introduce you to Luisa Navarro Kent. Joshua's wife.''

"His *wife!*" Beryl shrieked.

A stunned silence fell as all eyes centered on Kent. Patrick, irrepressible in his discovery, broke the quiet. "Now you see why he was in such a rush to marry you! He knew they'd follow and thwart his nefarious plans."

"You would have married me, when you have a wife already?" Beryl accused, her voice shaking. "Precisely what would that have made me?"

"It's not like that, old girl—"

"No?" snapped Patrick. "How was it, then? We're anxious to know."

"Aye, that we are," Mr. Bainbridge threw in, resting his hands on Lester's shoulders. Mr. Merriweather, forsaking all efforts at maintaining a professional detachment, edged next to them.

Joshua cast a frown their way and scanned the condemning faces before him. His gaze found Beryl's, and he spoke as if to her alone. "I'd no intention of harming anyone, you must believe. I married Luisa, yes, but that was when I didn't even know my own name. She was the daughter of the house where I was taken after the battle; these gentlemen are her brothers. When my memory came back, naturally I wanted to return to my old life and my first love. Can you blame me for that?"

"So you simply left her?" Beryl queried in a scandalized voice. "Without so much as a 'by your leave?' " She was so disappointed in Joshua she wanted to cry. How could she be so wrong about a person?

"No, you don't understand. We discussed it. I told her I must go home to England. She begged me to stay in Spain, said she didn't want to leave her family. When I spoke of a bill of divorcement, she would hear nothing of it—the Navarros are staunchly Catholic. So I came home—"

"Escaped, you said." Beryl's tone was scathing.

"I did, yes. They"—he nodded toward the brothers without looking—"were watching me closely. Had to steal away in the middle of the night—"

"You said you were starved and clothed poorly," she shot. "And had grown a beard."

"Perhaps I exaggerated a little," he said rapidly. "But my intentions were good. I meant to have my marriage annulled before you and I set a date, but when I discovered you were so close to tying the knot with Garrison, I lost my head. Thought I could go quietly about the paperwork, then you and I would say our vows again with no one the wiser. Don't see why I should be punished because a Frenchman knocked me mindless!"

Luisa Kent placed a delicate hand on Joshua's sleeve. "You—you don't love me, *amada miá*?"

Beryl saw the hurt in the Spanish lady's eyes and felt her heart grow colder toward Joshua. But when he lifted Luisa's hand to kiss it, confusion stirred. His expression was tender upon his wife as he spoke slowly so that she would understand.

"You know I love you, Luisa. But I loved Beryl first. She's part of my world, and my world is England. We've talked about this before, don't you remember? You said England is cold and damp, and that it rains too much. Sometimes it is all those things, but it's what I need. I belong here, where the earth runs green and the chimneys blow smoke even in summer. And you belong with your family, where the sun shines its own image into the trees and grows orange blossoms for your hair."

"Oh, gawd," snuffled the blacksmith. "That's beautiful, it is. I'm puttin' it to a tune if I can remember it."

"I will stay with you now," Luisa said, her accent delightfully exotic to Beryl's ears. "My brothers bring me here to remain. A woman belongs with her husband."

"But Luisa; the damp—you said you can't bear it."

"You will buy me a coat. I will be with you."

Seeing the perplexity in Joshua's eyes as he looked from his wife to her and back again, Beryl felt something within herself break. Joshua may have stomped headlong over everyone, but that was an inevitable result of his lusty pursuit of life. Even though his insensitivity could have caused her to lose Charlie, it hadn't—or she prayed it hadn't. She believed Joshua truly hadn't intended harm to anyone, but now he must bear responsibility for his actions.

"Joshua," she said, moving a breath closer to him, "You think you love two people. I can understand that; I have felt something like it. But I believe if you examine your heart carefully, you will find there is one you prefer over the other; one you wish to spend your life loving." Rapidly, she added, "And of course, that person is your wife. A part of you recognized that, even when you knew nothing else about yourself. Otherwise, something inside would have stopped you from marrying."

Distantly, Beryl felt the force of attentive eyes surrounding her, but it was Joshua's gaze that locked with her own. She saw arguments flaring within him, then acceptance, and finally, a soft regret.

"Of course, you are right," he said brokenly, turning from Beryl to Luisa. "Welcome to England, my dear."

A sunny smile broke across Mrs. Kent's features. She included her brothers in that smile, and they mirrored her happiness, clapping one another on the shoulder and talking rapidly in Spanish. Laughter bubbled from Luisa as she nodded and repeated, "Welcome to England, welcome to England!" and then, tilting her head upward at her husband, she said pointedly, "Welcome to England, *bebé!*"

Incredulity, then joy spread across Joshua's features. *"Bebé?* We're having a baby?" When Luisa bobbed her head rapidly, Kent swept her in his arms, lifting her feet from the floor. "I'm going to be a father!" he shouted.

Beryl pressed her hands, palms together, to her lips. Tears welled in her eyes. She was so happy for him—for both of them—she could burst. Everyone seemed to be talking at once. Mr. Bainbridge and Mr. Merriweather made their way into the hall, offering congratulations. Into the confusion, Patrick sidled next to her.

"That turned out better than I thought," he said. "Aren't you relieved they found him before the wedding? Can you imagine the disaster?" She nodded, hardly listening. "Now that you have your feelings sorted out, we can go ahead with our ceremony tomorrow. I bear you no ill will for your confusion."

He had her attention now. "What are you speaking about?"

"Well," he said, lifting a demonstrative hand toward the blissful couple, "what you said a moment ago about loving two people. About preferring one over the other. Better late than never, I say, and we'll speak no more of it. I'm not the sort of man who will remind you of the past two days. We'll simply consider it an attack of nerves."

"Oh, Patrick." She could not believe she was going to have to go through this with him again. "I wasn't—I'm so sorry, but it was Charlie I meant."

He stared. Long seconds ticked by. Around them, the sounds of chattering merriment continued; she was glad no one noticed them.

"Charles Longstreet? You intend to wed *him* now?"

She nodded, looking ashamed.

"You—you are terrible!" Patrick flushed at his boldness, then seemed inflamed by it. "You don't know what you want. Thank goodness I've found out about you before the wedding. Marry Longstreet—marry that large man over there with all that hair! Marry one of the Navarro brothers, for all it affects me. You are—you are a flighty woman!''

Having flung this barb, he pushed his way toward the door. "Patrick," she called halfheartedly, and followed. But she had only apologies to offer him, and her steps were slow. He was on horseback by the time she edged past the tallest Navarro brother and stood on the entrance landing.

She returned inside. For a few moments she stood on the edge of the crowd, smiling sweetly at their buoyancy but inwardly churning. She was a terrible woman; Patrick was right about that. But it wasn't because she was flighty, only confused. And now that she knew her heart's true desire, where was he? She could not stop picturing Charlie's body half-buried in a weed-scattered bog.

Unwilling to present a long face before the cheery inhabitants of the hall, she retraced her steps to the landing. She was contemplating starting her own search for Charlie regardless of Mr. Merriweather's advice when a horse with two riders appeared on the horizon. Ecstasy spread through her body as she recognized Charlie. And surely the lad with him was the smith's son. "They've arrived!" she called gladly over her shoulder. "Your son is safe, Mr. Bainbridge!''

The smith plowed through the crowd to stand beside her. "Aw, there he is, there he is, thank you Lord for sparin' him.'' When Charlie and Jess, whose breeches were splattered with mud, were within hailing distance, he bawled, "Get in here, boy! I got summat to say to you before you go to yer lessons!''

With a look of heavy dread, the lad slid from the horse. As he followed his father into the hall, Charlie dismounted and tied the reins to the post, befuddlement lining his face as he viewed the open doors and the people within. Beryl could restrain herself no longer. Like a projectile hurling toward its target, she flew to him and threw her arms around his neck.

"Thank goodness you're all right! I was so worried!"

"Good heavens, Beryl," he said uncomfortably, releasing himself. "The lad was no more than two miles away. What goes on? Are we having an entertainment?" And, softer: "Why is Joshua here?"

"Wait. Please. Stay a moment before you go in. I need desperately to speak with you."

The intensity of her speech fastened his eyes to hers. "All right." His voice was gentle, but the cool distance she heard in it pierced her.

"I've found out about your accident; about how Joshua tricked you, and why."

Paling, he made as if to step away, but she set herself in his path. He halted, his eyes intent on the hedgerow growing beyond the drive. "I never meant for you to know."

"Why not, Charlie? Why not tell me you cared?"

"Isn't it obvious? You loved Joshua. Why should I jeopardize our friendship by putting that burden on you?"

"I wish you'd said something. Our lives might have taken a very different path if you had."

A skeptical light entered his eyes. "Well. It's neither here nor there. You'll wed Joshua and be happy. And I— I've determined to set a new life for myself. I've decided to sell the school, to travel. Ireland first; that's where my grandmother's people are from. Then Scotland. Mayhaps the war will end and I can got go to France and Italy. After that, I'll—"

"Charlie, hush," she soothed, pressing her fingertips against his mouth. "I'm not marrying Joshua. I've just found he's already married to someone he met before he regained his memory."

A hundred questions looked ready to burst from him, and she begged he wait for Joshua's version. "Even before I knew," she continued, "I'd decided not to marry him. What I felt for him was like a dream. You know how dreams are; they dissipate upon awakening. But my heart is, and always has been, with you. You have been the steady flame that has warmed me throughout all my life."

A procession of emotions flared in his eyes as she spoke: shock, indignation, and hope tightly reined. It was this last that made her want to weep, and she did so silently, the tears trickling down her cheeks. "And now I beg you: Stay here. Please. Or if you do go"—her voice broke—"take me with you. Only let us not travel long. I want children, many, many children, perhaps an entire school full, to share the love we hold for one another."

"Beryl," he murmured, making her name a question, as though he felt *he* were the one dreaming.

In a trembling voice she added, "Am I wrong, Charlie? Do you still have a fondness for me, or has my ignorance and self-centeredness, for all these long years, broken your affection?"

When his eyes, too, flooded, her heart pounded as if it wanted to leap from her body into his.

"You can't love me, Beryl," he said brokenly. "I'm lame. I'm not wealthy like Patrick and I don't have Joshua's talent for making people admire me. I have nothing to offer you."

She moistened her lips, tasting the salt of her tears. Gently, ever so gently, she pressed her hand against his chest, above his heart. "Here, Charlie. This is the man I love and all I want in this world. The dearest man, the best man, I've ever known. And if you don't love me back, then—then my life will be worth nothing."

The hope of years was unleashing, she saw that in his face. "Are you sure? Really, really sure?" A twinkle entered his eye. "Because if you promise to be *my* wife, I'll not stand for your changing your mind again. A fellow only has so much patience."

She beamed through her tears. "As certain as I am of my own life."

Slowly, as one who wants to savor a long-withheld reward, Charlie enclosed her in his arms. When he pressed his lips to hers, she felt a wild desire to grow even closer; she longed to be always thus, within his arms, within the circle of his protection and love.

Applause sounded from the open doors of the school. They turned, startled. Joshua was clapping his hands and smiling. Luisa, too, began to applaud, followed by her brothers, Mr. Merriweather, and the blacksmith and his sons, beaming from ear to ear. And then, in the classrooms facing the drive, young faces began to appear at the windows, accompanied by curious teachers, who, observing the sight, added cheers to the bedlam of sound.

"How nice to be alone when I make my declaration," Charlie said with a delicious grin. "A foretaste of what lies in store for you, I warn."

Beryl's spirits lifted even higher with his. "I suppose this means you'll be too embarrassed to kiss me again."

"Think again, child." And he proceeded to kiss her thoroughly, an action that prompted a raucous response from their audience. He broke away, feigning fury at his observers. "All right, enough sport! Back to work with you!"

Muffled groans came through the windows as the students returned to their desks. Joshua and the others began walking slowly toward carriage and horses; only Mr. Merriweather and Lester remained inside. Before any well-wishers could reach them, Charlie seized Beryl's hand and hurried her around to the side of the house where several benches were placed.

"Here we'll have the illusion of privacy, at least," he said when they sat, and circled his arm around her. After a moment of blissfully exploring her lips, he murmured, "What a shame," and leaned his cheek against the top of her head, his body trembling with emotion.

"What?" She lifted her face, her teeth showing in an enchanted smile. "What could possibly be a shame now?"

"All those guests present at your home, and no wedding to attend on Saturday. Do you think they would be willing to stay a little longer while we procure a special license? Would Garrison protest?"

If she grew any happier, her shoulders would sprout wings. "Patrick has probably packed his bags by now. Judging by the look in his eye when I told him I planned to marry *you* he has no caring for what I do or when."

"Did you tell him that, horrible child? Before so much as broaching the subject with me? What if I'd confessed to loving another, as someone I know has done more than once? I'm too polite to mention her name, of course."

"I regret to say I would not have been as patient as you. I am a determined woman."

"That you are." Suddenly, he began to chuckle. "Now we know why your bridal dress hasn't changed color. It was waiting for *our* wedding!"

Beryl's smile froze. "Charlie, pre—precisely how important is that gown to you?" Her voice quickened with inspiration. "For I was thinking of starting my own tradition by wearing a new one. The dress I had made for the ball—the one I didn't wear last night; I've never worn it—would be perfect. Its lines are simple, but I think you will like it."

He kissed the tip of her nose. "Don't wear a new gown, my love. How could we neglect the opportunity of seeing another miracle?"

She was in agony. How many times had she disappointed him in the past? She didn't want anything to hurt him, ever again. "But, Charlie, if the legend doesn't come true . . ."

"Sweetheart, I'm not a child. What if the gown looks a little old?" A little old, she thought miserably. Ancient spiderwebs look better. "I knew one day I'd watch you waltz down the aisle in your heirloom gown, but I never dreamed you'd be wearing it for me. That's the true miracle, Beryl. That you love me."

"No, Charlie," she said, tears rising again. "The miracle is that your love has lasted through all my giddy childhood days, before I recognized the other half of my soul rested in you."

Several days later, in the small hours of the morning, the door to Beryl's room yawned open. She looked up from her work, her bleary eyes slowly focusing on her mother. Mrs. Carraday, attired in pink nightgown and a frothy cap, walked forward a few steps. Beryl moved suddenly as though to hide the acres of lace spread on the floor in front of her, then realizing the futility of it, smiled ruefully and shrugged.

"I saw the light beneath your door," Mrs. Carraday said, advancing farther into the room. "Is this my daughter with a needle and thread in her hand?"

"You should be asleep," Beryl said, pulling the waistband of the wedding gown closer to the candles on her bedside table, aligning the panel of lace along the seam.

Mrs. Carraday paced closer. "I could say the same to you, dear."

Beryl kept her gaze on the delicate fabric, her needle diving in and out. "I couldn't disappoint Charlie tomorrow. Of course, the gown still won't be perfect. I didn't have time to replace the satin, for that would be as time-consuming as making the entire garment. Surely the new lace will make it appear more brilliant, though. I didn't want him to have any doubts about us. He believes in the legend."

"You sound as if you don't."

Beryl gave the impatient laugh of the very tired. "You see before you how much I believe."

"Yes, I do," said her mother, moving to the sewing basket and rummaging until she found another needle. Seating herself opposite her daughter on the floor, she lifted one of the sleeves to her lap and began loosening threads.

"You don't have to do this, Mother," Beryl protested.

"Why not? My mother helped me."

Beryl's needle slowed, then stilled. "What did you say?"

Mrs. Carraday continued working without pause. "And her mother before her."

Beryl leaned across her gown and clasped her mother's wrists. "Are you telling me the legend has been a fiction all this time and you knew it? How—how could you deceive me so?"

Mrs. Carraday smiled. "Exactly what I said to my own mother, almost to the word, a week before I married your father. Unlike you, I didn't wait until the night before the wedding to take action on the gown. Perhaps I had less faith." A wry look came into her expression. "Of course, the circumstances were a bit different."

"But, Mother . . . *why?* Why perpetuate this . . . lie?"

"It's not a lie, Beryl. There *is* magic. Only love would lead a bride to *make* the miracle happen, do you see? Surely such love destines the marriage to happiness."

"But I thought—when you were twelve, you said the gown—"

"Oh, my dear, the powers of a young girl to see what she wants! By the time I was of marriageable age, I was no longer able to imagine the glow. But I knew Daniel to be my destiny, so I secretly began to work. My mother found me at it, just as I found you. And then she explained as I'm doing." She paused as she raised the sleeve closer to the light. "Rosa continued the legend with her firstborn daughter, after the gown worked so well in helping her choose a husband. She knew the power of one's own desires, and wanted her child to be certain of her heart. Thus have we all done with our daughters, as will you, if you think the test a worthy one. And there you have it, our family mystery across the generations."

Beryl pressed her hands to her cheeks. "So the gown . . . has never been enchanted."

"Oh, Zella cast a spell upon it, I do believe that," Mrs. Carraday said carefully, gauging her daughter's reaction. "But the true enchantment falls upon the bride."

"Oh, Mother," Beryl said, a slow smile crossing her face.

Mrs. Carraday's lips spread into a matching grin. "And now that we are done with *that*, may I take this occasion to say how very, very much I love Charlie? He was always my favorite because he loved you best and longest. Mothers sense these things. I believe you will be exceedingly happy."

Beryl leaned across the bridal gown to embrace her parent. "Is that part of the legend, too? The mother is always to endorse the groom, no matter what her feelings?"

Mrs. Carraday patted her daughter's curls. "That doesn't sound a bad policy, but I need no legend to love Charlie."

"Neither do I," Beryl declared. After thinking a moment, she amended, "But it didn't hurt. At least, it will help convince him."

"Fair enough. Now we had best hurry. Dawn is coming soon, and you will have dark circles beneath your eyes if you don't rest awhile."

* * *

And so it happened on the second Wednesday in June, Beryl Carraday floated down the aisle toward Crestinley Rock's only headmaster. With her brother to give her away, she looked so beautiful that for many years afterward the wedding guests spoke of her, their voices echoing the words first uttered that day.

"Her gown! It's so beautiful!" whispered Felicia, Beryl's cousin, to Aunt Aurelia as the bride walked by their row.

Overwhelmed with emotion, Caroline Garrison wiped her eyes and blew her nose. Despite Patrick's disappointment, she had insisted her mother remain with her for the wedding. She'd hoped a last-moment disaster might spell a second chance for her brother, but now she admitted her error. "Those are the two who should be married," she hissed to her mother. "That dress is whiter than blazes."

"Caroline, really," Mrs. Garrison replied mechanically, her gaze fixated on the gown as Beryl swished past.

On the back pew, Luisa Kent turned bright eyes to her husband. *"Su vestido de boda es tan blanco,"* she said in wonder, nestling closer to her beloved.

"Yes, yes," Joshua replied, a little grumpily. "I can see for myself. No need to go on and on about how white it is."

Beryl had almost reached her bridegroom. Watching her glide by, Damara Carraday murmured in disbelief, "The legend *is* true. The gown looks as if it were made yesterday."

"Why, so it does," said Mrs. Carraday complacently, and then, taking a second, longer look, added in awe, "even the satin is gleaming!"

Brian, formally handing his sister into the bridegroom's care, kissed Beryl's cheek, making her smile widen when he murmured, "The dress couldn't have looked better on anyone who's ever worn it, not even Rosa."

My heart is so full, Beryl thought, basking in the good will flowing toward her from every direction. She was thankful for each loving person present. But most of all, she was thankful for Charlie. She'd waited her entire life to adore someone like him, and to be adored. And he'd been there all along.

Thank God she'd had time, with her mother's help, to finish the new lace so that her betrothed would have no doubts. She dashed a look downward and saw a stitch they had missed at the waist. Hopefully, no one would notice it. But what was this? Was the gown . . . *glowing*?

Charlie was not mindful of her wedding raiment. He saw only a vision, the one for which he'd prayed a lifetime, the flame of Beryl's love shining from her eyes as she took his hand.